T0208815

THE
WATCHMEN'S
CHRONICLE

THE TOWER OF BABEL
IS RISING

THE
WATCHMEN'S
CHRONICLE

MICHAEL TSAPHAH

THE WATCHMEN'S CHRONICLE
THE TOWER OF BABEL IS RISING

iUniverse books may be ordered through booksellers or by contacting:

iUniverse
1663 Liberty Drive
Bloomington, IN 47403
www.iuniverse.com
1-800-Authors (1-800-288-4677)

ISBN: 978-1-5320-1771-1 (sc)
ISBN: 978-1-5320-1770-4 (e)

Library of Congress Control Number: 2017903666

Print information available on the last page.

iUniverse rev. date: 03/08/2017

This book is dedicated to the brave souls who are Christians and veterans of the armed forces, who are homeless and are making that journey home. You who are in Christ have the greatest mansion awaiting you. Nevertheless, I love you with all my soul. To Christ, my lover and strength, with all my love, I wait for your return.

This novel is dedicated to Matthew Kerr, LCSW, Michele Steever, PhD, Ronnie Michelle Ayers, and all of the veterans. All gave some, and some gave all. I pray that the United States of America will never forget the gift of liberty we gave to its people.

PRELUDE

June 10, 2063

To whom it my concern,

I will have you read some interesting things about the falling away of the church and how it happened, which is actually quite simple. As the Bible tells us, in first Samuel chapter fifteen verse twenty-three from the King James Version that reads "Rebellion is as the sin of witchcraft." The word witchcraft, which has crept into the church, comes from the Hebrew qecem (keh'-sem), a lot or by magical scroll, also divination (include its fee) by an oracle, divine sentence that seeks for a reward[1]. Notice the word divination, which shows up in Acts chapter sixteen verse sixteen in the King James Version.

The spirit of divination is rising to form an alliance with Satan, and many are coming into the church acting as if they are operating in the Holy Spirit. But Satan has perverted this free gift to a movement that is now turned into the church era of the Laodicea.

The epistle you are reading is not a witch hunt, but it deals with the spirit of divination and the new ecclesiastical

---

[1] Strong's Concordances #7081

form of the Catholic Apostolic Church from the eighteenth century. Paul ministered to a woman who had a demonic spirit, known as a spirit of divination. Most Christians are unaware that this same spirit has crept into the body of Christ, often disguised as oracles, miracles, works, ministers, and now gods who are wielding the deadly divine sentence of death in people's lives.

Some of miracles, signs, and lying wonders have been used to fool the elect of God into following their magic shows and paying a fee to be healed.

The scriptures say there shall raise false Christ's and prophets who shall show great signs and wonders with which they shall deceive the very elect. These lying wonders, as the Bible tells us in Second Thessalonians chapter two verse nine are only the start of the charismatic witchcraft movement. The hidden spellbinders are the prayers of people who think they are praying to God, when actually Satan is the answerer of their deadly prayers. Any Christian could be guilty of this praying-mantis type of prayer about death and sickness for their rebellious loved ones.

Once these prayers are offered, the victims find themselves much like people who are revived by a witch doctor in a voodoo ritual. What is the difference between this and a grandmother praying for her grandson to come to Jesus "even if you have to kill him, Lord"? Can you show me that Jesus prayed any of those prayers over the unrighteous of his day?

The famous oracle was found at the temple of Delphi in Greece. A female creature with a python-like figure, supposedly a diviner or soothsayer, would foretell a person's future in return for a fee. The python was a mythological giant snake in Greek mythology, the son of Gaea, known as

Mother Earth that was produced from the slime left on the earth after the great flood.

This belief surfaced after the philosophers had covered up their idolatry by making themselves the new order of priesthood. They started schools much like the school of the Heraclitus of Ephesus, continuing the search of the Ionians for a primary substance claimed to be the fire of the gods.

Many philosophers noticed that logos, another word for the "fire-like words" doctrine of Heraclitus, which identified the laws of nature with a divine mind, developed into the pantheistic theology of stoicism, which formulated the doctrine of metaphysics. This religious philosophy became a branch of philosophy concerned with the nature of ultimate reality.

The thirteenth-century philosopher and theologian St. Thomas Aquinas declared that the cognition of God, through a causal study of finite sensible beings, was the aim of metaphysics. The rise of scientific study in the sixteenth century soon brought metaphysics and other Greek philosophies into the church. These crept in as the new gods of the church, but notice that it was in the Roman Catholic Church where these heresies arose.

The Roman Catholic dogma of the Immaculate Conception holds that from the first instant of its creation, the soul of the Virgin Mary was free from original sin. This doctrine is not to be confused with that of the virgin birth, which holds that Jesus Christ was born of a mother who was a virgin.

The new mother religion, the Revived Catholic Apostolic Church, was slowly creeping into the worship of the church of our Lord Jesus Christ, which came from Scottish theologian John Duns Scotus, a member of the Catholic Apostolic Church. The thing that we, the body of Christ, must understand is that God doesn't need man to help him with false doctrines of devils and lying wonders.

This will bring together the oracles of Delphi into a new order of the mother religion and the revived Catholic Apostolic Church, which will have a form of belief in Satanism, with the Antichrist as the god. The false prophets will be the Black Pope, the Future Mother Religion, and the Revived Catholic Apostolic Church of Satan. This will be a church that worships witchcraft (Wicca), spiritualism, and mother goddess religion. It will be up to the hidden body of Christ to keep to the ways of the Bible and the spiritual laws of Christ.

Christians must also stay away from the denominationalists, who are the wolves and false prophets that follow the natural laws of mankind. We can believe in Jesus Christ as God without the fables and false doctrine that come from the flesh or the world's demonic system. Mankind needs only to read the true word to get the real picture of who God is. Beware of false prophets coming to you dressed as sheep, because they are actually wolves that devour.

These wolves, which are cowardly money grubbers in sheep's clothing, bring death and judgment. But they also believe in the Rapture and they will ask God for deliverance. Why should God deliver these wolves, who don't care for the sheep that are slaughtered? These false shepherds prowl, just like the wolves that sentenced Christ to his death, which leads me to ask, "Would they kill the Antichrist and play God?" This made me wonder, what would a person do if they saw the son of perdition face-to-face?

Sincerely, your servant,
De'Angelo M. Jonah

CHAPTER 1

🜋🜋🜋

The Revolutionist Rising

As the philosopher Plato once said, *"Only the dead see the end of war."* Working in this age of grandeur of the commonwealth of the New Western Republican Occupied Majority European States (R.O.M.E.S.) Empire, in what was once the United States of America in the North American continent; I can sadly say that I have walked a mile in the pleasures of life in this empire.

One time while I was working as the emperor's press secretary, I met with the online blogger-reporters. These young but mature candidates were eager to get their shot at being the next press secretary or a star reporter of the online blog the *Time & Warner Chronicle*. One particular reporter, Ted Edgar Allen Coppell III, really tried to make his mark. He raised his hand, smirking as he shouted from the crowd, "Mr. Moore, do you believe the rumors that there is a Vicar curse or a conspiracy about the family?"

"Yes, of course, Ted. We all have skeletons in our closets," I said, pointing at the next reporter. "But which one of you is willing to report on those newsworthy subjects?"

Hearing a roar of laughter, I moved on to the next reporter's question. I had a spooky feeling of satisfaction that I had given the right answer. The young reporter was ashamed and embarrassed; I could see his eyes roll and his tan face turn red.

I knew in my soul that I was lying through my teeth. You know the truth—that there was, in fact, a family conspiracy that reached all the way back to the bowels of hell itself. However, I lied and sacrificed my integrity to save my job and skin.

Giving the facts of the case, I wonder whether you would have done the same thing if you had been in my shoes. Think about that, before you throw the proverbial switch that would banish me to the lake of brimstone and fire. Before this major career move to press secretary, I had my humble beginnings at the White House. I was the director and chief steward of White House Affairs, a fancy title for the chief cook and bottle washer.

Moreover, much like the words found in the Bible, that day shall not come except there comes a falling away first, and the man of sin be revealed as the son of perdition Second Thessalonians chapter two verse three in the King James Version. In the White House, the seat of power for the United States of America, were both President Richard Vicar and his nephew Natal Apollyon Vicar, who would one day become emperor of R.O.M.E.S. I used to cover up the pasts of the leaders of both nations by inadvertently teaching good Christian values to Natal Vicar when he was a young boy. Now, what he did with those morality lessons—good versus evil, right versus wrong—was totally his affair, but I helped write Christian values in the heart of that little boy.

I cared for Natal much like he was my own son, and I continued to talk with him throughout his life. Those shared conversations kept him alive, and he will always know that I loved him enough to tell him the truth. Nevertheless, with every beat of his heart, his blood ran with the curse of the Vicars. There was something about Natal Apollyon Vicar's families past that needed to be reviewed. God created him a man, but it was mankind that made him a Vicar.

The Vicar family conspiracy did not start with a revolt or some government plot to take over a country in a distant land. It began naively with two people lying in bed and copulating, making love as people have done throughout history. But these were not just any run-of-the-mill people, even though they passionately sweated in the exotic affair of intercourse with each other.

These two lovers were in the bowels of sin because they were not ordinary people. Nor were they living in ordinary times, but instead in the dark ages of the fifteenth century, when they should never have been together. They belonged to a jealous almighty king, and they had vowed to be his bride, just as he was their husband and their God.

They had both taken a vow of celibacy, so the Roman Catholic Church would make them suffer for their secret, covetous affair. Becoming one in holy matrimony was impossible for them, because he was a priest. In fact, he wasn't just some monk—he was the abbot of the local monastery. And she was a breathtaking beauty, one of the fair maidens of the court of Jesus Christ.

However, my tale is not about them, but about the product of the sinful ways of this friar and another nun who comes later in the story. The real reason I wrote this story was to tell about the great Natal Apollyon Vicar and how he became the emperor of the world.

If they lived today, the nun and the abbot of the monastery would be hypocritically scorned by the media and ignored like last week's tabloids, but they didn't live in the twenty-first century. No, they lived in the good old days of plague carried by rats, famine, pestilence, death by sword, and beheadings by the ax men of the fifteenth century. In those times of lords and ladies, the days of lesser kings and their great castles, men fought blindly and died in their chessboard crusades. In the fifteenth century, the luxury of hypocrisy could cost you your very head—and your instrument of sin would be cut off as well.

Because they lived in such dangerous times, these two people did what any red-blooded hypocrites would have done, especially if they had religious authority over the huddled masses. The older abbot and the younger mother superior did their deed in the shadows of secrecy at night and while in a hidden underground catacomb where they often walked. There was a hidden chamber below the catacomb of the rich Villa of San Marco. In the old monastery, called San Marcos de Monumentos, was a long tunnel that ran under the graveyard and connected the monastery to the convent. The old abbot and the young mother superior took advantage of that tunnel for their passionate affair.

Dim torches illuminated the pathway of the tunnel, which held many unspoken secrets for centuries. If those tunneled halls had lips to speak, they would tell of infanticides and homosexual, adulterous, and unbridled affairs that were hidden from the pages of history. They would speak of the twenty-first century hypocrisy of empty apologies and papal confessions.

The sound of giggles, groaning, and moaning having come from behind the wooden door, which was bound by ropes of hemp. It was a lascivious setting of passion, starting with the fireplace that warmed the room and then moving on to the two wine-filled stone goblets and a basket of fruit on the table. The silhouette of a man and woman could be seen under the covers of the feather-stuffed, pillowed mattress with its covers in royal purple and gold tapestry. A beautiful young woman rose from her bed of iniquity, revealing only her tight breast, which was red from her lover's nibbling in their bed of fornication.

"Come, my love, let us go another round," spoke the muffed voice of the man as he pulled her back under the covers.

"Stop, my lord, I must protest," said the whiny voice of Angelina, the young mother superior, as she tried to pull away from the bed. "For alas, I must be about my devout duties."

Angelina Delacroix had been given, at the age of twelve, to the Convent of San Marcos by her father, Vincent DePaul Delacroix, to pay off the debt he owed the church. At only sixteen years old, Sister Angelina was the youngest nun to become mother superior of the Convent of San Marcos, and at twenty, Mother Superior Angelina was assigned her duties by a man who was twice her age.

Abbot Dominican and Mother Superior Angelina were not exceptions to the hypocrisies of their day, even though these two lovers could have been anyone back in the fifteenth century. These two were leaders in the church, and moreover, one of them would advance to the highest position of leadership within the church of their day.

The Roman Catholic Church was notorious for hiding its own sins. The church would make every peasant in the villa confess their sins every Saturday, but these two lovers would hide their debauchery of concupiscence in unbridled passion. As Angelina tried to clothe herself in her black robe to cover her nakedness, Dominican grabbed her again and pulled her back for one more round of making love.

She giggled as she said, quite poetically, "You devil lover of my fiddle, stop pulling the strings of my tart fruit to your lips."

"Aha, but I must play you, my beloved," he said with a grin.

"Don't strum me again, for I must leave with haste," she moaned.

Grinning, the man whispered in her ear, "Then if I am a fiddler, let me strum you again until dawn." Suddenly the erotic noises of foreplay arose, like a person would make after biting into a sweet Georgia peach and this peach was firm and ripe for Dominican's picking.

Angelina moaned again. "Wist thou drinkest thy fill of thy cup till thy cup durst be dry?"

He appeared from under the covers, licking her navel and kissing her thighs. As he began nibbling and kissing on her long legs, this gorgeous woman of the church began rocking back and forth, as she started to pucker her lips because of the erogenous action of her lover.

"If ye were honeysuckle and I were a bee, then would I suck that sweet nectar till noon," he said as he appeared between her breasts.

"It is almost dawn," she said. They began to cuddle, and he hugged her as they lazily lay in each other's arms. "And I must waketh the sisters to prayeth," she continued as they kissed each other in their bed of messed-up covers.

"Be done with thee quickly, because I must go," she said, pretending to don her black robe. Then he grabbed her again as she giggled, leading to another round of making love. The two lovers clothed themselves not only in black robes, but in a dark secret that could be revealed only by time.

The abbot would rise to power as a bishop, and one day the bishop would become a cardinal. If he played his political cards right, that cardinal could become the next pope. We know that absolute power can corrupt absolutely, and the man who loved God so much could have used his little power to corrupt future generations.

"One day we will be together," Abbot Dominican said, putting on his robe.

"And whist this miracle shall happen?" Mother Superior Angelina asked sharply. "When they release innocent souls from purgatory?"

"Well, my sweet," Abbot Dominican abruptly said with a grin as he tied his robe, "as soon as thy coin in thy coffin rings a soul from purgatory springs[1]."

The two lovers quietly faded into the shadows, and with a final secret kiss, they departed. Their lips would remain shut until they met, once again, in those same secret tunneled halls. Speaking nothing of their surreptitious deed, young Abbot Dominican walked away in his brown faded robe. He was quite slim from religiously fasting during the year, and the bald spot on top of his head shone in the candlelight. Much like Judas Iscariot, he knew that he eventually would betray her for a handful of coins. Rather than prove his love, he would one day watch her burn at the stake. Until then, they would remain lovers in their hypocrisy.

The morning was bright, though slightly cloudy, as the two secret lovers went about their playacting affairs. When they passed each other, they would sometimes do battle like opposing chess pieces. No one at the monastery or the convent could ever guess that the two were in a game of furtive, concealed pretense.

One brisk fall morning, as the sun shone through the clouds, a horse-drawn carriage appeared, accompanied by two armed guards with steel-plated chest armor that glistened in the sunlight. The carriage went riding down the cobblestoned road with two robed messengers toward the monastery with news for the abbot.

They passed many monks doing their chores—picking grapes to make the Communion wine, gathering wheat to bake the Eucharist wafers and the bread they would eat, and sweeping the steps and pathways to the sanctuary of fellowship.

"We shalt be at the monastery soon," the older monk said.

"Yes, indeed, and with great tidings of Abbot Dominican's promotion to bishop, which wilt be pleasing to him," the younger friar said. "With the many reports we hast received from Rome, Abbot Dominican wilt be missed here."

"Thou wilt do the same, my lad," said the old monk with a smile. "Thou wilt do the same, if not even better."

In the chapel, the sounds of monks singing their chants of worship in fellowship and prayers toward the Almighty God could be heard. It was like heaven on earth, and the pious Abbot Dominican watched the busy monks doing the work of the Lord, just as he had done so many years before.

At first the abbot didn't notice the horse-drawn carriage arriving, because he was thinking of his night-by-night furtive meetings with the voluptuous young sister from the convent.

As the messengers rode closer, they saw grapes being picked and water being drawn from the well in the cool autumn day. Neither the brothers herding the flocks of sheep and goats and gathering had the hay to feed the livestock, nor the riders in the carriage suspected any evil on the horizon as they approached the gate. Looking through the latticed window, Abbot Dominican saw the carriage approaching, knew it must contain important visitors, and went out with two of his monks to greet them as they arrived.

As the well-dressed priests rode into the courtyard, the abbot went to greet his guests from Rome. Hoping they would inform him of a promotion that would give him more power, he realized that he had to stop thinking about seeing his beautiful young woman.

"Greetings and peace unto thee," the older priest said.

"Greetings and peace," said the abbot.

"Art thou Abbot Adrian Dominican?" the older priest asked.

"I am."

"We comest to thee with a letter from his holiness Cardinal Franco," the older priest said as the younger friar handed Abbot Dominican the letter.

As he began to read it, the abbot asked, "Am I to be a bishop?"

"Thou must movest at once and come with me," the older priest ordered. "The friar who is with me wilt takes over in thy stead."

"Where goest I?" asked Abbot Dominican.

"Ye goeth to Isle Britannica, to the Synod of Clement," the older priest answered.

As Abbot Dominican entered the coach, he looked back and watched the younger friar entering his former home. He knew that once he became bishop of the Synod of Clement, he must kill Sister Angelina of the Convent of San Marcos and cover any tracks of his ever having been involved with her. That night at the monastery, when Mother Superior Angelina went into the tunnel, she found herself alone in a cold room. Little did she know that she would soon feel the cold fingers of death wrapped around her heart.

Meanwhile Bishop Dominican came up with a scheme for her demise. He knew of a nun—a mother superior by the name of Anna—who would love to run this convent, or maybe in return for some midnight rendezvous would take care of his little problem. Mother Superior Anna would keep her mouth silent for the gain of his love and affection. They had known each other before he went to the monastery, and now he was bishop of the Synod of Clement and she was mother superior of the convent. He knew she would help him move forward his plans for advancement.

When he arrived at the Synod of Clement, he spoke to Mother Superior Anna and asked her to deliver the following message:

> Dear Mother Superior Angelina,
>
> It is with great importance that you are being given an award for your service to the Convent at San Marcos. This letter is to request your immediate presence, for you are to receive your letter of commendation before the monks and sisters of the Synod of Clement.
>
> Sincerely in Hope in Christ Jesus,
> Bishop Adrian Dominican

He gave the letter to Mother Superior Anna, but she was no fool. She knew in her heart that this note would mean either her own undoing or the death of the other nun. She knew that the young Mother Superior Angelina was the bishop's concubine, and Superior Ann loved the bishop and was willing to let Angelina pay for her sins. One cold, dark night, a horse-drawn carriage rode through the Spanish villa toward the convent at San Marcos. In the courtyard, Mother Superior Anna met with the unknowing sacrificial lamb,

Mother Superior Angelina, and gave her the letter from the bishop. As Angelina read the note, a smile warmed her heart and replaced the heartache she had felt upon being left alone in the cold, dark tunnels of the catacombs.

"You will be rewarded for all your hard work," said Mother Superior Anna with a smile. "I promise thee, the holiest of angels shall sing thy praise."

"Wast there any personal message from his eminence?" Mother Superior Angelina asked.

"Yes, my dear, there wast."

Then Mother Superior Anna gave the unsuspecting woman a kiss on her forehead, and smiled as they both walked out of the office of the convent. Little did Mother Superior Angelina know that she had been condemned to death.

Many weeks later, Bishop Dominican met the carriage with a smile, knowing that his deed was done and that Mother Superior Anna had kept his hands clean. Mother Superior Angelina had been condemned to be burned at the stake for being a witch. When she was taken to the spot of her execution, Angelina had been bloodily beaten and whipped by her jealous sisters, as penance for her sins.

Bishop Dominican's former lover was like the woman in the Bible caught in adultery. The mother superior and bishop had sent her to the stake, but no stones had been hurled as judgment against that lamb now turned scapegoat. Instead, Sister Angelina was burned for her sins. "And when will this miracle happen?" Sister Angelina had screamed at her murderers, as the flames rose higher. "When wilt thy Lord release the innocent souls from purgatory?"

Closing the shutters, the bishop said, under his breath, "As soon as the coin in the coffin rings, a soul from purgatory springs."

The bishop couldn't have cared less about justice and truth. He dared to call himself innocent, when both of them should have died that day for their sins. The one who called himself "the innocent" was not really deserving of that true name, which is the reason I begin this tale. The mother superior of the Synod of Clement would make sure that he paid for burning one of her nuns. Mother Superior Anna would trap the bishop in a web that would suck the very life out of him, and her plot would start a chain of events that would continue for centuries to come. The true meat of this tale starts when he was just Bishop Dominican of the Synod of Clement.

Mother Superior Anna was from royal stock. As she watched the burning body of Sister Angelina turn to ashes, she remembered how she, too, had been burned—by her father, the Duke of Wendover, because she had refused to marry Baron Von Shannon. Anna had once loved the same bishop who was a pauper, and was not a prince of royal blood. So Anna's father had sent her away, while still a young girl, to a convent.

Anna remembered looking out at the night sky as she traveled to the convent in a horse-drawn carriage with her father. She was reading a book in Latin and praying with her rosary, "*Domino espiritus Santos ectecta Santos Maria, Amen.*" She moved a rosary bead and began another prayer, "*Santa Padre halo Dé espiritus …*"

Breathing heavily, the duke looked at his daughter and then pulled down her prayer book. "Thou knowest that ye dost not needeth to goeth to this convent, my love," the duke yelled at Anna.

"Ye knoweth I doth not love that Baron Von Shannon," Anna said. Then she continued to pray, "*Santa Padre halo espiritus …*"

The duke spoke sharply. "Thy head is as hard as thy mother's."

"*Santa Padre halo espiritus ...*" Anna repeated. "Dost thou not remember my mothers wast a peasant who much loveth Adrian Dominican?"

"But I wast a duke, while he hast not any royal blood in his vein."

Anna challenged her father, "Then canst thou make him a knight, since thy daughter loveth him?"

"Thou knoweth that answer," the baron said sharply.

"*Santa Padre halo esprit ...* 'Tis why I wilt not marry thy companion, the baron," Anna cried.

From the day she turned thirteen years of age, Anna's father had begged her to marry the baron, but she was never to answer her father. The Black Death arrived in Wendover, England, and wiped her family out because of the curse her father had brought on young Anna.

Mother Superior Anna, thinking that God had answered her prayer because of her father's injustice, would capture her mate with the stealth of a black widow, and her prey would be the new bishop of the Synod of Clement.

Mother Superior Anna came to realize that not fate but *God* had brought her lover back to her. She knew that if she had married the baron, then the fate of her father and the baron's death from the Black Death plague would have come upon her head as well. She began to pilot her course as a master chess player moves his military pieces on a board. When the pious and privileged man and woman secretly passed each other, like two warships in battle, they played a game of iniquitous passion. As the bishop and the mother superior walked toward each other, cannons at the ready, the shots of words began.

"Good morning, mother superior," Bishop Dominican

said, smiling. "Today is a beautiful day to speaketh to our Lord."

"Good morning to thee, bishop," Mother Superior Anna said as she led the nuns to morning prayer. "Prayer in the morning is always good to clean the soul of wicked feelings, my lord. Come, sisters, let us not keepeth the Lord waiting."

Nobody in the monastery could ever guess that these two were engaged in a furtive game at this holy site at the Synod of Clement. One night, down a secret corridor, the sound of two people giggling, groaning, and moaning in lustful passion came from behind the door of a dimly lighted room.

The two bodies were locked in throngs of passion, and the woman with blond hair and green eyes was seated on a now older man in his late fifties. He looked like a bright red old beast[2], and she drank her fill of him. When he wanted more of her, she kissed him with hidden venom that made her beast sleep. Then she would slip away into the night.

This game went on for years, until one day a letter arrived, addressed to the bishop of the Synod of Clement from the College of Cardinals in Rome. He was to report to them at once, and he was gone several years. But when he returned, having been promoted from bishop to cardinal, Mother Superior Anna came to him again, just like clockwork.

Three years later, Adrian Dominican was crowned Pope Innocent III and moved to the Vatican at Saint Peter's Square in Rome. Two years passed before he would even speak to Mother Superior Anna again at the convent of the Synod of Clement. Then one day, Pope Innocent III said these fateful words in front of Mother Superior Anna and the priesthood of his court: "Since thou, priest, art supposed to be God's temple, a vessel of thy Lord, and a sanctuary of the Holy

Spirit, it offends thine dignity to lieth in thy conjugal bed and liveth in impurity.[3]"

Anna muttered to herself, "Thou double-minded hypocrite, if I hast to goeth to the stake, he wilt goeth to the grave." Mother Superior Anna looked him straight in the eye as she thought, *Now God wishes for me to repent and payeth for my sins, and then I wilt not goeth to the flames alone.*

Ten months later, as the clouds of night ended another day, a rather large crowd of men, women, and priests started to be blown about by the winds of revolt. As one would rake leaves in the winter, this time the fire was set to roar on his grace at the estate. Starting as small crowds, the revolutionists began to gather into larger gangs that broke into jeering and shouts of insults, gathering strength in the ripened fields of the countryside outside Rome. Men and women were pointing at the crest of Pope Innocent III, and they started to gather straw and tie it around wood to make torches as the crowd grew into a fuming mob.

"Thy pope is a sinner and hast a baby with a woman," yelled a woman as she threw a rock at the crest. Then a hailstorm of rocks was thrown at the crest as the crowd grew in number and strength. A priest shouted, shaking his fist, "Thou double-minded hypocrite!" The riotous mob moved forward with their weapons—pitchforks that were once used to gather grain. Now they would harvest a riot as they gathered more stones, torches, and people from roadside hovels near the surrounding villages and towns. The people grew more and more angry as the revolt grew in strength, and looked for something that would fan the flames of the inferno that burned in them.

"What about thine own offended dignity?" yelled another monk. "If we canst not lieth in a conjugal bed and live in impurity, then thou canst not lieth in one either."

Another priest screamed, "It offends our dignity that you lie in the conjugal bed.[4]"

The crowd continued to grow in fury, throwing more rocks at the crest of Pope Innocent III until it came tumbling down. Then as some cheered, the crowd grabbed the splintered crest, along with other wood and rubble, and set it all on fire. The Swiss Guard lined up to form a barricade to stop the bonfire from spreading, but the riot got bigger as the crowd grew larger.

A carriage sped toward the newly finished Saint Peter's Square and arrived at the courtyard just outside the gate. The tall Swiss Guard stood there, ready to defend the Vatican, with their sharp, curved spears at the ready and glistening in the daylight. The sergeant of the guard opened the gate and let the carriage through. Pointing their spears at the riotous people, the guards began to move the crowd back as the carriage entered the Vatican.

When the carriage stopped, the dark silhouette of a fat cardinal, wearing a red beanie could be seen. The cardinal spoke to the sergeant of the guard as he looked at the mob and then at the wrought-iron gate. The sergeant nodded, and the carriage rolled forward into the courtyard.

After a knock at the large double oak doors, the squeaking of the hinges announced the entrance of a small, frail, old man dressed in traditional priestly robes into the papal office. Shuffling over to the pope, the elderly priest bowed graciously to him.

"Your Grace, Cardinal Giulio Dé Medici and Cardinal Antebellum desire to see thee," the priest said sympathetically. "Will you needeth anything else, Your Eminence?"

Depressed, the pope sauntered over to the window. Looking out at the balcony, he sighed and said, "No, brother, not at this time."

Their royal red robes glimmered in the sunlight as the two cardinals, Medici and Antebellum, entered. The pope peered out the window, hearing the shouts bellowing toward him.

"The pope hast sinneth. He hast a woman with a baby," a woman's voice yelled from the crowd as a rock was hurled and broke the window.

"It would seemeth thy chickens hast cometh home to roost," Cardinal Medici said loudly.

"How canst we hideth this disgrace, Your Holy Eminence?" Cardinal Antebellum asked.

Cardinal Medici spoke again, in a piercing voice, "We needeth a sheep, not our chief shepherd in sin."

As both cardinals continued questioning him, the pope, who was still looking out the window, turned to them and spoke sternly. "He that art without sin among ye, let him first casteth a stone, for I am sureth that we all hast hidden bones in our closets."

Then, as if Cardinal Antebellum got the message, he replied, "What doeth ye needeth from us, Your Grace?"

Suddenly Cardinal Medici spoke, shockingly, "What is this dreadful thing?"

"Destroy this temple, and in three days I will raise it up," Pope Innocent III said, in a challenging riddle. "If I go down, we burn together, Cardinal Antebellum."

Cardinal Medici spoke up in a prophetic voice, "Your blood wilt pool in thy veins. A mystery must findeth its abortive strain." Then he left the room in a huff, slamming the door behind him.

Mother Superior Anna, now in her late twenties, had been stripped of her habit, crosses, and robe. Six months pregnant, she stood in front of the jeering crowd in a dirty sackcloth peasant's dress.

"Herest is thy papal whore," one of the angry people yelled.

There was silence as the crowd waited for the verdict. His eminence decided he would not have her burned at the stake, for he loved her. This time he would make right the wrongs he had done in secret, so he decided to marry the damsel in her disgrace.

"Release my wife and I will go silently," the pope said, clenching his teeth.

Years later, Pope Innocent III died of an unknown blood disease and was quickly buried. His death was riddled with mystery, around the same time as the marriage of Count Charlimas DePaul Vicar and Lady Roseland Andante Rothschild. A baby in the cradle was rocked by two nuns while a priest conducted the ceremony.

Meanwhile, back in Saint Peter's Square, an aide to the pope was walking down the secret halls of the Vatican. The former Cardinal Giulio Dé Medici—now Pope Clement VII—called for one of his aides to do a task for him. The door made a creaking sound as the elderly priest entered and shut the large double doors behind him.

"You calleth for me, Your Grace?" the priest asked in a soft tone.

Pope Clement VII motioned for him and the priest shuffled over to him. The aide was dressed in a black robe that came down to his ankles as he stood in front of the vicar of the church. The priest had on a highly visible, thick white collar with long ribbons of purple that hung around his neck and shoulders, with elaborate golden-colored Latin scribbling on the ribbons and three gold tassels at the ends.

The pope was scribbling something at his desk and then gave the letter to the priest to read. As he read the message, the priest had a confused look on his face.

"I want you to transcribe this letter into French and

giveth it to Lord Gideon. Have him killeth the bishop and all of the monks at the Synod of Clement."

"But Your Eminence, Lord Gideon is to rideth toward Jerusalem in three months," the priest said.

The pope yelled, "I sweareth by the gods of our fathers, I wilt hunteth down all of the snakes of the bishop and his monks of the Synod of Clement!"

Meanwhile, at the monastery at the Synod of Clement, Bishop Thomas Waldensian was transcribing a biblical manuscript that would bear his name. The bishop's Bible was being transcribed by the monks of the Synod of Clement. Thomas walked into the scribe's dimly lighted room. Candles flickered as the wind blew in while the door was opened and shut, and the smell of sweat and body odor peppered the air as the monks were all busy writing.

"Well, how is my favorite friar today?" Bishop Waldensian asked.

"Tired, Father," the friar said as he pinched the bridge of his nose. "Brothers, goeth now and taketh a break from thy work."

As the brothers and young lads of the monastery left the room, the rather round friar began to stretch and yawn as the day ended. Wearing the typical friar's halo bald spot, this humble man of the cloth was very well versed in the biblical arts. Friar James Madison was an English squire who had traded in his tutelage. After his master of twelve years died in the first crusades, during the reign of King Richard II, he had vowed never to carry arms against another soul.

"How many doth we hast, Brother James?" Bishop Waldensian asked.

"We hast six hundreth finisheth," Friar Madison replied.

"From the six thousand already done," Bishop Waldensian responded with a smile. "Amazing!"

"Well," James said in a meek tone, watching the monks

and young men working and playing in the distance, "I cannot taketh all the credit, my lord."

As he watched Friar Madison close the room down, the bishop said, "The bishop's Bible will be a great tribute to the late Pope Innocent III."

As they spoke, on the distant horizon loomed an evil presence that would disrupt their work, as Lord Gideon and his men rode toward the gates of the Synod of Clement. The Knights Templar would kill all who stood in the way of Pope Clement VII's new Latin Vulgate Bible, being translated by his monks at Saint Peter's Square. Nevertheless, from the ashes of the Synod of Clement would rise a group of monks who would keep the bishop's Bible close to their hearts.

These unorthodox missionary monks would swear to give their lives, if necessary, to protect the Bible they had translated. The men who arose from the ashes of the Synod of Clement would call themselves the Waldensians. They would carry the bishop's Bible, even if that made them sworn enemies of Pope Clement VII, who was murdering them only out of revenge.

Lord Gideon stood over the ruins of the burning Synod of Clement as the Knights Templar piled the bodies of the dead monks into a heap to be burned. The knights dragged Bishop Waldensian over to Lord Gideon.

One particular knight came to stand beside the bishop. The knight's armband wasn't like the others, and his armor was black with Spanish insignia. Known as the Black Knight of Spain, the young man's name was Louis El-Deon Ignatius. He was sent by Pope Clement VII to help midwife his order to destroy the former Pope Innocent III's namesake monastery.

Smirking, Lord Gideon said, "Bishop Waldensian, I hope that you have enjoyed your stay here."

"I have pity on your soul," the bishop said in sorrow.

"Then pity this," Gideon yelled. Then Ignatius pulled out his sword and beheaded the bishop, whose body fell to the ground. "Now, Ignatius," Gideon instructed him, "Takes that head to Pope Clement and tell him we will need his support in Jerusalem."

As the men rode off, a boy cradled the scrolls in his arms as he shivered in the bitter cold and wept. Making sure that the riders were far away, he ran into the forest. Buffeted by the forest branches and bitter wind, he fell several times. The last time he fell, he was picked up by Friar Madison.

"John, 'tis me. It's okay, lad," the friar said, holding the crying young boy. "Go now, John, and stayeth at home. Do not tell a soul what thou hast seen until tomorrow."

The followers of Bishop Waldensian at the Synod of Clement came to be known as the Waldensians, who brought about the birth of the Watchmen, sworn guardians of the word of God. These men would lay down their lives to protect the body of Christ, serve all ministers of the flock, and minister to all who were lost. It was for these reasons that I became a student of peace with them, and I now serve as their leader. At first I thought we met by accident, but I learned through their teachings that there are no accidents with God.

You know those days when the sun is shining, the birds are chirping, and kids are playing jump rope and hopscotch outside as you walk along a wet sidewalk, passing the mail carrier and other people in the neighborhood?

You would never think it was going to be a bad day. Furthermore you'd never think you'd be labeled a traitor and shot at dawn. Moreover, you develop the opinion that things couldn't get worse with age. You think your old bad back is a better weatherman than any highly specialized and degree-toting meteorologist. But then again, you begin to think instead of listening to some weatherman and staying in a comfy bed. You decide to go out the door, and you go to start your day.

First, you will have to find out that your bad back was right, and the weatherman Ted Edgar Allen Coppell of Philadelphia's channel six Action News was wrong about it being a gloriously sunny day. Instead you are stuck in the rain with a wet newspaper over your head. I gave you this rather long narrative of my life today, which could not have taken a turn for the worse if I were a blind man walking into a bar fight.

This particular rainy day I was doing my normal e-mailing, sending press releases to the various online news services There was the Time & Warner Chronicle, the *World Review*, the *Roma Press*, the *Vicar Journal*, the *Boulder Review of Nevada*, and the *Watchmen Chronicle*, which was yours truly favorite.

The young man beside me was Chuck Cummings, a local youngster in the Parr Boulevard Jail work release program, and I was at the Reno Palace territorial branch of the emperor's summer home. Chuck was an easygoing, hardworking daydreamer who wanted to be rich but had never been given breaks in life. Chuck was from Catoosa, Tennessee. However, there was in the local jail, and he was in the work release program from Reno, Nevada. He was arrested for assault and public drunkenness. He never talked about how long he would be in jail, and I never would ask.

"Chuck, hand me that last disk and we'll be done," I said.

"Do you want me to stay a little bit longer to clean up?" he asked.

"Sure, why not?" I said with a smile.

"We can send everything in one shot."

"Oh, don't forget to send the First Amendment disclaimer, Chuck."

As I was sending the last e-mails, the door suddenly flew open. Some palace guards burst in and hit Chuck over the head. "Hey, did you have to do that?" I yelled.

They slapped me and dragged me out of my office. The first guard yelled at me, "You rebel scum!" My face felt swollen, and as I looked in the mirrored walls of the hallway, I saw redness around my eye. My body was definitely feeling its age.

Everything was swirling around, and I felt like a swarm of bumblebees were buzzing around in my head. I couldn't see what had happened to Chuck. I found myself in a small room with one bright light, and I was thrown into a chair. A Secret Service agent came in and yelled at me, "Don't speak another word, you damn traitor."

I was slapped again, and then a rather tall figure came through the door. All I could see was his collar, which beamed like a bright, incandescent, sixty-watt bulb. From the shadows, the dark figure spoke slowly in a low voice. "So, Raymond, do you waive your right to counsel?" Then, smiling broadly, he stepped into the light. It was my nemesis, the Reverend Maximus Coven. Until then, I had not realized that he was gunning for me. "I hope you will decide to represent yourself," he said, still grinning.

The charges against me were not explained. Instead, I was picked up, like an old sack of potatoes, and carried by elevator up to the main floor of the palace. Then I heard the Reverend Maximus Coven say in a singing tone, "Ah, but I do have one head, my lord."

The door opened to the room, Natal looked up, smiling. When his eyes met mine, however, his amused grin turned to an angry frown of distrust and unbelief. When I first saw him, I had thought for a moment that my freedom was at the door. Surely this was some cruel joke, and everyone would jump out and yell, "Surprise!"

"Is this some cruel joke?" Natal asked. "You want me to fly into some rage or tyrant's fit, right?"

"This is your traitor, my lord," the Reverend Maximus said, calm and smirking.

Natal asked softly, "You mean he's?"

"The notorious Naba Zaphah, better known as the Watchman Tsaphah."

"Take him away, then," Natal screamed.

I was quickly dragged to the lower prison of the palace to await my trial.

CHAPTER 2

🏭🏭🏭

Dark Trials of Justice

January 14, 2058

This is my final journal entry, and I am glad to see this day. I can wait, for I am one hundred years old. Besides, I am praying that the trial will be quick, and I will be done with my life. I have seen many sorrows of life, even though my pain is more in soul than in body.

I wish that my heart could say the same. I am going to be led outside, instead of being put to sleep in my chamber as a hero should be. I will be shot, as if I were a real criminal. I will have etched my last message on my prison wall. How was I supposed to know that freedom of the press had been outlawed in the thirty-fourth edition of the New Constitution of R.O.ME.S?

I think back on the horrible day of my trial, which left a bitter taste in my mouth. I was looking out the window of my cell that day as the rain slapped on the outside glass. The tolling bell in the distance wasn't ringing the sound of liberties. Instead, it was ringing death to freedom of speech. I was going to be hanged for my crimes, and I began weeping for my old America.

"Mr. Moore, my client is in no way connected to the infamous Naba Zaphah of the Watchmen," my court-appointed lawyer proclaimed. "And I will further prove that he was framed by outside forces under the gaze of the emperor."

"The counsel for the state may give their rebuttal," Emperor Vicar said as all eyes turned to the Reverend Maximus Coven.

"Clearly we would not want to believe that Press Secretary Raymond Moore could possibly be a traitor," the Reverend Coven said piously. "But the imperial state will prove that he is the infamous Naba Zaphah. This former member of the Marine Corps is a trained sniper with a record 105 confirmed kills. He is fully capable of executing his plan to overthrow the former United States of America by attempting to assassinate the former president Richard Vicar."

"Objection," said my lawyer. "Those charges were dropped, and Mr. Moore was vindicated of those charges."

"Well, your excellence," the Reverend Coven said calmly, "the notorious Naba Zaphah was foiled in his attempt to overthrow the empire."

"The witness may take the stand," Emperor Vicar said.

As I took the stand, I could feel the hatred and shock from others in the courtroom as the emperor looked down at the computer screen. The Reverend Coven turned on the projector to show an excerpt from the online blog posts that I had sent the previous day.

"Press Secretary Moore, is this one of the many articles sent out from your terminal three days ago?"

"Why, yes," I said. "Yes, it is."

"Did you realize that article five, subparagraph two, says that all e-mail, electronic documents, and their attachments must have approval of the emperor before being sent out?" the Reverend Coven asked calmly. Pulling out a copy of some documents, he then yelled, "This was an illegal transcript."

"Nobody gave me the new memo," I said, staring at Natal as he turned to Maximus. The crowd giggled as he continued.

"Objection, your honor," the Reverend Coven said sharply.

"On what grounds?" my lawyer barked. "The defendant answered the question."

"Sustained. But a word of caution, counselors," Emperor Vicar warned. "I will not have this court drawn into a fight to the death. This trial has caused my country to weep a downpour of tears. Now proceed, but I am warning both of you."

I should have stayed in bed, because the anticipated rainy days of my life had turned into a thunderstorm. The storm was this trial, which was creating a flood. The Reverend Coven had me trapped in this kangaroo court.

"Let me read a portion from the defendant's infamous writing," the Reverend Coven said. "And I quote, 'The leviathan is none other than Emperor Caesar Apollyon Vicar.' End of quote."

"Objection," my lawyer exclaimed. "That piece of manuscript hasn't been reviewed by the defense."

"Now comes my question to you, Mr. Moore. Did you send this e-mail?" the Reverend Coven asked. "The evidence is there, so there is your guilt, Raymond Moore."

Even now, those words are echoing down here in this cold cell as I wait for my day of reckoning. I had been willing to march into work like a true titan. All I was trying to do, as press secretary for the New White House, was save the world.

I should inform you of some things before I start my story, because I have only six weeks until my execution by firing squad. The old ways of the Republic of America, and they themselves, will die by fire like wormwood, as I will. The deadly meteorite will hit the planet. The will of the new empire makes this world's waters blood red and bitter, as was predicted in the book of Revelation. Where will you hide when judgment come calling for liberty? No cave, missile silo, or Rocky Mountains fortress will hide you from the coming judgment when the troop comes to call. Still I secretly write this epic to call for poetic justice. I would call you to war if I was getting shot next year.

Emperor Natal A. Vicar, mighty warrior of R.O.M.E.S, became emperor of the Western Hemisphere, and we are no longer the great United States of America. We flushed our constitutional rights down the toilet for the sake of security a long time ago. It all began on September 11, 2001, when terrorists plowed those planes into the twin towers of New York City's World Trade Center.

Standing in front of a firing squad is not among the top ten things that would make my day. Even if I lost my job, house, and wife or girlfriend all on the same day that would never suck as much as standing in front of a firing squad just six weeks before my hundredth birthday.

I would prefer a surprise birthday party where the guests all jump out and yell, "Surprise!" At least that way I would die of a heart attack. Instead, I get six bullets to the shot to the head, leaving me with a goofy open-eyed and openmouthed look—a brainless stare.

If I had known that writing an article and pressing Enter would launch this plight of poetic justice … If I had known my day would end like this, I would have never left Orlando, Florida, to become the White House press secretary for the emperor. Those articles never won me a Pulitzer Prize, but they will be close to my heart when I die. Then my article will be with me when they bury me.

In His Service,
Raymond Moore

CHAPTER 3

🏭 🏭 🏭

The Poetic Justices

February 27, 2057

Dear Abba,

Ah, the pain of being ninety-nine and knowing I won't make it to one hundred. This burden can be a nightmare, bringing up all kinds of fears. A man on death row sits there in his cell and contemplates his misbehavior over the past hundred years of his life.

I was the victim of critically bad actions of judgements of making moral decisions of good and evil, whom I was graciously given the name to the Moore family by God. I can't blame my parents, because they were doing all they knew. Nor did I at first blame God for things I now think. My biological father, Richard Anthony Moore, had his demons of the night, but they seem to run in the family. When I was a little boy, I had nightmares of biblical proportions, and those nightmares would leave me in a cold sweat. The terrifying dream of my childhood would start like this …

In my dream, I saw a seven-headed dragon appear from out of the dark, shadowed clouds. The seven-headed beast was in colors of purple, sea green, and blue. He came to steal, kill, and destroy all that had the sign of death marked on their forehead.

The monster's scales of sea green and blue had armor-like plating to protect him. One of the monster's heads was wounded, which seemed very odd to me. Nevertheless, the seven-headed beast would continue to war against castles, nations, and villages, devouring all that he saw in mere minutes.

The beast would start its attack by luring the weak-minded into an impenetrable, dense, and forbidding miasma. The mysterious miasma would call to the people and enslave them. People would be lulled to come toward a box that had one eye, and the box would hypnotize them and cause them to slumber. Meanwhile, the beast with seven heads would roar and howl heartlessly, and it would blaspheme God Almighty, which made it grow even larger. Then the leviathan would continue its war over the nations, saying deceptively, "Peace, peace. I grant no conflict, but peace."

Meanwhile, I saw my real father trying to escape the seven-headed dragon. He was looking in the distance as a young virgin woman with blond hair and green eyes was coming up this hill. As she struggled up the hill, the beast, who was far away from her, saw that she was trying to escape the city, which it was attacking far below her.

The seven-headed leviathan would blast fire, and the inferno blew up near her and flames almost swallowed her whole. Moving out of the monster's way, the young woman skillfully avoided the flames, but failed in her struggle to escape her fate.

As the beautiful woman got closer to the top of the hill,

my father tried to save her. She called to him in panic, "Help me, please." As he reached to pull her up, my father saw a red mark on her forehead. The character looked like a Hebrew symbol for death. It was crimson red, as if it had been burned into her flesh by a branding iron.

The seven-headed beast was breathing fire, in addition to a fog of smoke and flames. The seven heads could not always be seen, because the leviathan would hide itself from sight in the foggy flames. Each head of the dragon had a name on its brow. The first head was named *Mayhem and Chaos*, Each breath from the seven-headed beast caused confusion, and the village people would walk around dazed and confused. Adding to the confusion, the first head of the beast began its attack.

The nation of humanity would never fight the beast, but instead would attack each other in civil war. The sea of humanity would begin in chaos and then burst into years of wars and rumors of wars, bringing confusion and fear into the nation, cities, and villages that destroyed the very fabric of any continent rising into growth and strength. The seven-headed leviathan would bring death, destruction, and doom.

Nevertheless, in the midst of the thick fog from which this great leviathan emerged, the figure of a man appeared. The man's eyes were black as the night, and his voice was like the voice of a dragon, but when he spoke, he roared like a lion.

Behind him appeared a crimson letter that read, "And I stood upon the sand of the sea, and saw a beast rise up out of the sea, having seven heads and ten horns, and upon his horns ten crowns, and upon his heads the name of blasphemy."

The man laughed as he turned away and went back into the fog. The woman and my father saw the leviathan come out of the fog again and charge toward them.

I screamed, "Father, run! It's behind you. Run."

Then Raymond A. Moore arose from this nightmare, screaming and crying like he had done many nights before. This was the first of many nightmares that I would have about my father. I would share and inherit his prophetic dreams as a boy growing into manhood.

* * *

On February 27, 1958, I was born in the city of the Hampton Roads area called Port Norfolk. We came to know this city through our transit travels. My family had moved there from the small, seafaring town of Swansboro, North Carolina. My mother, Carol Betty Smith, was a beautiful, fair-skinned, African-American woman. She was a haunting beauty who looked more Caucasian than African-American, with her black hair and hazel eyes.

This African-American woman, fair to gaze at, had captured the heart of my real daddy. Their families both moved up north to another old Southern seaport town. But before they all moved to Virginia, he asked Carol to be his bride and loving wife, and I was born six years later.

"Richard," Carol said, "I need to go have the baby."

"My Lord, girl, I got to get ready to for work," whined Richard. My dad was a worker in the Norfolk Naval shipyard, and he struggle all his life to keep a roof over our heads. But my mother couldn't have cared less, because it was my time to come into the world. "Richard, please call my sister Jenny. She'll get Mama."

"But baby …" he pleaded.

"Damn it, Richard Moore, the baby will be here before you leave for work."

"But …"

"But my ass, man. Call my mama."

As an African-American in the 1950s, Carol's only two options were to either rush to Norfolk General Hospital or give birth at home. Norfolk General was one hour away by ferryboat, because blacks did not ride the bus. In addition, you might as well have been born out back in an outhouse. An outhouse would have been cleaner than a ferryboat, in fact, since we would have had to ride in the back of the boat. So my mother's options were actually to take a taxicab to the hospital or give birth at our home in Port Norfolk. As far as a baby was concerned, whether I was black or white, I was coming into the world.

I was born at home. Mother sweated some thirteen hours to push me into the world, assisted by my grandma Amanda, who died before I was two years old. She and Aunt Jenny were the midwives who helped bring me into the world.

I was not born into a family of rich nobility, famous athletes, or motion picture stars who had a way out of poverty. Nor was I considered a "favorite son" by my father, because he had wanted his first child to be a girl for some reason. My mother loved me, however, and she gave me a name that means "beloved" in French.

"Girl, he sure is a cute little devil," Aunt Jenny said with a smile.

"Mama, what do you think I should call him?" my mom asked.

"Every child I had was only beloved by me," Grandma Amanda answered.

Then my grandma Amanda saw the baby-naming book and opened it to the letter "R". She gave it to my mother, who saw my name as if God had beamed a light on it. I was born Raymond Benjamin Moore. Benjamin was my great-grandpa's name.

I grew up in the slums of the little shipping towns of the Tidewater area of Virginia. Among drunken sailors, pool halls, whiskey, and the stench of cigars, I learned to fight just to stay alive, In Port Norfolk, I found myself at the crux of the melting pot of America, which was showing signs of coming to a boiling point.

"Raymond Benjamin Moore, come in the house for a minute," my mother yelled. I was playing outside with my friend. I ran to the house as fast as I could, because when children heard their full name, it either meant something was wrong or they were in trouble. I was stunned to see my daddy drinking a beer as he stared aimlessly out the front window. Daddy's duffel bag was packed. As tears streamed down her face, my mother folded her arms and looked away.

"Raymond, say goodbye to your daddy."

"Bye, Daddy," I said in a shy, heartbroken tone.

Without saying a word, Daddy gave me a hug. Then he picked up his duffel bag, got in a taxicab, and disappeared from my life for the rest of my childhood. My dad had joined the army, and he was to become one of many living casualties of the sixties and the Vietnam War. My mother had enough of him going off to fight some other man's war, so they got a divorce when I was six years old.

Later that year, Mom married a man named Keith "Woody" Douglas and our family was happy again. He added six more children my half-brother De'Angelo and five half-sisters, Imani, Tabitha, Phalisha, Samantha, Riana to our family, and he did what all good dads do, taking the boys crabbing and fishing. Keith—or Daddy Woody, as he told us kids to call him—was more of a dad than a stepfather, and I will always love him.

"Hey, boy," Daddy Woody said sharply, "watch your baby brother there."

My brother, De'Angelo, was leaning too far over the edge of the pier, looking at small guppies in the thick mud and oily waters of the Elizabeth River. I had to grab him quickly, before he fell in.

Both Daddy Woody and my brother looked at me, stunned that I got to him so speedily. As the oldest kid, I guarded over the younger and weaker kids. My step-brother and sisters didn't think life was bad, but I always watched for the worst-case situation.

"Doggone it, De'Angelo," I snapped. "You want to be crab food?"

"Hey, boy," Daddy Woody said sternly, "watch that mouth. If you can replace dog with damn, then don't say it at all. It's still cussing."

"Yes, Daddy Woody," I said humbly.

"You ever saw a dog making a damn?" Smirking, he looked at my mama.

I laughed as he grabbed me and hugged me. "Ha ha! No, sir."

We were crabbing on the bank of the Elizabeth River. Mama was having a picnic with my noisy sisters on the other side of the train tracks. My sisters and Mom had on matching jeans and white T-shirts that seem to glimmer in the sparkly river below as the girls ran and played in the muggy Virginia summer air. Daddy Woody said that Mama was wearing those pants that could make a lion whistle before he eats her up.

Little did we know that a two-legged lion was prowling nearby, watching us as we tried to enjoy our day. I noticed the man, who had a dark complexion and ashy skin—but it was his eyes that I remember most clearly. He looked at my mama like he was stalking her, and his eyes were cold and empty. Then he seemed to disappear like a phantom.

We had a good life, growing up in the sixties and seventies in the small town of Portsmouth. There was school on the weekdays, crabbing on Saturdays, and church on Sundays at Ebenezer Baptist Church on Effingham Street. The church mothers dressed in white dresses and fanning themselves to relieve their hot flashes, would be tapping their feet to the rhythm of the upright piano.

As the pastor raised his hands to bring us all to the saving feet of our Lord Jesus, neither those church members nor their neighbors in the little town of Port Norfolk had any idea of the danger that was coming to that seaport. The church elders and the Reverend David P. Williams never foresaw the evil that was coming to that little town.

Sitting here today, in the latter part of the twenty-first century, I *can still see that man's ashen face, black skin, and ghostly, charcoal-black eyes. He had murder on his mind, but I never understood why he came into our lives.*

As I await my execution, another meal of rotten flesh is slid under my cell door. I try to stomach what may come through the door next. However, this isn't the first time I have had to confront death in my little life.

In a most memorable way, my life changed on a hot and humid summer's night. I was the oldest of seven children. My sister Imani was three years younger than me. She had inherited my mother's hazel eyes and black hair, and she would play mother hen when Mama was away. When Imani smiled, it would light up the room. Tabitha, with her curly hair and chubby round face, was about eight. Long-legged Phalisha was about six, Samantha was five, and then there was Riana, was two years old. We ate dinner that night—the crabs we had caught—and then went to bed on that warm evening.

My younger brother, De'Angelo, was only four, and we were all sleeping in what was thought to be the sanctity of our home. My stepdad, a shipbuilder by trade, was a short round man, but he was as powerful and solid as the Plymouth Rock. Daddy Woody never had to fight in a war; my real dad and I were the family members who fought in a war.

The warm summer breeze gave no indication of the thick atmosphere of butchery that was coming to our home. At that moment, the aroma of death roamed through our house as noses and eyes were being rubbed and slumber overtook the whole house. As I was sleeping, I again had a nightmare, which started like this: The seven-headed leviathan rose from the sea. Its second head had the name Republicus engraved in bright, blood red scales. The being had the names of long-gone emperors engraved in smaller letters on its seven heads, and it was worse than any other beast in my nightmares. Intended for deception, the leviathan would be engulfed in its flames as a tornado-like cloud was blowing. The second head of the dragon, Republicus, could be seen striking lightning to scare others away. When he spied me looking at him, he turned to strike a deadly blow toward me …

Suddenly, I heard a shot ring out. I sat up in my bed and looked around. Then I tried to go back to sleep, but the excitement of having heard the shot kept me awake. So I sleepily dragged myself out of bed, rubbing the sleep out of my eyes. De'Angelo, my four-year-old brother wanted to tag along, because we shared the same bed.

"Hey," my brother whispered. I just waved my hand at him, but he called again just a little louder. "Hey, Raymond."

"Shh! You want to wake the girls up?" I whispered, gritting my teeth at De'Angelo as the girls tossed and turned in their beds. "Stay in bed, little brother."

Then I heard the thud of feet running over to me, so I just held out my hand and De'Angelo's warm hand grabbed mine. I did not want this burden, but for the moment I was chained to my loving, pain-in-the-butt brother. Our bare feet flapped on the cold floor of that two-bedroom home. In the country, our house might have looked like a shack, but in the heart of crime-infested Port Norfolk, it was a castle under siege.

Mama used the tactic of us sleeping together to keep me alert to my brother's bed-wetting problem. After he had a little bathroom break, I planned to flush the toilet and take him back to bed. But then I heard another sound, like a muffled scream, and something inside me said to move forward quietly.

As I was just about to call out to my mom, a spirit of fear in the air took my voice away. As if a samurai had cut out my tongue, I could not speak to call out to my mother. As I held tight to my brother's hand, I started walking through the open door into our parents' room, where I saw my mother being violated by a strange man.

As I watched him rape my mother, I saw that my dad's head had been blown apart. Blood and brains covered his pillow, and my beautiful mother's face and gown were covered in blood. She was no longer looking at her rapist, but she stared at me and my brother with eyes glazed over with pain and fear.

Standing there, in the cool of a summer breeze, I watched the rapist assaulting my mother. A chill ran down my spine like cold steel and numbed every nerve in my body. I couldn't speak or move, except to grip my brother's hand tighter. I stood there empty and dazed, with my bare feet on the cold, pine floorboards.

When the man saw me and our eyes met, I grasped

my brother's hand even tighter. I pulled De'Angelo behind me as the rapist paused to look at me and I stared back at him. De'Angelo and I were frozen in that horrific moment, and I could neither attack nor run away from the perverted hoodlum.

I stood still, watching his every move, and to this day I do not know what was in his evil heart. But I know what was in mine—revenge. Every fiber in my body wanted revenge, but I was too scared. So I just stood there and prayed, "Our father which art in heaven, hallowed be thy name. Thy kingdom come; thy will be done on earth as it is in heaven. Give us this day our daily bread; and forgive us our trespasses as we forgive those who trespass against us. Lead us not into temptation, but deliver us from evil ..." But then I couldn't finish the prayer. In my heart, I felt that nothing in that room was finished. I needed that nightmare to be over right then, so I just stared at the man and waited for him to go away.

I wanted to believe that it was just another bad nightmare. I wanted to wake up in my bed with my mother comforting me, as she had done so many times before. Even as a man, I was having a nightmare that was worse than any war in which I had ever fought. And those nightmares were my real reason for drinking. That man, that barbarian, was killing my dream and my family—and I wanted him dead.

The hope that he would disappear faded into the reality that the man standing before me was not a demon. He was alive, but he didn't kill me. He stood there watching me with empty, glassy eyes, and I just stared back at him.

He was holding one hand over my mother's mouth and pressing a pistol into her temple with his other hand. But then he let my mama go, got up off of her, and pulled up his pants, which had been down around his ankles.

To my surprise, he was still looking at me. The only sound I could hear was the sickening sound of the clasp of his belt hitting against the buckle, and I wanted something to quiet that sound.

There he stood, not moving a muscle, and I felt like a cobra hypnotizing a rat before I struck him. When I was a scout sniper in the Marines, looking through my scope to make a kill shot, my spotter said that the look on my face revealed my killer instinct. I felt the power of a killer rise up in me that night. I could have told that man to do anything, and he would have done as I commanded.

The rapist could have shot my baby brother and me down, but he paused just for a moment. In that moment of silence, I don't know whether he saw the error of his ways or he feared the murder that he saw in my eyes. Just then, my mother slipped out from under her rapist, crying, and tried to cover De'Angelo and me, although it was futile of her to try to protect us.

Time seemed to stand still. Judgment was at the door, however, like a lion ready to pounce. All at once, a loud bang startled me and I heard a thud. My mother jumped in nervous fear. As the gunshot cried out its judgment, I knew that I had been robbed of taking the rapist's life. I became angry at God, looking at the dead body of my stepdad's killer lying in a pool of blood.

As that shot rang out the window and through the neighborhood, dogs in the distance began barking, echoing a distress call for help. Bleeding and covered in the blood of my stepdad, my mother wept bitterly as my sisters raced in, crying and terrified from the noise of the gunshots and the sight of two dead men.

Lying on the cold floor in two pools of blood were my stepdaddy and his murderer, who had taken his own life. I didn't make a sound.

"It's okay, babies. Mama's okay," I heard my mama say as she stroked the back of my neck to comfort me.

"Mama, what's wrong with Daddy?" My sister Imani was crying.

Phalisha asked, "What's wrong with Daddy's head?"

"It's okay, babies. Mama's okay," Mama said as she quaked in nervous fear. "Daddy is just sleeping."

My mom held it together as best as she could as she watched them cover Keith. The police arrived and wrote their reports, mopping up what that leviathan of war had done. As my stepdad's body was being wheeled away, Mama realized that the man who had been her security for the past six years was leaving her.

The detective asked, "Mrs. Douglas, did you know the man?"

"No."

"How long had you and Mr. Douglas stayed with each other?"

"We've been married for six years," she said nervously. "Can I take my children to my sister now?"

I watch the second detective walk up, holding the gun. He was a fat slob of a man, and his suit looked like it had been slept in. "Here is the weapon that killed Mr. Douglas," he said. "It's a thirty-eight special. Did you know Todd Benton? He's a local boy down at Drake's Bar and Grill?"

"As I said, I had never seen the man who raped me and killed my husband."

"We need some more information about him, since he was found dead in your house."

"I said I don't know him. He raped me," Mama cried.

The mother I had known was gone. Her soul was being wheeled away, along with the man from whom she had gotten her strength. They both were gone from us forever. When my mother saw her lover and friend being lifted into an ambulance, she began sobbing. She had a nervous breakdown. And as I watched my mother crack like an egg, that image was permanently ingrained in my memory.

Our house, the neighborhood, and our lives were casualties of those beasts who needed to feed on the blood of their daily sacrifices in our country. My brother, sisters, and I were all taken away and put into the powerful system known as Child Protection and Enforcement. I haven't seen my brother or sisters since that night.

Nobody would have imagined that a member of the 1958 through 1998 generation would have my kind of experience. I bounced from foster home to foster home, gradually leaving behind any hope of ever being normal. Finally I landed in a home that at least resembled my home in Port Norfolk, although at first I didn't care to make it my home.

There were no exceptions to this rule when it came to being digested in the belly of the beast head called Famine. I was finally settled in a place that taught me some level of peace.

When I started living in Virginia Beach, about ten miles from the place of my birth, the principalities of bondage began sending their impish, demonic thugs of religion to me, and I began to wonder if God had a plan for my life. Demons of self-righteousness judged me by the natural laws of humanity. The spiritual laws of God tried to free me, but I was locked in by my own version of the two hundred and fifty commandments in the Levitical and sabbatical laws,[2] which were engraved on the tablets of my heart. They spoke their own condemnation to my heart and told me that I should have all of humankind.

I grew up in the late 1960s, which were like the year of

---

[2]   p. 84 (Tsaphah 2008).

the tornado with smoke and mirrors, and nobody cared that I was a casualty of the invisible war that was being fought. It was a time to go to parties with sex, drugs, and rock and roll in the heartland of these intercourse games of the spirit of whoredom. The queen of heaven,[3] a goddess called Columbia, captured those she could entrap in her covetous web.

The Tidewater area of Norfolk, Portsmouth, and Virginia Beach was a bustling mix of commerce and debauchery. The goddess Columbia would pull her marionette-like strings on the people as they danced off to work and play for the queen of heaven.

Children watched a huge television screen as a news anchorman began his report: "The nation symbolized by liberty, justice, and the Statue of Liberty is now becoming, in the seventies, the world of which Dr. Billy Graham spoke when he said, 'Christmas, instead of a celebration of the Savior's birth, has become only a feasted debauchery of shallow hearts at work.' In this nation, in this time of inflation, we care more about produce and product. Today the Dow Jones Index rose fifty points and the unemployment rate is twenty-five percent. For ABC News, this is Ted Koppel."

The channel on the big, thirty-inch screen changed again. "Christmas is now a worship of the goddess of Columbia. As she pulls humanity's strings, people spend their hard-earned money on the toys that she gave them, except that the toys and money were given for the worship and tributes. Humanity is worshipping the dragon of the Chinese prophet, who has become a resident in its cave, waiting for the captives. They will be devoured, as if they

---

[3]   Jeremiah 44:17.

were raspberry-filled cakes that were put in the nation's breadbasket.

"Now, the queen of heaven is beautiful, but we should not be worshipping her. No, the savior is the reason for the Christmas season. Well, my time is up. Until next week, this is the Reverend E. B. Hill saying, 'Goodbye and Merry Christmas.'"

"Can we please watch *Frosty the Snowman*?" a round-faced girl asked with a sigh.

"Fine. You take the remote and find it," the little boy replied.

"That is enough fighting over the remote. Give it to Raymond. He knows where it is," remarked Miss Smith, the foster caretaker. Miss Smith was the person who put meaning into my life, and she would have taught me about why I did what came naturally.

Miss Smith once told me a truth I will never forget. "A smile wouldn't break that face of yours," she said.

I was coming home from school one day. The birds were chirping a song of spring, the bees were buzzing around the red, white, and yellow rosebushes, and the smell of honeysuckle perfumed the air. The only problem with this after-school picture was that I was not singing any songs toward the heavens. It was not that I did not have a good singing voice. I was a very good singer in the Ebenezer Baptist Church junior boys choir, and I had a gift for the piano when I was in Port Norfolk.

However, no words, song, nor laughter came out of my lips for the simple reason that I was mad at God. Nobody at the funeral—none of my aunts or uncles—had been able to successfully answer my questions about why my parents had had to suffer the way they did. This question did not come up all at once, but my anger, pain, and deep sadness built up over a period of months and turned into a desire for revenge.

Michael Tsaphah

One day I was in my mother's kitchen, still waiting for the Commonwealth of Virginia's Child Protection Agency—of which my siblings and I were wards—to finish our case. Aunt Jenny was my favorite person in the whole world, because she reminded me more of my mom than any of my other relatives. She was cooking my favorite dish of collard greens, yams, turkey, and stuffing. It was like Sunday dinner on a Saturday.

I had to know the truth about why God had made my good parents suffer. As an eleven-year-old child, I had to get out my questions and speak what was on my mind. The question would cause me to explode if I didn't ask it. However, when I asked my aunt Jenny, she rejected my question and shut me down. Moreover, I did not receive my answers to this truth, which were woven in the confusion of my scared consciousness. That puzzle would later be unraveled by the Watchmen and God, but I had to suffer with my aunt's words for many years to come. African-Americans walk in the unsure footing of separation of taboos and traditions.

And yet these separations have foreboding taboos. Men, women, and children traditionally walk in these unspoken mysteries. Sadly, we must walk in miry clay with our unanswered questions. As it is said, "Misery loves company, and we are a happy, miserable lot, as a race of people." Mine was the one question that we should avoid asking. The question I asked my aunt about God and his authority was one of those taboos from which drunken men struggle to stay away.

"Auntie Jenny?" I said.

I heard her humming one of those old field spirituals, "Take Me Back." Her humming came from the back of her diaphragm, and it was pushed out of her throat so strongly that you knew she believed every word she was humming.

Aunt Jenny might have been made of "sugar and spice and everything nice" when she was a little girl, but as an adult, she could leave you thinking that she was nothing but just spice.

"Yes, baby?" She was cutting up the onions for the collards.

"Why did God kill my mom and dad?" I asked innocently.

She slammed down the butcher knife with a snap of the blade on the counter. Her face started to swell up and get darker, and she looked like she was about to blow. Aunt Jenny was getting mad at her little Ray-Ray, and the blood vessels in her head looked like they were going to pop out. The devoted churchwoman was about to explode, and the aftershock would vaporize my hope of ever finding out the truth.

"Where did you get that garbage from, and who made you ask such a question? Boy, get out of my sight before I lose my religion."

As I slumped out of the kitchen, I could hear her muttering and cussing under her breath, and I was thinking about the question more and more. Nevertheless, the answer she gave me had only made my aunt mad, and it got me madder than hell at God, more and more. I didn't know whom to turn to, because I couldn't trust anyone with that particular question ever again.

In a similar kitchen setting at Miss Barbara Smith's foster home, love was the only force that could guide me to stay and behave. My aunt Jenny meant well, but so does a sump hole in the ground from an outhouse until you fall into it. It may give you a warm feeling, but the smell is the killer.

The smell of Aunt Jenny's solution to my problem hurt me and made me not want to talk. I wasn't talking anymore because of the anger building up inside of me, but Miss

Smith never pressured me to talk. However, there were times she would gently say some funny thing to get me to smile. "Raymond, a smile only means that you are laughing on the inside," Miss Smith said, smiling as she continued cooking. "So you just keep smiling. After a while, a giggle will slip out, turn into a laugh, and then that laugh will turn into a pure joy fest."

After that, I didn't want to laugh. So I started talking again, and I have been that way ever since. However, Miss Smith always worked on me, and she harvested the seeds she planted. One day, in the quietness of her garden, I gave my heart over to God, even though I didn't want to laugh. A whirlwind of hurt overcame my heart that day, and the seed of peace was planted in my garden by a gray-haired woman named Miss Smith.

The way I saw it, if you're busy talking, you won't laugh at all, so I became a talker. Talking a lot was the reason I became a Marine. It helped me to tell people the truth about themselves, or to tell a joke without even cracking a smile. Having a painful soul hemorrhaging inside of me, with the throbbing memory of dead parents and a mother in the crazy house, wasn't funny to me.

These facts in my life never allowed me to laugh my sorrows away, and they kept everybody around me busy trying to find reasons to get away from me. However, I came to know the name of my pain in later years to come. I was a broken child on the inside, hidden from view by the hard shell of a warrior.

That hard shell allowed me to have girlfriends while I was in high school, but I never could keep them because I had what everybody called an attitude. Wendy Jones was a soft-spoken girl with hazel eyes and silky brown hair that gave her cream-colored complexion a glow that made you want to hold her forever. We made love one Saturday under a blanket in a field behind a Chesapeake dairy farm.

Every Saturday, I would park my car miles away and we would walk to that farm. I wanted Wendy and she wanted me, too, as the breeze blew the smell of wildflowers and fresh-cut grass. We played in the straw in her uncle's back forty, which gave me a reason to start talking about life. Wendy lay there baring her soul, and I felt on the inside a parental comfort when talking to Wendy. She gave me love and an ear to listen.

"No matter how I tried to look at things, whether good or bad," I told her, "it was always God's fault."

"You take life too seriously sometimes, Ray," Wendy responded. "Everything can't be God's fault."

"Well, who can you blame?"

"The truth always comes out," she said. "Only twenty-five percent of what we do, whether right or wrong, is our fault, but we look to blame everything on someone else."

When she said that I tried to blame someone other than myself, it got me to wondering who God was. How could I sit in my carnal flesh, playing a role in this theatrical production of life, and judge the creator of the universe?

The more I opened myself to women in my life, the more I believed that each woman would give me what I needed and wanted, without the addition of a family that could be taken away. Wendy was one of many women who would try to fill that void.

One time when I was younger, I became a disruptive class clown at school, and I was labeled a troublemaker from that point on. I was running around and around a boy, Tommy Morgan, who was rolling around on the ground and holding his stomach. I would yell, at the top of my lungs, "Is God dead?" When Tommy would reply, "No, he still alive," I would kick him in his fat belly.

"Is God dead?" I repeated louder, running in a circle around him.

And Tommy answered, "No, he still alive."

So I kicked him again in his fat belly.

"Ray, stop it!" Wendy yelled, running up to me. Then she turned away in anger.

It was against student policy to talk about God in public, but that was not what got me into trouble. The real reason was that I kicked Tommy Morgan in the stomach to keep him from saying that God was dead. That's what got me sent to the principal's office. As I sat there waiting for Miss Smith to come through the door, I knew she would express to me her disappointment. Standing there at the threshold, disappointment would begin to appear on that old wrinkled face when she came to rescue her wayward son.

"Raymond, my boy, you've got a lot to learn about life," she said. That was all she had to say as she drove me home. I guess that is why I am so inclined to have women with depth and wisdom in my life.

I missed my mother, who was a very kind and wise woman, and I looked for those same qualities in a lover. I didn't want a barefoot, pregnant housekeeper for a wife. After all, having a wife had only brought drama into my stepdad's life. I would quickly grow up and stop being the class preacher or disruptor when I got to high school, where it wasn't cool to be the class clown. I was an actor on this stage, willing to take responsibility for only 25 percent of my mistakes, but God has to take all the blame for my poor choices. I would be a fool if I tried that in real life, but will the emperor who has condemned me to death see the error of what he has done? The answer to that question will be brought to light eventually, no matter what my fate.

I remember someone once asking me a question that

would have stumped even the slickest city lawyer. President Richard Charles Vicar II, the twin brother of Rebecca Carolina Vicar, was president of the United States of America at the time, and I was given the task of caring for Natal, his nephew. The only son of Rebecca Carolina Vicar, the orphaned boy was full of questions, much like any young child. And like most little boys. Natal had a small problem with lying to his auntie.

The item of suspicion was a two-thousand-dollar Ming lamp, which was broken in the sitting room of the common area of the White House. Natal had broken it while playing ball in the house. The full story was told to me, so I was well aware that he was the guilty party. First Lady Ann Thelma Vicar was a tall, astringent woman of refinement. In her careful investigation of the crime, Mrs. Vicar talked with White House staff members, as a spider traps its prey, and then she went right to the only person who could have done the deed.

"Natal, how did this lamp get broken?" she asked.

Natal snapped back at her, "Why is it I get blamed for some lamp I didn't break?"

"Don't you stand there and lie to me, young man," First Lady Vicar yelled back, waggling her long slider finger. "I know you did it, because I asked the upstairs servants."

"Well, I didn't break it," he said, pouting. "They might as well lie to you about the lamp because of the way you are acting toward me."

"Don't you get smart with me, mister," she shouted. "A liar is good for nothing but …"

"But what?" he asked. "Where do liars go?"

She said, scoffing, "Ha, smarty-pants, that is for me to know and for you to find out."

Then she walked off in a storm as Natal thought about

what she had said. Later I was making him a peanut butter and jelly sandwich, which has been my all-time favorite since I was a kid. I was unaware of what had happened between those two, but I became the first lady's religious voice and helper in solving Natal's problem.

"Uncle Raymond," he said in that high-pitched soprano voice of his, "where do liars go?" He began swinging his legs under the chair and busily picking at his sandwich. I stalled for a minute, because I didn't have an answer to that question. I knew where thieves, murderers, and rapists went—to prison. Then they got out of prison on good behavior, but some repeated the same offense.

"Well, get your uncle's Bible from his study and let's see what it says," I said.

That gave me a few minutes to think while Natal ran from the table to get the Bible that his uncle Richard read from time to time. He came back with the Bible—an old, worn, gold-leaf Bible that later sat on a stand in the glass case in the Oval Office. It was the same Bible with which his uncle took the oath of office. Turning the pages very carefully, I went to the only scripture I knew that talked about lying, and I set it down in front of him.

"Now you read it," I said. "What does it say?"

I knew I had to be careful with this impressionable boy, since I really didn't know the answer to his question. Because of that, I opened the Bible, a book that I had not looked at for years, since I was at Miss Smith's foster home. Ever since I was a kid, it had been the only book that I knew would give the truth. In addition, the Bible couldn't care less if you beat it, burned it, or threw it across the river, never caring if you ever picked it up again.

I opened the Bible, the tool I would use to speak to this young boy. As I thumbed through the pages, I turned to the book of Revelation, chapter twenty-one, verse eight. He read the scripture aloud, slowly and with the intensity of a lion stalking his prey.

"'And to the fearful, and unbelieving, and abominable, and murderers, and whoremongers, and sorcerers, and idolaters ...'" He paused and asked, "What's an idolater?"

"That's like when your uncle tells your aunt that he's having a meeting with the chief of staff, when he's really staying home to worship with the Washington Redskins and watch them play football, instead of going to church, baby," I responded in a sarcastic tone. "How he loves those Redskins. Keep reading, Natal."

Then Natal asked, "But don't you love the Atlanta Falcons?"

"Yeah, but you don't see me missing church, do you? Now keep reading, smarty. Boy, you're going to make one hell of lawyer one day."

"'And all the liars, their part [is] in the lake that is burning with fire and brimstone, which is a second death.[4]'" Natal stopped reading as the word liar jumped out on the page. Then he began to think and asked softly, *"All liars."* So Uncle Raymond, is Uncle Richard not only an idolater, but a liar too?"

"And if you don't quit lying to your auntie, you and your uncle will go to a lake of fire, a flaming lake," I said. Smirking, I turned away from him. However, I noticed out of the corner of my eye that his legs stopped mid-swing. As he took another bite of his sandwich, I asked him, "That doesn't sound like a place you'd want to go for a vacation with the relatives, huh?"

"No," Natal said softly. He gulped down his last bite

---

4   Young's Bible Translation New Testament 1863 Version, translated by Robert Young.

of sandwich and then looked at me, dumbfounded but with a fearful look on his face. The look on his face was, as MasterCard puts it, priceless. The scripture that he read might not have cured him of lying, but that little boy thought about it for a good while that day.

My story might give us all something to think about, especially how one word can change our lives and destiny. I can truly say that I loved that little boy deeply. I mentored him, whether for better or worse, into the man he is today, through all of the things we talked about to each other when he was a little boy. I will never regret that, no matter how ugly my future may turn out. It has been my journey home, finding rest for my soul in being a Marine.

CHAPTER 4

🔭🔭🔭

My Journey Home

April 22, 2057

Dear Abba,

The stories of my conviction of being a guardian of the truth of the Watchman and of my infancy have been told. Now the tale of my journey to becoming a soldier must be told from its beginning. Being a scout sniper in the United States Marines Corps turned me into a warrior. However, God had other plans for my life, which is how I found myself in this cardboard box. Even as I came to be the man of honor that I am now, so this was my training added with the seven elders of the Watchmen.

    I was in the Marines Corps for some twenty-five years of my life, which helped point me in the direction of this walk of faith. I saw a light from which I couldn't turn away, that of becoming the Watchman of the City in North America. And although it was as foggy and unclear as the San Francisco harbor, I marched onward toward that mark.

Michael Tsaphah

I came to disciple the son of perdition when he was at a young age, and my journey was with a man who came to define himself as an infamous rebel with a cause. Knowing nothing at all about who Christ my savior was, or who I was at that time, led me down a twisted and dark path.

Constantly he was tested by my love of both the creator and his creation as I danced with the devil's delicacy, in his indecisive change of heart. However, he made his run after the lunar paradises of jewel. The son of perdition was like the false illuminations of power, money, and sex that are the heart of all the great leaders of this world.

Moreover, finding myself in a whirlwind of pain, afterward I played the concerto of the fool's dance with the prince of Hades, which bounced me from one crumbling pillar to another, nearly dropping me to melt in the lava pit of agony. The first time, I was homeless and at the beginning of my journey.

I began walking down the dimly lit alleys of being a soldier, homeless, and an assassin long before I even knew what homelessness was. In my fragile, orphan's mind, I didn't think of myself as destitute. Nonetheless, I was waiting on my mother to get better and marry another daddy, but she never did come back.

I was only eight years old. In my mind, my unpacking was temporary, because I expected to eventually rejoin my mother, brother, and sisters. But the truth was that I was to be proven to do Abba's will. Although he was not the cause of my parents' deaths, he allowed it to happen because of the sinful and evil world in which I was living. That truth drove me to this path of being a warrior of righteousness.

I was born Raymond Benjamin Moore, and many times in my hometown of Port Norfolk, Virginia, the truth of this ugly world was all around me. But it was the death of my parents that hit me dead in the face.

However, my life as a child wasn't bad in the beginning. I can remember lying in the front yard most of the day until the nine o'clock gun would sound off from the Norfolk naval shipyard. For me the early sixties were not a worrisome time.

The war in Southeast Asia was just starting, young lions roared at God. The seeds of rebellion were sprouting new growth among the flower children.

Meanwhile, on August 28, 1963, a Baptist preacher named Dr. Martin Luther King Jr. stood at the foot of the Lincoln Memorial and delivered his "I Have a Dream" speech to the world. And our nation grieved the loss of our beloved President John Fitzgerald Kennedy on November 22, 1963. However, I was unaware of all of these historical events, since I was very young.

My life was all about watching ants form lines to their anthills, catching and freeing lightning bugs from my mother's mason jars, and eating the bowls full of cherries that life had to offer. As I watched the clouds roll by like little puffs of whipped cream, I could do no wrong. In those days, I swung by like Batman, the caped crusader, and fought imaginary enemies alongside the Green Hornet and Kato.

The world I lived in back then gave me hope that life would never end. But that was then, and this is now. I am stuck like chuck in this body as a Marine. Lance Corporal Raymond Moore was in a foxhole, nervously waiting for Charlie to cross the Thailand border for the fifth time in the year of our Lord 1984.

No, that was not the Vietnam War. I was much too young to fight in that era. This was a coup d'état that the Vietnamese government attempted to launch against the Thailand monarchy, which they did every year.

In the eighties, someone named Prince made the movie Purple Rain, *and Michael Jackson was crowned the new king of pop. I was a Cold War veteran in the force recon company, pulling sniper duty on a hill far away from home. One day when I am old and gray, I will write my memoir, but for now that is a letter to my first wife.*

While I am soaked to the bone in this bloodsucking leech-infested mud hole, I'm praying we never see Charlie. Because I guess if I die, no one will ever read the tale I have written in this letter home. I joined with my comrades-in-arms, veterans of countless other wars before me, while the Thai marines would have to ward off this take-over attempt by the Vietnam government. Nevertheless, we are trying to lure the haughty Vietnamese into an ambush, because we are the same weak, imperialistic, capitalistic Americans of the sixties ...

"I never should've rebelled against the call of God in my life," I said in a whining voice.

"Oh, for crying out loud, Moore," Lance Corporal Graham snapped back, "you big-ass, cammy-draped baby. 'Whayah!'

As I waved off the only spotter who could talk that way to me, I knew better than to preach at him about who I was in Christ. Even though I was raised in that foster home, my local church in Norfolk taught me, along with Miss Smith. As a teen, I became very outspoken and rebellious. As I began to grow into a man, I didn't need a gang. My stepfather was dead, my real father was walking around like he was dead, and I was turning into a lone thug.

Because of the death all around me, I could only define death as being separated from everyone whom you loved and everyone who loved you. All the bereavement in my life added one more pain that would haunt me.

Years later, my mom committed suicide in the mental hospital. The winds of fate kept me safe from that news, or I would have joined her while I lived in Miss Smith's foster home. I found out this grim news when I was graduating boot camp on Paris Island. By then, however, I was a Marine, so I forced myself to be battle hardened and never cry for her loss.

A man came running down the center of a single squad bay toward me. He was dressed in a short-sleeved shirt and green slacks, and he was wearing a drill instructor's hat with Marine Corps insignia, which is an eagle, globe, and anchor. "Moore," he yelled, "are you eyeballing me, maggot?"

"No, sir," I yelled.

"Well, ladies, since Maggot Moore likes to diddly-bop back on the block," the drill instructor yelled, "we are gonna climb."

"Yes, sir," the platoon yelled in unison.

"Get down and give me fifty," ordered the drill instructor.

I missed being in the foster home because at least Miss Smith never made me do push-ups when I messed up. A member of the local Assembly of God church in Virginia Beach called the Rock Church, Miss Smith was fair about allowing me to go to Ebenezer Baptist Church in Portsmouth, because a van would come to the house and pick me up.

The Reverend David P. Williams never trusted wild-eyed boys like me. Nevertheless, the women of the church took the place of my lost mother. Being nursed by those mothers of the church helped me maintain my mental health.

"Mother, that boy is a train wreck waiting to happen," the Reverend Williams whispered to Mother Grace, who was pouring punch at the youth social. "He got too much fire in him."

"I seem to remember the same thing was said about you as a youngster," Mother Grace responded quickly. One time when I was home on leave, Miss Smith told me that the Reverend Williams had been charged with having sex with an underage teenage girl in the church, and that three days later he went into his office and blew his brains out.

I fought for neither God nor country. Every time I was put in a foxhole in a foreign land, I fought so that I could live to see another day. This philosophy didn't always ring true in my brain, until I was drawn like a prizefighter into every great and small war in which this country got involved between 1982 and 2005. For the sake of amusement, I'll say that they were all fought in the name of freedom.

All the same, at least I enjoyed the opportunity to see the world. And my imperial republic could relax, knowing that countless volunteer pawns, such as me, were fighting for their freedom. Because of us, the elusive upper-middle-class masses could eat, drink, and play their Xbox games. I stand here, like a sitting duck, with the muzzle of my rifle pointed at an embankment. Meanwhile, down below me are Bravo Company and Recon Platoon with the Thailand Royal Marines setting up an ambush to draw the Vietnamese into our little trap.

They were stringing thousands of feet of wire, along with fake and real claymore mines with flares, which would lead them to Lance Corporal Graham and me. We were pulling double duty as forward observation and sniper's watch. We were dressed in camouflage, known as a ghillie suit, which is netting with burlap and camouflaged rubber leafing on it to help the wearer blend into the background. I couldn't see anything except what was in front of me because of the damn heavy rain. Lance Corporal Graham saw and heard everything, but I couldn't see my hand before my face because of the downpour.

The ideas was for Lance Corporal Graham and me to draw as many Vietnamese officers and soldiers to us as possible and then kill them. Rather than allowing them to go to Bangkok, they would stay here in Pattii Beach and die in our ambush.

Lance Corporal Graham was a funny character from a Montana reservation, and a descendant of Sitting Bull. I felt very comfortable with him as my spotter and scout. We had been partners for some two and a half years since we got out of boot camp together. Our platoon sergeant said that Graham and I were a mismatch, because I was raised in Port Norfolk, a naval town, and Graham grew up on an Indian reservation. But our differences seemed to make us the perfect match to watch each other's back.

Lance Corporal Graham was a community college dropout who had decided to see the world from the end of a rifle instead of a textbook. Graham's parents had taught him to hunt, track, and listen to the wisdom of his spiritual guides, which wasn't typical, because many Native American families suffered from drug and alcohol abuse. But his parents chose to teach him to follow the ways of his ancestors and stay away from trouble. Graham joined the young buck's tribal youth, and then the leading tribal council made him an honorary member. He was a tribal police officer while also attending community college, until he shot and killed the chief's son-in-law for selling drugs.

Meanwhile I was learning how to stay alive on the gang-infested streets of Port Norfolk and Virginia Beach. We made the perfect team. I was no lone ranger, however, and Tonto was a bum compared with Graham.

"What the hell do you mean, 'Whayah'? I ain't a crybaby."

"You been bitching like this since boot camp," Graham said, laughing.

"You should know. I would have to dig in the rose garden for the shit you pulled."

"It made you the bad-ass, locked-and-cocked Marine you are today," Graham said.

Sergeant Kensington barked from his foxhole, "If you

damn ladies are done bitching at each other, can you keep an eye on the gooks coming soon?"

The sweltering night air was suffocating as the sweat dripped off my nose, and the mosquitoes were bombarding more than the Vietnamese that night. My heart was racing, up in my throat, in anticipation of what was to come. Meanwhile Graham had his ears open for the sounds of the enemy's advancement. I could hear nothing but his breathing, which was very shallow. The night was still as a graveyard with death riding above us. Graham took first watch, and I, of course, fell asleep.

When the Royal Thai Marines gave us the signal, by flare, we had only a few seconds to shoot down the enemy. My job was to kill the staff officers at the Vietnamese command post, at a distance of a thousand yards. There were five hundred Vietnamese soldiers against one hundred and fifty U.S. Marines and two hundred Royal Thai Marines, who were there to ambush the Vietnamese as they crossed the border. I was fifteen hundred yards away from the border where Bravo Company and Third Recon Platoon were based.

The company commander, along with Lieutenant Manson and Gunny Featherson, put Bravo Company and Third Recon Platoon in foxholes five hundred yards away from us. Meanwhile, the Thai Marines were enveloped in the jungle along the border, silently waiting, because the Vietnamese Army had set up surprises with trip wires of claymores and flares. A mile away from the border was the First Thai Marine artillery regiment. They had fire support with three 105-mm howitzers in tow and waiting in the rear echelon, one thousand yards out from Bravo Company and Third Recon Platoon. However, time was creeping by for Graham and me as it started to rain lightly.

As we tried to maintain the visual of the night watch,

I could hear no movement from the Vietnamese. Finally, I drifted off to dream under the thousands of stars in the sky ...

The leviathan called on me for another nightmare. Republicus was spawned from the womb of the pit of rebellion, which was a violet sea of the abyss. It had the flaming face of trillions of tormented souls. This was my childhood nightmare, come to visit me again.

I saw the beast come from the sea of humanity and disappear into a boiling melting pot of the sea of the huddled masses. Republicus was not seen until a thousand years later, when the course of history was complete.

The United States was exploding into a nuclear blaze, and the beast emerged from the lava lake like a Phoenix reborn. Now that this hideous beast had appeared, it would only turn back the furious dragon slayer who was screeching and calling for our doom.

One of the seven heads of the leviathan, which looked like a skull, was called Scarcity. This head would bring down the strongest of men in repulsive sickness and disease. It had a swarm of flies and maggot-filled sores around its mouth and nose, which dripped puss and slimy acid on the babies and young children of the United States. The acid would kill all the firstborn, whether rich or poor.

Screams were heard coming from the cities, towns, and villages as people suffered from the wrath of war and wept for the loosed unborn. Every time the beast raged in war, these two heads would feast most heavily on the carcasses of the unborn and the dead. The sight of this beast would make any person who called for help or crossed the threshold of the cloud have to pay tribute, in response to the dragon's call for charity.

"Give more. Give more," the dragon from the cloud would call.

The dragon would call the poor of the world into this cloud. And as the people would come back out, chains of poverty would be attached to them by the spirit of bondage. Those victims of famine would drag the long chains of addiction around, like slaves, until they died. Then the tail of the beast would crush their bones into powder ...

Then suddenly I awoke to hear a branch break—or maybe it was Graham slapping my head. Suddenly, sixteen of them came out of the brush and straight at us with muzzles blazing. Grahams pointed his M-16A2, which had an attached M-203 grenade launcher, and sprayed a small burst into the squad of Vietnamese. He also fired from his grenade launcher two concussion grenades and one smoke grenade, which forced the charging squad of Vietnamese to move up the hole we gave them into our kill zone.

One bullet whistled by and grazed my ear, which burned like a flesh wound. Another round hit Graham's shoulder and then his rifle. As my own rifle jammed, I grabbed my pistol and began shooting frantically, but the firefight got too hot and heavy. Then another bullet shot the pistol out of my hand, jamming it and making it useless. Doing a belly roll, I grabbed the muzzle of an AK-47 from one of the dead Vietnamese. Meanwhile Graham used his M-203 grenade launcher to chuck a grenade between two Vietnamese men, blasting them apart. Body parts and blood sprayed my face. As Graham continued to pitch grenades and smoke at them, I quickly turned and fired, hitting two or three more Vietnamese soldiers who fell just in front of me.

Then before I could get out of the way, the Thai Royal Marines and the Marines from Charlie Company shot crossfire at the rest of the Vietnamese troops. When the smoke cleared, five hundred of Vietnam's finest soldiers lay dead, plus the sixteen that Graham and I had wasted. When

I looked at Graham, I saw that he was bleeding from his shoulder.

"Looks like we got them," Graham said, shaking but laughing. "Yeah, but my damn shoulder hurts."

"Okay, hero, before you go charging up that hill, let me patch you up," I said.

As I leaned over to grab a thick bandage from my first aid kit to patch up Lance Corporal Graham, we faded back into the Cold War. One day at Camp Lejeune, as I watched some television, I saw the result of the little part that I did in Thailand to help stop the coup d'état by the Vietnamese government, which we helped the Thai monarchy beat back that day. The coup d'état of Thailand and the bringing down of the Berlin Wall were many miles and years apart. I didn't get a Congressional Medal of Honor for bravery that time, but Graham and I did receive our first Purple Hearts. Sometimes when I was sleeping on the streets of Orlando and suffering from my nightmares, I'd ask myself whether it had all been worth it.

I realized that the fall of the Berlin Wall was a sign of freedom, but as the years passed, I started asking myself whose freedom we were protecting. One cloudy day—August 12, 1990—the first Persian Gulf War was over except for the mopping up, which was usually left to the army. However, Charlie Company 2/6 and I were left to finish engaging Saddam Hussein's Republican Guard, but instead we found ourselves in an all-night sandstorm.

Finally the storm lifted the veil from the approaching millions of miles of wasteland, with the Second Marine Division's two sixes, Alpha and Bravo Companies, in the lead, followed by Second Force Recon Platoon in the rear. As dawn barely cracked the sky, we began moving up toward our flank while the other companies swept those areas we missed. They were going to meet us at a technical land zone foxtrot at 0900 hours.

We appeared like scorpions out of the cool sands of the Kuwaiti desert. As we moved left of the other companies, we slowly advanced on a bunker in front of us. I was then a combat marine staff sergeant. Gone was the innocent child, turned into someone whom Miss Smith wouldn't have even recognized. Now a little more tanned—or more accurately, slightly red and peeling from the hot desert—I stepped forward to another battlefront to watch over my men as a platoon sergeant.

Thinking we would advance on a sleeping enemy, or maybe piss off one ready to fight, we had two of our riflemen advance forward. However, as we approached the bunker with caution, we saw that it was empty.

You might think we would have been disappointed, but I wasn't. It would be an easy day, with no dead bodies to mourn over or wounded to tend. Nevertheless, the bunker didn't sit right with me and I was very leery about going near it. Just a couple of weeks earlier, Bravo Company had tripped a booby trap in a bunker that had killed three men and wounded five.

I sent in two of my men from my second fire team to investigate the bunker. Assault Rifleman Lance Corporal Peterson and Rifleman Private First Class Singleton were in the second fire team, which was piloted by Corporal Gates, a blond-haired, blue-eyed Marine who used kindness to keep his men in order. Corporal Gates whispered, "Peterson, what is it?" Later, as they walked back from the bunker, they motioned for us to go over and talk with them.

"We noticed that there were barrels," Lance Corporal Peterson said. He drank some water and then passed the canteen to Private Singleton.

"They have some kind of foreign writing on them," Singleton said, returning the canteen to Peterson.

I told them, "Okay, go back to the corpsman and get more water and chow while we find out what's the real deal." Later, when I got the all clear from the bunker, I went inside and noticed that two of the barrel tags had German and French writing on them.

"You two get back to your fire team," I said sternly. "Corporal Lewis, call HQ and tell Captain Morgan or Lieutenant Summers that we might have a live one here." I moved away from the bunker several feet, and then yelled to another Marine, "Corporal Gates!"

"Yes, Sarge?" answered Corporal Gates.

"Tell everybody else to stand fast. I don't want anyone playing in that bunker."

Corporal Graham came up behind me and asked, "How far of a perimeter do we make around this bunker?"

"Twenty—no, make it fifty feet," I said. "But get all the men watered down first."

We radioed back to headquarters that the bunker was abandoned and filled with strange barrels marked in German, Russian, and French. It was hard to make out the words, because the barrels were rusty. Apparently they had been in the bunker for a long time, and the desert conditions had worn down the markings.

As Corporal Lewis gave me the radio, I put out the cigarette that I had just lit and cleared my voice to speak. Being a hard-core smoker, I had never thought that I would be one to put out a cigarette. But I didn't want to look or sounds like some shit-bird Joe Blow who was back on the block.

"Yes, sir, this is salute Mike echo six to Charlie Mike Oscar three. Be advised that we have an unidentifiable hot pocket in an empty nest of possible chemical agent inside the hot pocket. Be advised that we need to meet up with Delta Company at 0900 at the TLZ Foxtrot," I continued. "Sir, I understand that we'll stand firm until they arrive. Roger Lima two-six out."

Corporal Lewis asked in disappointment, "So we're staying put?"

Corporal Gates replied, "Damn, the same game. Hurry up and wait."

"You know the game. Until the army ordinance guys get here, I need a perimeter around the bunker," I yelled. "So let's move it, and give me a one eighty."

As the hazy, hot day slowly moved toward 0700 and the dawn of a new day appeared, the boys and I grew weary of waiting for the men from army ordinance to arrive. Watering our tired bodies in the blistering heat nearly emptied the water bull as the sun beat down into the dirt from which we were created. We knew that we would be relieved as soon as the army showed up, but we were anxious to be away from that bunker.

The spirit of fear was blowing like a sandstorm among the men of Charlie Company, almost as if we all knew that something in those crates inside that bunker wasn't good news. I had to reassure them that they'd be out of there as soon as the army ordinance arrived.

By 1000 hours, the heat was taking its toll. Two of my men had heat exhaustion, and the corpsmen were working on the suffering. Suddenly the army ordinance truck arrived and was greeted by the men of two-six, who were happy to be relieved of that bunker. The army ordinance people wasted no time unpacking their gear and sent three men in to blow the bunker.

I wasn't in a good mood to deal with a know-it-all staff

noncommissioned officer. "Staff Sergeant, we were told not to blow that bunker," I said to him roughly. "There may be chemical weapons in there."

He replied calmly, "You have your orders and I've got mine. So if you don't mind, Staff Sergeant, stand back."

"Okay, fine. Fellas, let's get moving." I walked away and continued barking, "The army's here now."

Suddenly the bunker blew up. Even though my men were away from the explosion and jumped for cover, the bunker was blowing its toxic tornado toward us all. The scene of chaos was like a slow-motion picture. I yelled to my men to get their gas masks on, but for some it was too late. I watched some of them overtaken by the whirlwind of toxic gases from the bunker. It was just as I had feared.

As the sands blew up before my eyes, there arose a demonic force from hell that had one red eye like a cyclops. A flaming mouth started moving toward wounded and unconscious men. The demon that rose from the sand cloud began grabbing my men, killing them one by one, and devouring them.

I struggled to get my gas mask on before the sand demon came toward me. Otherwise I, too, would be gripped by the Grim Reaper's deadly mist. I saw the demon coming toward me, and it blew me to the ground. I cleared my gas mask with only seconds to spare, and then I took my pistol out and shot wildly in the air as it came whirling toward me. The demon tried desperately to grab me as it scratched at my exposed hands.

Then I came to my senses, knowing that this couldn't be real, because the demon was only a reaction to the toxic chemical and biological gases I had partially inhaled. So I took two atropine hypodermic needles and shot them into my thighs as I tried to avoid the toxic chemicals. As the atropine rushed to my head, my hands began to shake.

As I tried to avoid being exposed, I stuck my hands into the sand. Right at that moment, the sand turned into a whirlpool and began to pull my dead comrades into the sand with me. As I was sucked into the whirlpool, I began to scream, "Nooooo!"

This nightmare was one of my flashbacks from the first Gulf War. I did make my journey home, but many of my brothers died that day. I will never get past the horror of my dreams or the nightmares of my childhood.

CHAPTER 5

🏯 🏯 🏯

The Birth of the Lynx

As I fell through the sands of the hourglass, I saw a beautiful woman running up the side of the mountain. I tried to reach for the woman, who was in my dreams from time to time. "Take my hand," I shouted.

"Please, help! It's going to destroy us," she yelled, looking up at me.

As I saw the symbol and its evil glimmer, which nearly blinded me, I tried to save her from near death. "Hurry! Take my hand," I called out to her. "I can't go any farther or I will fall over the cliff."

Then the monster, seeing that her deliverance was near, grabbed her as she screamed, and devoured her whole. I could not believe my eyes when I saw the judgment that came upon that woman, and I fainted from the ghoulish way in which she was destroyed. As my life began to flash over this long walk I was taking, revenge rose in my soul. I prayed that the kingdom of heaven would keep me safe.

Suddenly, as the monstrous beast that had devoured the woman tried to continue its rampage, it began to get sick and threw her back up. The leviathan hiding itself in the clouds threw up the remains of the dead woman, with blasts of flames that landed right in front of me. The remains of the dead woman formed into a white cocoon that became her crystallized tomb, and the leviathan continued his rampage. Meanwhile the cocoon began to grow and change from white into a black diamond.

Suddenly I saw the cocoon begin to make cracking and peeling sounds as the woman began to emerge in front of me. At first she was naked, but as she came closer to me, a black scaly garment appeared on her body, and a red hourglass tattoo could be seen on the lower small of her back. As she turned away from me, I could see the red hourglass more clearly. Scarlet sands seemed to move inside the tattoo. Then the beautiful woman moved away from me and toward the remains of the cocoon. She bent over, reached into the cocoon, and pulled out a black crown with a diamond that had an eye in it.

Placing the crown on her head, she walked over to the cliff and whistled for the great leviathan. Ending its destruction of the cities, the monster came over to her and the woman leapt onto its back. Riding off, the woman cackled, as she saw the mayhem of the fallen church that was devoured by the government that made its war on my own country and people. Moreover, the whorish church that was united on the side with this beast for a time lay destroyed and in ruin.

I jumped again, under my covers, when I felt someone touch my leg and awaken me to the truth that it was nothing more than another nightmare from my past. When suddenly I felt someone grab my foot and shake me, I jumped up and startled the short elderly security guard who was standing there.

Jeff was a fat butterball who did that every morning

for two years. I knew him as the park ranger and security guard. Officer Jeffery Ramirez knew me because he was a Vietnam veteran and felt sorry for me, so he would let me sleep in the bushes at the Orlando Historic Center. I wasn't Staff Sergeant Moore in the United States Marine Corps any more, and that wasn't the Persian Gulf War or any other war in which I had served. It was February 2006, some twenty-five years later, and this is where my story begins.

"Ray! Hey, man, get up. It's time for you to go," said Jeff. "Man, you okay? Did you have another nightmare?"

"Yeah, yeah," I said grumpily from behind the bushes. "I'm up."

"You okay, bro? You look like shit. You need to go to the Saint Pete's veterans' hospital?"

"Good morning to you, too, Jeff," I said, scratching and stretching. "What time is it?"

"Come on, Ray," he said. "The same time I wake you up every day ten to five. Now come on, before that battle-ax boss of mine decides to calls the cops on you, like she did the last time."

Trying not to ignore him, I gathered my things and put them in my backpack. I looked at the scar on my hand that had healed over from those days in Desert Storm. The navy doctors said it was a reaction to the chemical and biological toxins in the bunker, but I knew better. I got my 50 percent disability check after Afghanistan and after a shot to the back that nearly crippled me.

After I came back to the States, I was given a desk job at the Marine Recruitment office at Camp Lejeune in North Carolina. But when I was awarded my second Purple Heart and the Bronze and Silver Stars for bravery, I chose to be booted out of the Corps.

They gave me the Silver Star for saving the lives of sixteen of my men and three of the army ordinance specialists, including the know-it-all staff sergeant. To this day, I still cannot remember anything I did that day to save us from death—actions that the base doctors attributed to my "animal instincts." I was awarded one Bronze Star after the Gulf War and the other for my service in Afghanistan. The Medal of Honor was awarded to me when I tried to save the many wounded by sniper fire—an action that also earned me the nickname of Staff Sergeant El-gato (that means the cat).

No medal, however, will ever cure my constant headache, the nerve damage, or the heartache of losing Graham, Lewis, and Singleton. Even though Peterson and Gates made it out alive, the meds they have to take have turned them into the walking dead. But they will always be in my heart.

I started my day, just like every other human on the planet, by getting up with a long stretch and a yawn. Even I could smell my armpits, and—oh, yes—my cottonmouth-biting viper breath. Nobody wants to start their day with breath smelly enough to knock a bear to his knees. I couldn't go out with breath smelly enough to be worthy of being arrested by the Orlando police.

I put on my green army jacket and rose from my little warm spot from my night of rest. My jacket had the Marine Corps seal and destination patches from every place I had been in the world. My jacket was as warm as a child's security blanket against the winter breeze that blew from the nearby lake. But when I slept on the steam vent in the bushes that kept me warm all winter and cool on those hot summer nights in Orlando.

With my goatee and long hair, I would be considered a dirty mess of a medium-build man. Nobody who saw me would think that I was a hero, because I never wore my shit on my sleeves or chest, as if I wasn't proud to have served. I keep my medals in a White Owl cigar box in a safe deposit drawer for safekeeping, along with my smokes and personal stuff like my Marine Corps lighter.

Moving out from a shadowy alley, I began my daily trek for shower, smokes, and food. I needed to find a good washing facility, where I wouldn't attract any attention. I would get up every day and do the very same thing, with the help of my butterball alarm clock, and that was the only thing that was routine about my day.

I would go down through Central Florida Historical Park toward Lake Eola Park, to a large water fountain on the northern side of the park. Moving stealthily, I would strip down to my shorts and move into the center of the fountain. As the fountain sprayed water and curtained me from the view of the public, I would shower with soap in one hand and scrubbing sponge in the other. That cold shower would kill any lice infestation, bugs, and even the desire to ever mate again. Then I would towel off behind the bushes, dress quickly, and walk out of the bushes as if nothing had happened.

Survival was the name of the game. I didn't have a home to go to, so I made do with the surroundings I had. The living nightmare of being homeless was an unfortunate fate that I shared with many other war veterans.

The streets of Orlando soon became my playground where I honed my skills. Being an ex–Marine Corps staff sergeant of twenty years in two of the Gulf War's theaters and Afghanistan gave me the edge I needed to do the job over there, but being in the streets of Orlando was just a boring daily game. Being homeless on the streets would be no different, but only time and old age were my enemies on this side of the Atlantic.

When it came to dumpster diving, hiding in the bushes

to sleep, or showering in the cold-ass fountain, it was my catlike reflexes that kept me alive and from being caught—except for that one time, when I surprised a female jogger while naked as a jaybird. I had to leap over the wall with my clothes and all I had. I landed in a pool that broke my fall. After getting out of the pool, I was lucky to creep into the laundry room at some condos next to the pool, where I was able to dry my clothes. I just walked through the lobby as if I owned the place.

That was the only excitement I had in my life since the days of being a marine—although now it was more fun to have a slow-acting hazard to my health like rolling my smokes. Because I never did the drug scene, I had only two vices: Crown Royal Canadian whiskey and rolling my own cigarettes with the tobacco called Midnight Special in menthol once in a while.

I would go down to the smoke shop on Orange Avenue to get that brand. It was only $1.40 plus tax back in the good ol' days, and it would last me for two weeks, unless four of my hobo friends hit me up more than once or twice. I was trained in the martial art of Shotokan karate, and other than that the occasional rude encounter at the Salvation Army with the first-class pimp and his only white trash crack ho when they tried to cut in line.

My days of trouble started when I began thinking I could handle it with the knife and some muscle on my part, but that didn't happen too often. Mainly my life was uneventful, mundane, and very boring, until that too changed me. I believe God brought her down my path so I would think about someone else other than myself. Meeting Jessica Swan was truly an act of God, but I somewhat got in the way to meet her.

The day I saw Jessica, she didn't even know my name,

but Jessica was timidly walking toward me, trying to muster up the courage just to say hello. I was looking at a newspaper on the ground that got my attention as I picked it up and started down Wall Street.

Jessica had ducked into the Subway Station Sandwich Shop next to Wall Street. While she was getting a bite to eat, the day was going well, which gave me a comfort, but it almost got me killed because I wasn't paying attention to my surroundings. The newspaper I was looking at read August 5, 2006, and it was the Saturday edition.

As I was looking at the newspaper more closely, I noticed a picture of a Hispanic-looking man of medium build with a stupid smirk on his face. I had seen the man before, but I couldn't place him. Maybe I had seen him in the bread line at the Salvation Army or maybe around the Mexican consulate or somewhere nearby, but I couldn't place the face.

Suddenly from behind me, an explosion of powerful force ripped through the crowded streets of Orlando, pushing me up in the air like a rocket and landing me on a table just to the left side of a bar called El Casa Mai. I rolled under another bar table, hoping nothing was broken. To keep the jagged flying glass and debris from cutting me to shreds, I pulled the thick tablecloth over me. I was in a hurt locker of pain as I heard the whoosh of thunder and silence over my eardrums as they tried to come back to normal. The last thing I remember seeing is the look of horror on Jessica's face.

As the debris totally covered me, I just lay there motionless. I couldn't move because every bone in my old body screamed in pain. Then I passed out, only to be awakened by some rough ambulance attendant slapping an Ace bandage to my already pounding head.

"Here, hold this, Mack," he said, wrapping the bandage

around my head. "You'll be okay, but you picked a hell of a place to sleep."

"Dave, get over here," another ambulance attendant yelled.

"Yeah, he's okay," the first guy yelled back. "Okay, buddy, I've got to go."

The other ambulance attendant exclaimed, "Is he okay? Because we had gotten some really hurt people all over here." *Okay*, I thought to myself as I took the stupid bandage off my head and threw it on the ground. *Then why is my head ringing like a four-alarm bell at a fire station?* I watched him run off to help the other emergency workers with the wounded.

I wanted to smack the shit out of the fool, but I was still too dazed to go there. I thought I saw Jessica looking for me, but in the confusion of the crowd and the fire trucks, I lost sight of her. Nevertheless, I began to stumble, dazed and bleeding with small cuts, feeling a little unbalanced on my feet.

I looked at the picture in the *Orlando Sentinel* still gripped in my hand, tore the picture out, and put it into my pocket. Somehow there was a missing link: I couldn't remember the man in the picture. His ugly face must have meant he was responsible, but he wasn't on my priority list at the moment. I was bleeding and needed attention right then.

I reached into my backpack and took some of my pain meds and walked on, still thinking of that man's ugly face as my head still reeled from the explosion. I walk on, dazed and confused, and went to the hospital emergency room. They sent me to Saint Petersburg veteran's hospital with a concussion, and I was there for about six months for my injuries.

I didn't see Jessica until about a year later in the library.

I tried to say hello to her, but when she came over, talking was too much for my head to take. I acted like a cold fish that day. I waved at her as if I was busy, typing away at a computer terminal in the Orange County Central Library. I wish now that I had kept her closer, or maybe I should have been a little ruder to her and she would still be alive.

Nevertheless, she kept coming to me, wanting more than I wanted to give her. Then she would still be alive, but she saw something in me that she needed, and I soon fell in love with her. I loved her and she knew it, which was why she kept bothering me. I had my stupid intense look as if the whole world was a mission from God.

Jessica used her beauty to attract my buddies but would get info from my bumming buddies with a pack of Marlboros for my informants, which meant two for three (that's two cigarettes for every three question). She stopped seeing them after she was working with me.

Jessica's beautiful ways came into play; she was a mix of Jamaican, Latino, and French, which gave her a creamy skin color much like my mother's that, was smooth to the touch. The way she would look at you would make any man melt. Those doe-brown, chestnut eyes could look into your soul.

Later, when Jessica and I were together, I invited her to my apartment and made a candlelight dinner for two. The cool breeze of Lake Eola and the soft music of Nancy Wilson gave us a romantic evening together. I wanted her to be in my life forever and maybe work with me as my spotter, but I had to see if she was good enough to be my partner. As I carried her into the bedroom, she just melted in my arms. We made love for the first time, and I was stuck on her after that.

I hadn't been with a woman or felt like that since Lynette, my wife, and I had been together some six years earlier. Lynette had left me because of my nightmares and abusive drinking, taking the kids and going back to Pine Bluff, Arkansas. When I had released all my love into Jessica, I began to quiver. I didn't know then that she was a virgin and that I was her first. As I began to lie on my back and she cuddled beside me, she felt me shaking.

She asked, "Are you cold?"

"No, I do that only after I've made love with someone for the first time," I said.

"Was this your first time?" Jessica asked while kissing my arm.

"No, I was married about six years ago," I said, but then continued. "But I haven't done that since my wife divorced me."

"You were my first," she said as I wrapped my arms around her and she kissed my chest.

I said, kissing her forehead, "I have something I need to tell ..."

"You're not gay, are you?" she exclaimed, raising her head to look up at me.

"No, I am not, but I work for the CIA now," I said calmly.

"How can you, an old-ass man, be working for the CIA?" Jessica asked as she inched up on top between my legs and appeared out of the covers while kissing my chest.

"It's simple," I responded as I reached over with my left hand and opened the drawer and grabbed a piece of paper. She began reading it. "'I know who the man is that did the bombing on August 6, 2006, and in exchange I will be happy to be of service in finding him.

Signed, Fire on the Altar."

"What did they say?" she asked.

"It's not what they said," I said. "It's what they did. Remember when you were in the park and you started asking my friends where I was?"

"Yes."

"That was the day they came in the park and asked Don where I was …"

"He told me he saw you get into a black Ford Exposition," she said.

"Right, and that's what happens …" I said to her as I began telling her the story.

A black Ford Exposition picked me up three days later, and no one saw me for three months. The agents drove up behind me just as I pulled out the picture of Mustafa. Something wasn't right about the whole scene. The day was cloudy, and even the birds had stopped singing. I told you that the squirrels, which normally came up to me, fled. This let me know that my gut feelings were right. Something was about to happen that day that would change my life forever.

I turned to meet the people who would later become my guardian angels the whole time I was with the CIA. Agents Davis and Jones were their names. They dressed in casual attire with Ray-Ban sunglasses.

"Mr. Moore," Agent Davis spoke softly, "Mr. Raymond Moore."

Jones followed her lead. "Sir, can you come with us?" Pointing at the Exposition as they came toward me, trying to cut off any path of escape. I mean, it wasn't as if I didn't know why they were coming. I had called and had been expecting them for two hours. I didn't like tardiness, which is a no-no in the Marines. It was always hurry up and wait.

I said to them while rolling a cigarette, "I e-mailed and called you to see if you had an answer about the offer."

I later told Jessica one time that I had been in New York sending them an e-mail and a picture of Mustafa, saying, "This is who you're looking for … Give me a call and I'll take care of your problem." This was the one time I knew they were coming up behind me. I could feel the tension in the air as the agents came close with the SUV. When the doors opened, they both smelled like trouble, which was government trouble.

As they motioned again toward the SUV, I did not attempt to run because this was my chance to help track down the person who had tried to kill me. All my hobo and street friends watched with curiosity, but they made no effort to rescue me. Maybe if I had left a trail of lighted cigarette butts, they would have come and rescued me.

Those clowns couldn't fight their way out of a wet lunch bag with a plastic butter knife. They all knew I was in trouble with the law, and the only thing on their little minds was there goes our free cigarettes, the bums, so they only watched from a distance.

They drove me to a federal building at 20 Hughey Avenue. It was a very tall white building every bit of ten stories, and I know. I counted them as I went up the elevator to the ninth floor.

We went into a very well-furnished suite with trophies and pictures of buddies from Derrek Coltrane's college days with three degrees from Colorado State University and Harvard Law. In some other pictures he was shaking hands with the current president and the CIA director. Standing there motionless and somewhat moonstruck by the whole scene, I looked at a man who didn't strike me as a common CIA agent.

He was more like a well-groomed, clean-shaven CEO of a Fortune 500 company, with the name tag on his executive desk reading *Derrick R. Coltrane.* On the desk was a box of cigars—Havana's, from the looks of them. Looking at me while he talked on the phone with a shitty smile on his face, he waved his hand, beckoning me to come in, and then hung up the phone.

"Come on in, Mr. Moore," Agent Coltrane said jovially. "We've left the torture room for the movie people in Hollywood."

"That officious, huh?" I said nervously.

I meandered over, embarrassed, slumping down into the chair to embark on this new adventure of my life. We talked for hours about my career in the Marines and their agency, and they even bought lunch from a Chinese take-out restaurant. I had chicken teriyaki, and Deputy Director Coltrane had beef teriyaki. Agent Davis was a vegetarian, and Agent Jones had moo goo gai pan. They slipped in a couple of jokes and then went in right for the kill by asking me my thoughts about who had done the bombing of the Wachovia Building. Then I showed them, for the second time, the Mustafa picture I'd torn out of the newspaper.

"This man I think is responsible for the bombing," I said.

"And who is he?" Agent Davis asked.

"Why do you think that?" Agent Jones asked.

I began to explain how there had been many bomb threats in the area in the last couple of days—three, to be exact, although there was usually about one every month. Then I got professional on them, saying, "This is common with terrorists. When I was in Afghanistan, the Taliban and Al-Qaeda would do the same thing to us, and every time, it was for many reasons. Nonetheless, the terrorists would do it mainly to confuse the authorities and to keep the citizen in a state of panic until the real one did hit."

Deputy Director Coltrane took a lot of notes; they all wrote down everything in the conversation that day. Agent Davis asked, "Do you think this was just one man?"

"Nope," I responded.

"Did you see anything unusual that day?" Agent Jones asked.

"No," I said calmly. "Hell, it could have been a suicide bomber."

When I said that, Agent Coltrane stopped writing and looked at Agent Davis as if I was on the right track, so I started telling them my thoughts. They listened to my opinion, which surprised me and seemed kind of strange, because no one ever listened to my opinion while I was on the streets of Orlando.

Agent Jones questioned, "Why do you think that?"

"Because it felt like somewhere, someone was watching me," I said.

Most people would never listen to a homeless person, for that matter. It made me feel like I was a professional soldier again. I began to feel somewhat more at ease with them because they made me feel like I had answers to their problem. The meeting ended, but they said nothing else about hiring me on as an agent and put me back out at the park.

Everybody wondered about what the five-o talked to me about, but I just ignored the moochers for the rest of the week. I went to bed that night and never thought about it again. I guess I felt I had done my duty for them and that was the end of it, or so I thought.

Then two months later, Agent Davis came up to me in Gator Park—that's another name for Central Florida Historical Park, which has three statues of alligators, so the bums call it Gator Park—while Jessica was cleaning up. You see, she got caught smoking pot and had to do community service for a month, so she was picking up trash, and that's when I started talking to Agent Davis.

I went to a restaurant on the lake known as The Lakeside.

I remembered the place because that is where I would shower at the fountain in the center of the roundabout and hide my things in the bushes. We ordered light because I was going to watch my manners. I knew it was a little different this time because Agent Davis was a woman, and I wasn't going to blow my chance of getting a date with her. I would joke with Jessica about it, and I knew it would either get me a slap upside my head or we'd laugh about it when I'm old and gray.

I was going Hollywood if not crazy for sure, from thinking I was a James Bond type to thinking I would be in bed with Agent Davis. She was built like Wonder Woman, with reddish-brown hair. She had gone to Yale and was a tough woman, by the looks of her, and even though she looked soft in demeanor, I could tell she could take care of herself in a pinch. Agent Davis didn't waste any time but went right to the point with me.

"Well, let me say this. We need to know if you're interested in taking care of a little problem for the agency." she said.

"What kind of problem?" I asked.

Then as if it was some business deal, she opened a laptop computer and showed me a portfolio-type file of the agency's problem, and as it booted up, she took a sip of herbal tea. Her slender fingers stroked the keys of the laptop quickly, and she showed me a picture of a well-dressed middle-aged Asian man with jet-black hair and a wide smile. He was sitting behind a desk of some foreign bank.

I studied every detail of his face and said calmly, "So, who's he, your little boyfriend?"

She smiled but ignored my stupid comment and kept working, never looking up at what I was doing. I was feverishly nervous, fidgeting with the table forks as I waited for her to get to the point.

As she worked, the keys again showed his lifestyle, his cars, and even his children. She noticed my nervous behavior and smiled, but continued showing me more of this man's life and other things like what he did with his millions as she continued explaining. "This is Lee Tiá Mohammed, a very important man to us." She continued, "He's the front man for the man you say is responsible for the bombing of the Wachovia Building and other sites around the world."

Agent Davis gave me a copy of his picture and said that Lee owned the Grand Marquis hotel in Cajun, Mexico. I looked at the picture and handed it back to her as Agent Davis continued, saying, "Mr. Mohammed has also chains of convenience stores all over the United States in Latino and African-American neighborhoods. He runs drugs, is involved in white slavery in Asian houses, and is into the importation of Mexican illegal aliens, which we believe are Al-Qaeda operatives.

"But he mainly funds Mustafa with weapons, and Mohammed is helping him smuggle many of Mustafa's terrorists into the country by passing them off as Mexican illegals." As she continued, I notice something about the restaurant that I hadn't noticed before. There was no one else in the place but Agent Davis and me. Not that I was going to try something stupid, but the simple fact that I was actually in a secret briefing meant only one thing: that I was going to be hired. As I leaned back in the chair, I got a little childish and began to think that I was somewhat important. In a real serious tone, I said, "So will I be your version of 007?" as I raised my eyebrows.

When I did flirt with her, Agent Davis noticed it, but she only shook her head and smiled slightly. But she kept typing while going on with her presentation. She started to focus on her job, which made me feel somewhat sheepish again. I came back to reality.

"Well, are you done playing deputy, Barney Fife? Or maybe you'd like to play the James Bond character one more time," Agent Davis said smiling, "I really like that one."

Then she pulled out a plane ticket and a credit card for me to get a room in a hotel. I took the ticket, and Agents Jones and Davis drove me to the airport. She told me that I was only a contracted mercenary employee for the CIA, and it should be keep secret.

While both of them were walking me to my plane, she said, "Once you leave here, you must understand that you wouldn't ever be an agent, so be careful. This means that if you are ever caught, we would deny your employment. You can be on call at any time. Welcome aboard the CIA." The agency was sending me back to an old familiar place where I had to be trained in some weapons that they have in Quantico, Virginia.

Agent Davis also told me that once I passed some prequalification testing, I would be briefed on where I needed to go for my next assignment. From that point on, I didn't see Jessica for two years and when I returned, I never again went back to the park.

The chain of nine lives linking me to Jessica was dangerous, but she was the only altar at which I worshipped back then. She was my only hope of staying alive, and I needed her later on, but that came later and was the only reason why this story had the ending it did and why Jessica knew so much about me. I finished my training in weapons and explosives in one year. It helped that I was a trained combat engineer and scout sniper in the US Marines, which gave me an edge right from the start.

I had a final meeting like Agent Davis said, but this time Jones and Coltrane were there in the briefing room with me. The setup was like boardroom meeting, and very businesslike. I guess it was a business, even if we were going to kill a man.

I was instructed to go to Cajun, Mexico. That's where Lee Tiá Mohammed vacationed sometimes with one of his girlfriends. I would have to assassinate him before he got to his hotel and then leave quickly and come back to the States. I was given fifty thousand dollars in cash to spend in a bank account in, of all places, the Bank of America—oh, how patriotic.

Then they explained that I would need to know some other details, like the location of safe houses and rendezvous in case something went wrong. The meeting ended, and we got up from the big board-meeting desk. Agent Jones came in and said, smiling, "So what do we call you, now that you're a spy?"

I had always liked the car called the Lexus, but that wasn't good because it sounded too girly for a spy. I often rode on the Orlando free transit bus, which was called the Lynx after the wildcats that use to roam in that area, and it was my catlike reflexes that saved my life more than once.

I yelled proudly, "Alexander Lynx. Change my name to that."

Once the briefing was done, I went back to my suite in Washington, DC. I was staying at the Watergate Hotel, and the agency was footing the bill, or should I say the American people were paying for my stay at the suite. Suddenly, I heard a knock at the door.

"Who is it?" I asked, standing there in my bathrobe.

When I looked through the peephole, it was a young Caucasian boy with a package in his hand. I put my small pistol in my bathrobe and answered the door. When I opened the door, he stood there smiling. It was the first time in a long time I had felt human, as if I had a purpose in life.

"It's an envelope for you, Mr. Moore," the bellboy said.

I took the envelope from the package and gave him a ten-dollar bill. "Thank you, sir," the bellboy said as I closed the door. The room was garbed in gold and brown colors. I sat down in my white robe with its gold trim. I looked at the envelope, which had my name, Mr. Raymond Moore, typed across it.

When I opened the envelope and dumped out the contents, I saw a passport and credit card with the name Alexander Lynx on them. Smiling, I knew that I was finally in a job that had my name written all over it.

As I boarded the plane, a feeling of fear came over me—not about what I was going to do, but about the fact that they were using nobody to kill somebody.

Suddenly I started thinking of all the wars I had fought in the same manner, thousands of nobodies fighting to get rid of a known government dictator. Death was now a price too high for me to pay. Plato said, "Only the dead see the end of war."

Nevertheless, I would do this war on my own terms and come back to fight another day. When I arrived in Cajun, a taxi drove me to the hotel where I was supposed to do the job. I saw in the alley that there was two hotels link together, which had some Mexicans taking a smoke break in the alley. The first hotel was the Hotel Casa Domino, which I was going to and the second was Casa Montoya where Tia Mohammed was supposed to be checked in. After I had checked into my hotel on schedule, I looked under the bed and said to myself, *"Let's see if the cleaning lady left me a vacuum cleaner to do some dirt removal."*

Opening the case, I made sure that the rifle, which was a Remington 30/30 modified with an Arma-sight .223/5.56/7.62 Vampire 3X Tactical Night Vision Rifle Scope "CORE"

IIT, was clean and ready for what needed to be done. As I began to load the weapon that night, the thought of being indispensable kept haunting me, and I picked up the phone and ordered room service. I dyed my hair jet black and used a straightening hair kit, and shaved my goatee off to look like the bellman I had seen earlier. I pulled out a Robo-Vac, which started doing its job while I field day that means to clean a room or, for you civilians, uncontaminated the room from top to bottom.

Fifteen minutes later a young Hispanic man came to the door with a tray of food. When he offered to bring it in, I spoke to him in Spanish and waved ten hundred-dollar bills in his face, then picked up the Robo-Vac and put it in my backpack. Then I walked out of the room in the bellman's uniform and with the cart.

Going down to the service elevator, I went down to the basement floor, which linked the two hotels together, and went up the other elevator. I went through the other hotel servants' quarters, grabbing a master key that was hanging in the security room, which was open, and went up to the eleventh floor on the west wing—one floor above the tenth floor of Mohammed suite, and I turned off the light so I couldn't be seen from his room. I was positioned in front of Mohammed's suite and bedroom, and then so not to get gun residue on the jacket I took it off.

As I looked through my scope I could see Mohammed coming into his suite through the open door then he and his girlfriend came into his bedroom. They were about to make love to each other. However, Mohammed did something very strange: he opened the window. I guess he didn't want to be hot and smelly after all that exercise.

"All the easier," I whispered. "No broken glass."

I quietly and patiently waited, like a lion would wait for

its prey. I started to focus my scopes. I looked through the scope. I watched for both of them to get into bed and start having sex. Right at the moment when they were about to climax, I pulled the trigger, and the rifle jerked back and the scope fell on my quarry.

Looking through the scope, I saw the blood pouring from the center of Mohammed's back from one shot. The bullet went into the girlfriend's head. I had killed two birds with one gunshot.

In a deep whisper I muttered, "His wife will thank me later."

Quickly I packed up the rifle and put the uniform back on. I had rushed to clean the room of the brass shell casing, not to leave a calling card. I went through the room with a fine-tooth comb so that no one could trace the assassination to me. Meanwhile, in the floor below, across the street in the room, the two guardian angels assigned to make sure I did the hit right watched for me, thinking I had blown my chance.

"Mohammed's already gone up into his room," Agent Davis said.

"Well, where in the hell is he then?" Agent Jones asked.

They watched the camera, but it showed someone asleep in the chair with what looked like a rifle. They sighed angrily and turned the camera off. Complaining to each other, they walked toward the elevator to go upstairs. I was moving to finish this one-act play as I destroyed and disposed of the weapon.

Then I called for a taxi before going underground in the service tunnel where they told me to stash the rifle in a gutter in the alley one block down. I went up to my room while Agents Jones and Davis were coming down to the room. I told the man while giving him his white coat to keep quiet about the whole thing or he'd lose his job.

I jumped into the other elevator going down to the lobby and checked out of the hotel. There I jumped into a taxi in the alley, and was at the airport in minutes. Both Davis and Jones had just walked to the room. After knocking on the door several times, Davis and Jones left and got on the plane going back to Washington to report on what had happened.

On the plane, they got a call from Deputy Director Coltrane just as they were arriving in Washington early that morning. "Sir, we're sorry you had to hear about your boat. It sank." That meant that the sniper had missed the target, or worse, that he was killed. They tried to explain in detail about how I had been asleep.

"What are you talking about, Davis?" Agent Coltrane said, laughing out loud. "Did you see the CNN report about our boy killing both Mohammed and his girlfriend while they were in bed?"

"No, sir, I don't understand," Davis said. Then she yelled, "He caught both of the fish."

"Huh?" Jones said, looking confused.

Coltrane, laughing, continued, "Yeah, they're blaming it on the wife, saying she did it."

Well, that must have been a kick in the head for both of them: seeing the success of the mission, but not in the way they expected. But then again, the main thing about the murder was that, as I said, I was coming back alive no matter what. The only thing bad about the whole situation was that of me killing one of the members of the Syrian Hamas Assailants Militia Insurgent Army terrorist ring that the assassination was out within two years in the terrorist ring knew my appellation. A report leaked out that an assassin named Alexander Lynx was the architect behind the vigilante hit squad that had done the unique job.

I was watching the breaking news story from a female

news reporter on the "World Report" on Fox-News.com. The woman, who was of Asian descent, started describing the story as she stood in front of the Cajun hotel: "This just in: The murder of Lee Tia Mohammed wasn't the result of a lover's spat but an assassination by a terrorist mercenary named Alexander Lynx. According to Arrai TV News network, a price is being put on Lynx's head by some of the KGB's old bounty hunters, who are offering a million dollars to find and kill him."

My life as Alexander Lynx was turning deadly. Like an old western movie, it went from good, bad, and then got very ugly after a while. However, in all, Alexander Lynx's name became known as the terror for the terrorist.

I came back to Orlando in hiding and resumed my identity as Raymond Moore on the streets, hoping I would be able to live my life as just another bum on the street. I was going to the Salvation Army food line, laughing, and joking with my friends as if nothing had ever happened, but I knew life would never be the same. I would always have that nervous feeling of looking over my shoulder, because inevitably, the day would come when I could no longer be Raymond Moore but would have to embrace the name of the monster of my design.

Although I only wanted to help the agency for a wrong that was done to me, for now I was a mystery to Jessica, the only woman I loved. As my lover and friend, Jessica would have to be willing to help, but for now, I could not have anyone in my life. I am writing about the woman of my dreams. I wish Jessica was here to share our dreams, but that is another story.

I had been living in Orlando just shy of five years when I got an e-mail from President-elect Vicar to come to the White House to take care of Natal, and I asked him how he had gotten my e-mail address that rainy day. The president-elect was looking for a nanny for his nephew and needed a male figure to toughen him up. He had been told about me after I quit doing work for the CIA some five years later.

"Do you remember this e-mail?" he asked. Then he showed me an e-mail that said, "I know the man who did the bombing on August 3, 2006, and would be happy to be of service in finding him. Signed, Fire on the Altar."

"Okay, but I'm a hit man," I said. "Why do you want a hit man to take care of your son?"

"Well, I think you and he will work fine, plus he is my nephew."

These letters from President-elect Richard Vicar told me that I could take care of his nephew, and protect him and anything that was thrown at me. My background with the Watchmen was never known by the Vicars. I would have to change my name again centuries later as a reporter for the Watchmen's Chronicle *blog and was known as Naba Zaphah.*

This is my journey home, and I can only wonder what I will see in the years to come in the coming home to the White House. Their family came from a dark past of conspiracy, but will it end with a government plot or revolts to take over some country in a distant land? Innocently it really started with just two people.

Throughout the history of man, Satan has used ordinary people to turn the world upside down with just one affair, the intercourse of two lovers in the bowels of sin. Ordinary people like the Vicars have a family tree with a passion for power, money, and sex. I am now taking care of someone who may look ordinary on the outside, but on the inside, he will try to take back what his father lost in the garden.

These were not ordinary times anymore in the twenty-first

century, because in these times since the fifteenth century, these two could never imagine the soul they created for Satan to fit his claws into to judge the people of the twentieth- and twenty-first centuries. Becoming one in holy matrimony, he was a priest and not just some local abbot of a parish, or a bishop. He was the pope. Now his ancestor Caesar Natal Vicar is in my care. I could kill him and only God Almighty would know, but then again, Natal Vicar made this journal happen for his purpose.

CHAPTER 6

🕯🕯🕯

The Birth of the Watchmen

0219 hours

July 1, 2057
Dear Abba,

The dreams of my childhood seem to come to me when I dream about Republicus. Now because, you see, many men lay down their lives for our country in the name of Republicus. Therefore, we have become the very things that we as a nation fought against when thinking about freedom. Those things we forever contemplate have brought us to ruin. We are the fools of what we have fed upon in the ashes of past wars of Granada, Iraq, and Afghanistan victories that formed the empire of the United States of America.

We as a nation believed this false sense of bravado, which made me realize that we must look for gold on mounts or hills to give that country liberty. We as Americans began thinking that the grass is truly greener on the other side. I kept thinking, foolishly, that there truly was gold in them hills of foreign soil.

As I stood in front of this assumed vision that brought my knees to quake, I saw this vision of a bright glowing light surrounding this illumination. The enrapturing glory was all over him, and I asked him, "Who are you?"

When he responded, he sounded as if he were in a waterfall that made his voice echo. "I am the one who was and is to come again. But you may call me Master Emmanuel."

"Who is covering and watching this regime or trying to stop this great beast from killing off the innocent?" I asked. In addition, those who were assigned to watch over this deadly beast as it rose its heads were all in a deep slumber, and when they awoke, it began its pursuit of me, which dumbfounded me even more. I was betrayed and left to deal with the emperor when I refused to backslide and be a murderer for the Watchmen.

To the left in my cold, stainless-steel cell is my desk and stool, with a keyboard to write my thoughts. To the right my home has a bed that is cold and uninviting, with two blankets and a pillow. In this cell I suffocate, waiting for death's winged liberation. The meal is slid under the metal chamber as the rusty hinge creaks down the hallway.

"Here's your dinner, traitor," the guard outside scoffed.

"How's the traitor today?" Emperor Vicar asked.

The guard, startled, snapped to attention and replied, "He is being treated well, Your Excellency."

"Are you monitoring his e-mail?"

The other guard said, "He has made no transmission as of yet, sir."

"Good," Emperor Vicar said. "If he does anything peculiar, inform me at once."

I could hear the tone of disbelief in Natal's voice, and then I envisioned him looking at my cell door and wanting to open it. I could see his shadow just outside my door, and I was hoping to talk with him.

Natal sighed hesitantly and turned, the dirt underneath his shoes grinding as he turned away and left. I could hear the clicking of the guard's heels as they saluted him, and then the sound of the elevator doors closing.

As I turned away, I heard the rats scampering toward the feasting on the floor and then the ticking of the clock while my jailers played cards, gambling, talking, and joking with each other about the prisoners. I sat there somewhat stir-crazy, waiting for the Almighty's hands to comfort me in my time of need.

The comfort I felt came in an odd way as I began to remember beginning my training with the Watchmen. I hoped that they would be my rescuers and deliver me. As a baby bird safely waits for its parents' return, so do I wait for my death when I return to the dust of clay?

I couldn't think in that depressing state, so my mind began to remember the days of being trained by all twenty-three elders of the Watchmen. Each elder taught in his or her own different way how I was too soon the protector and holder of these truths. They taught me spiritual laws that have governed this universe, the earth, and the Watchmen for more than ten centuries.

Chief Elder Maximus Coven, who later betrayed the Watchmen, was the only one who refused to teach me anything, but in his silence he taught me patience and love. The elders were the only ones of this body of senatorial spiritual leaders of both men and women who helped me clear the cobwebs of this world. These mentors showed me my spirituality in a way that changed me for all eternity.

They knew I had full knowledge of self-defense, so they began my training in the seven spiritual laws but used my martial arts knowledge to teach me these spiritual principles. The first five elders who were my teachers were

Elders Quirinus, Zarepath, Makoto, Juniper, and his wife. Everyone had different backgrounds and began to stir the ingredients of this carnal stew, and then added their own flavors and spices to make me into a humble servant of the Watchmen.

I am not saying they never had challenges in this sometimes-foolhardy soul who thought and reasoned that he was an unstoppable machine. I can only say they took the clay, which God created, and turned me into the protector of the truth.

The raw metal of combat that the Marine Corps made me was only a tool for the Watchmen, but first I had to be a vessel that was broken, and they allowed my sorrows of iniquity to shape me. Moreover, each elder individually took out the metal in this clay. Besides, then the Watchmen would have shaped me into a minister of justice and walked me through the fire to make me into the vessel of honor for the master's uses.

There was first Elder Quirinus, a Latino man from South America who was brought to the full knowledge of the savior by traveling missionaries from Japan. Miguel Antoninus Quirinus was born during the Peruvian civil war, one of many revolutions in 1985.

However, when Elder Quirinus stumbled upon the Lord, he was only a twelve-year-old boy who fell into an open street meeting in the streets of Peru. He and his friends were running and playing around the local village. The dirt road was busy with activity, and Miguel was doing what most boys do: he was fighting.

As the fighting boys drew closer to the crowd of older adults, Miguel was on a collision course with his destiny with God. The young boys were drawing closer and closer to the adults' crowd, and Miguel's brood of street thugs, who were pushing and shoving little boys, got too close to the adults. Miguel was literally pushed into the hands of the Lord.

The Japanese missionaries who came there only used the opportunity they were given, and he was pushed right in front of a live street evangelism meeting where a man was preaching to the crowd of people in the village that hot summer day.

The man was Dr. Nakahtomia, who was a short man, although you would never know it from the way he preached. Elder Quirinus told me later that the short Japanese man was standing on a milk crate in tan jungle shorts and sandals. I fell right in front of him, and he pointed at me.

"You could be one of his chosen," said Dr. Nakahtomia as the other missionaries helped me up. "Don't think that your coming here was an accident, young man."

Well, Elder Quirinus told me it was an accident, and if it hadn't been for my big feet and my friend's pushing me into the crowd, I wouldn't have ever found salvation that day. Twenty-one of us gave our lives to God in that meeting.

"'Jesus, therefore, said unto the Jews who believed in him,'" Miguel said, reading the Bible out loud while resting on a rock by a river, "'if ye may remain in my word, truly my disciples ye are, and ye shall know the truth, and the truth shall make you free.'"

Then Miguel began to ask himself questions about his faith, and these questions made him think of problems of faith, and he would think on these problems for solutions much like solving math problems, using the Bible as his algebra book. He searched for solutions in the Bible as if they were math problems that needed answers.

One day we met on the streets of Orlando and went to a coffee shop on Wall Street. It was a sunny day and I was still working for the CIA, although that day I was on vacation.

I asked him, "Did these unanswered problems ever make you feel condemned?"

"Well, I was a child who never understood why I was afraid of death."

I asked again, "How did you get free of death's hold on you?"

He said, "Well as I can remember … they gave me a Bible and then left me alone. I began to think to myself that it was wrong to still be poor and running the streets of Peru, but at a young age I had a hunger for the words of that Bible.

"Meanwhile, I would read the word of God at home, and on the streets I learned to read my new book. One day while walking and reading in an open field at the age of fourteen, I fell in an old abandoned well and broke my neck.

"The last thing I remember reading was the scripture in Romans: the eighth chapter and the first and second verses of the Younger's translation in Latin. 'There is, then, now no condemnation to those in Christ Jesus, who walk not according to the flesh, but according to the Spirit, for the law of the Spirit of the life in Christ Jesus did set me free from the law of the sin and of the death.' Meanwhile, I was paying no attention to where I was walking and fell into a hole in the ground. I lay there trying to move, but there was a painful reminder that my neck was broken as a numbing and feeling of deadness of my lower body came over me. I tried to scream, but nothing came out, and then darkness suddenly overshadowed me.

"I felt myself falling into a hole, and it felt like one of those nightmares where you are falling forever. I got up, seeing a tunnel as I looked at my corpse. I had never seen myself dead. I decided to go down the tunnel that was before me, and I took the strange trip into a place that looked like the cathedral in the city.

"Walking into the midst of this large temple over in the far corner I saw an altar of burning coals with a cloud of smoke bellowing from it, which covered the entrance of the temple. Moreover, I walked over toward the left and saw a seven-bowled lamp holder that had two very green trees coming out of the candelabra. A man came toward me with a bright glow about him, and was clothed to the foot with a bright white robe—whiter than any priest robe I had ever seen.

"The man had a crown of a pure white dome and a golden band around the crown with strange writing on it, and he was girded on his chest with a breastplate with twelve beautiful stones on it. He wore a golden girdle around his waist, and his beard and hair were white like white woolen snow. His eyes were a flame of fire. His feet were like fine brass or pure gold. When he spoke to me, his voice was like a sound echoing and reverberating like a storm or a raging river or a waterfall. The sight of the man made me quake, and I fell face forward to my feet. However, he picked me up and spoke to me softly.

"'Don't fear, Miguel,' the man who was known as the First and the Last said. "I am the first and the last and you are my friend.'

"'How can I be your friend, my Lord?' I asked doubtfully.

"'Greater love has no one than this: to lay down one's life for one's friend,' Jesus Christ said as he pointed at me. 'You are my friend, Miguel, because I did that for you.'

"I said, crying, 'I can't do anything for you. I am but a boy, my Lord.'

"'Oh, but you can, Miguel. If you do whatever I command you, no more do I call you a servant, because the servant has not known what his lord does in the past. And you I have called my friend, because all things that I heard from my Father, I did make known to you,' Jesus said.

"'But I am just a boy. No one will listen to me,' I said, weeping as I fell to his knees.

"'Miguel Quirinus, don't say any more that you are a child.' Jesus raised his voice as he picked up the young boy. 'I will give you the words to speak, and I will be with you until the end of the age.'

"'Forgive me, my Lord,' I said.

"Then he asked, 'What can I do to help you, my friend?'

"'I want you to go into the streets and sewers. You will find four boys who will follow me,' Jesus Christ said. 'I will draw them to you, and then you will take care of them and build an underground church from these boys.'

"I asked, 'Will I need to go to the other churches in my country for help?'

"'Keep away from all denominations, and don't go the way of Balaam the false prophet or Jezebel the harlot,' said Christ Jesus as his voice echoed. 'Your church will be as a blood red stone, so call her Sardis.'"

When Elder Quirinus woke up and turned his head, he said, he saw someone looking down into the well, right into his brown eyes. Not knowing if Elder Quirinus was alive, the man was about to leave.

"Help me. I am hurt and I can't get up," Miguel Quirinus yelled up to the man.

"I see you. Let me go get a rope," the man called back.

Then the man went and got help from some of the people from Elder Quirinus's village. His two brothers came and called down to him, and they rescued him by letting his oldest brother down to him.

"Miguel, is anything broken?" Róguery asked.

"No, I don't think so," Miguel Quirinus yelled.

Miguel's broken neck was totally healed, but he had been without water and was dehydrated because of the hours he had been down in the well. When Elder Quirinus came back from the country where he had fallen into the well, he told his family what Jesus Christ had told him to do; however, his family thought he was sick. As a result, Elder Quirinus thought he would have to leave home, and started preaching in the streets of Peru. As he began to preach to his mother and siblings, the Spirit of Christ filled the room and they all gave their lives to God.

Moreover, from that point on, Elder Quirinus began to go into the city streets and the sewers, and four boys were drawn to him just as Jesus Christ prophesied to him. The younger boys received Jesus as savior and Lord, and Elder Quirinus discipled them.

As the years went by and the four boys were disciples, he built four large huts in different parts of Peru and put each of the four men as pastor over those churches. Elder Quirinus had to put pastors over the huts in the villages. Years later the pastors in the villages were killed by the revolutionaries called *Sergeí El Lūminōs*, and Elder Quirinus replaced them with five other men and started another church that made five churches total.

Finally, he took the churches underground and ordained five new pastors. The revival spread out into other parts of South America. Because of the blood that ran red in the Peruvian churches he had built, he called the assembly the Church of Sardis in memory of the four precious stones whose blood ran red from the civil war.

This same Elder Quirinus was the man who taught me their seven supernatural (spiritual) laws of Christ. The elders had three to seven years to teach me, and according to the Watchmen, all of them were responsible for teaching me.

When they were finished, I had to go through a test called the "walk of fire" to prove I had the call to be a prophet.

I was asked by all twenty-three elders a series of questions that would prove whether I was called to be a protector of the elders of their prophetic group.

I found myself in the Hall of the Watchmen Intercessory Council after my girlfriend Jessica was found dead, and I came afterward, fighting her murderers. It was a blood cult of vampires calling them the Dregs. I remember waking up bloody and bruised after fighting them for hours, and thinking Mustafa the terrorist had put a hit on me. I was after him when I worked for the CIA, and I thought it was Mustafa who had killed Jessica.

When I woke up kind of dazed and sore in a room, two men in robes greeted me and escorted me to the boardroom where the elders were all seated. I was still kind of punch drunk from the beating. I thought I was a dead man when I passed out from the beating the Dregs gave me.

"So, my fine gentleman," Elder Quirinus asked me as he folded his hands, "how are you today?"

"Well, for the first time, I entered life feeling like a sack of shit," I said. Then I stopped myself and continued, "I am okay, I guess."

"Why?" he asked.

"Well, I feel like God's watching me with a big bolt of lightning, ready to fry my ass the first time …," I yelled. Then I stopped and put my head down, trying to correct myself. "Oh damn." Elder Quirinus, laughing at me, looked at the others, who came over to me. Then they stood me on my feet, and he did something that I didn't think he would do.

Elder Quirinus just looked at me with tears in his eyes and hugged me at first. I didn't know what to do, and then he held me tighter. He patted me on my back while crying but never saying a word until I felt something come over me like a mighty wind. It overtook me and broke my hard-core frame of mind until I couldn't control myself. I felt like a little boy again. This was the same little boy who had seen his stepfather die right before his eyes.

Melting in the arms of this old man was not normal for me, but the more I tried pushing away, the more the feeling of peace came over me. I couldn't resist the feeling that came inside of me. I saw not with these physical eyes, but with the eyes of my spirit that little boy who was angry at the world. I was watching him coming closer and closer to me.

This old man kept holding on to me tighter and tighter as that little boy came closer and closer, until he came right on inside of me. While I stood there in front of everybody in that room, I began to cry out. "Abba, why did my daddy and mommy have to die?" I asked in a loud sob.

Elder Quirinus kept holding me as I cried louder and louder. At that time, the answer came to me in a still, small voice on the inside of me. Then the aura of light shone around me. You could hear a pin drop in that place as I heard a voice speak to me.

The minute that voice spoke, all the elders of the Watchmen fell on their faces as if they knew who it was. Even Elder Quirinus fell on his face, and out of the mist a cloud moved toward me and formed into a man. The voice sounded like many voices and was loud but soft at the same time as he spoke to me.

"Do you remember the first time we met, my beloved?" the voice asked.

"Lord, is that you?" I asked in a childlike voice.

"Do you remember in Afghanistan when you died?" the voice asked.

Then my mind went back to when I was in Afghanistan going after Osama bin Laden and the Taliban. I was back in my unit in a mountainous region of Afghanistan, being a staff sergeant over a platoon and talking to friendly tribal leaders. One day my platoon was searching for an Al-Qaeda sniper named Mustafa and his band of Al-Qaeda rebels who were taking out villagers.

I was working on the Intelligence and Communication link to do airstrikes on the Taliban and Al-Qaeda position. My scout snipers and First Force Recon units kept on me about not being visible because the Taliban and Al-Qaeda had put a bounty on me for fifty thousand dollars to kill the Medal of Honor winner known as Staff Sergeant Raymond Moore. It was on leaflets that were given to me by one of my scouts. I laughed about it that day and lighted a cigar with the paper out in the open. The tribal leaders thought it was bad to laugh at the Angel of Death, but I had no fear then.

Meanwhile, my platoon was out in the open looking for this notorious sniper named Mustafa. He was hired by the Taliban to kill tribal leaders and their people who were sympathetic to Americans helping to free Afghanistan. The sniper Anwar Mustafa was the same man who tried to kill me in Orlando. Well, anyway, he and I have history together, and that is another story.

This particular day Mustafa was slaughtering village girls who were out getting water at their wells. The people were dying of thirst and needed to get water, but they wouldn't send the boys because of their custom. We told them that the Marines would give them water if they wouldn't send their girls out to get slaughtered, so we had to enforce a curfew to keep the tribal leaders from sending their women and young girls out to get killed.

I looked up in the hills with my binoculars and saw Mustafa sighting in on something; meanwhile, one teenage girl got sent out disobeying the curfew, but rather obeying her parents instead of the curfew, and I saw her out of the corner of my eye. I saw Mustafa looking through his scope to see whom he could be sighting in on. Then I saw this young girl just a foot away.

Suddenly, without thinking, I jumped out in front of the girl. I was hit in the back, and a bullet pierced my left lung. I was going fast, and suddenly my body was sucked through a tunnel. I found myself on a gold-and-pearl-white bench with two books on it in a great courtroom.

As I was sitting on the bench in the courtroom to watch this trial, I saw a dirty, smelly, sinister-looking man. The man seemed to be guilty of a great amount of sins in his life, and he was in center of the courtroom. However, in the center of us all was a great chair with a large figure of a great man. There was light around the chair, and its back was away from both of us, which gave me a false sense of security because I wasn't that wicked man being judged.

To the left side of me was a sinister black figure of a man with blood red eyes. When I looked at the man, I felt a freezing chill in my being. The being moving toward me was as black as night, and it moved out of the darkness. The murky shadow of darkness seemed to move like a human figure dressed in a pinstriped suit.

The suit was blacker than the cavern's of hell, and the pinstripes were golden in color, and the suit moving like a shadow that covered him like a robe as the thin strips ran all the way to the floor. The dark human figure could only speak curses and foul language to me and the dirty wicked man in the courtroom, but would never speak anything but poetic psalms to the judge of light behind the chair.

I began to notice there was another man to my right, who was dressed in a white garment that came to his feet and a coat of many colors that he wore under a breastplate.

On his head, a domed crown with a signet read, "Holiness to the Lord," and he had a breastplate with twelve stones on the front. He wore shoulder pads of precious stones with a sash of pure white with gold trim, and in gold letters it read, "King of Kings and Lord of Lords." The light and the hope of glory surrounded him, and he had an aroma of a sweet smell that, when you inhaled its essence, gave you a sense of peace and loving-kindness from him.

In front of me was the wicked man who was being judged for his grievous crimes. There I sat on the bench, and he was kneeling down weeping. I could feel only sorrow for him as I sat behind him. I was seated on the bench, and the more I looked at him, the more I began to weep for him, sitting on the pure stone of clear gold. I noticed again the two books on top of the seat, and when the Lord of Darkness came over to the bench where I was sitting, he picked up the first book and opened it.

"This malefactor of sinful birth came into your honors pure earth," the Dark lord bellowed and hissed. "These are the crimes doth this wicked creature commits ..."

The dark lord of the court began to read the man's sins from the time he was conceived, shaped, and born into the world, calling out thoughts and actions nobody but the master accuser saw even though he was in the innocence of his childhood. No crimes of unrighteousness ever escape the eyes of the court.

All of this familiar wicked man's life was displayed on the screen of the clouded skies. Everything that was a reflection, dreamed, or spoken word was displayed as if the evidence was underwear on a clothesline by the prosecuting lawyer of darkness, who showed it for all to see.

"For this man was lover of himself, lusting for money, boastful, and proud," the lawyer said, singing the charges.

He continued, "He was an evil-speaker, very disobedient to his parents, unthankful, unkind, without natural affection toward the creatures of you, my Creator."

He continued his railing accusation, spewing venom in his poisoned report. I felt rather sorry for the wicked man in the court. "My master, this man was the worst of false accusers, unclean in masturbation and lewd behavior." The accuser of the wicked man went on: "Furthermore, all this unrighteousness of this malefactor was the fiercest hater of men that would make him a murderer, and the worst but my favorite of all a liar."

I could not believe all the wicked things this man did, but the man who was before him seemed very familiar. Moreover, I was thinking to myself that I was glad I was not this man. I whispered to myself, "Why, if he doesn't get justice by going to jail or prison, I will be surprised."

"Hereafter when his parents both died, he was heady, lofty, a lover of pleasure until that moment that he fell and came before you, most Honorable Most-Highest Judge of this courtroom."

Then I heard a rumbling from behind the chair as if the judge could not have cared less about the evidence the dark lord gave, and then with a bellow the dark lord cried, "My Creator and Almighty Judge, he belongs to me."

Nevertheless, he never stopped in his accusation, and the dark lord of the court reached over and picked up the other book. As he opened it, blood came out of the book. The man was being covered in the blood from the book as it poured on him from head to toe.

I started feeling funny, like something was being poured on me, and when I looked up, I was no longer in the seat. Transferred from the seat to where the wicked man was kneeling, I knew the wicked man was me. The dark lord came against me like a pit bull charging at a mail carrier. The devilish prosecuting attorney threw the books behind him as all hell cried for my soul.

"He belonged to me," the dark lord and all of hell's demons cried in a chorus of hissing and jeering.

As I knelt down, sobbing and weeping for my crimes against humanity, I looked over at the other man, who was dressed as a Levitical high priest. Nevertheless, the man said nothing to me. "Did you hear what he said to me?" I screamed. He never said a word, just smiled and began to move toward the judge's chair and position himself between the judge and me.

The room was quiet with a reverential silence. The high priest turned the chair slightly and showed him a hole about the size of a railroad spike, saying with authority, "Father, look."

The priestly man showed him the other hand, saying, "Father, look." Then he showed him different scars: in his side, in his feet and finally on his head. Each time the high priest showed the judge one of the predominant scars on his body, he would turn the chair. After all this, he turned and pointed at me and said, "Father, look."

As the judge's chair turned slowly to pronounce the sentence that would separate me from my fellowship with humanity, these words echoed in eternity from the Father of us all. "I saw you as a babe bathed in your own blood," and again he said louder, "I saw you as a babe bathed in your own blood." I hid my face in fear of the judgment I knew was going to come from God Almighty.

"I saw you as a babe bathed in your own blood," the judge proclaimed. "I commanded you to live."

Upon the third time of the voice's proclamation, I was thrust into another part of the temple. The soft words of the master spoke to me: "Be not afraid." From the mist of the smoke-filled curtain that was like deep purple and crimson drapes there entered two rows of angels. They came out wearing the same man dress as the Levitical high priest, and then I knew it was Christ Jesus. He said to me, "The reason you were delivered this day is my blood."

I fell to my face in tears. As they streamed down my face, I said screamed again at the top of my lungs, "Abba, why did my daddy and mommy have to die?"

"Because the world is full of its cup of iniquity," Christ Jesus said as he held me. "That's why, my beloved, but I took that pain for you."

There in that room with the twenty-four elders of the Watchmen Intercessory Council, I felt peace for the first time in a long time. I didn't have to look for peace in a bottle, a woman, or a job because it was holding me right there among the prophets. And then he was gone. As for my life, fading into what Christ Jesus did that day, I did not care whether I lived or died. In addition, nobody could tell me to search the truth of what I desperately needed but the one who held me that day.

CHAPTER 7

♟ ♟ ♟

The Trial of My Training

The first day I met with Elder Quirinus, I wouldn't call him by his first name, and the reason is that he wouldn't allow me to do so because he thought I had to earn his respect. As I said before, I found myself taking on a whole new type of training, one that was not like any type of boot camp I had ever experienced before. I heard a knock at the door of my room after dinner and it was Elder Quirinus. When I opened the door, there stood the elderly Latino man whose long gray beard flowed to his chest.

"I hope I am not disturbing you," Elder Quirinus said.

"No, not at all," I said.

"Well, then I just came by to say that I will begin your training tomorrow," he said politely. "If there is nothing else, then I will see you later. Good night."

"Well, yes, there is," I responded as he turned to go out the door.

"Yes, what is it?" Elder Quirinus said.

"What is your name?"

"Why, it is Elder Quirinus," he said as he closed the door. "Good night."

The next day Elder Quirinus came to me while I was in their prayer garden. The headquarters of the Watchmen was an old abandoned warehouse that had been converted into a sanctuary and monastery for the elders and those they trained. I would go to the one place in that warehouse in Orlando where I could look at the sky and lie on the grass like I had when I was a kid.

It was a Garden of Eden with springs and dogwoods, orange, and cherry blossoms in bloom. The fountain babbling in the background of the prayer garden they had created gave it a mood of serenity. As I watched the koi swimming around in the pond, it made my mind spin with thoughts of who I was. In Florida, spring was longer than the summer in Orlando, and I would mostly stay out in the prayer garden to sleep and pray to God.

"I can't understand why I feel nothing about who Christ is," I said.

"Religious experiences can sometimes move you to misunderstand how Christ walked on earth," Elder Quirinus said to me softly. "But they are never intended to make you a god."

"I never thought I was trying to be a god," I said, turning to him.

"Before Lucifer became Satan, he didn't think he was being God either," Elder Quirinus said to me. "He just thought he should be with God too."

I said, "I keep having this thought, and it never goes away."

"What is the thought?" he asked.

"Well," I explained, "I kept thinking that when I was a little boy, God could have done something to stop my dad from being killed."

"Do you know what that is?"

"No," I replied.

"You are determining a standard of conduct for God,"

replied Elder Quirinus, "judging God, while expecting him to operate in your attitudes and actions."

"I would never judge God," I said, shocked.

"The first principle that we must lay in your foundation will be the law of the spirit of life."

"I've heard of the law of gravity," I said with a questioning look, "but I have never heard of the law of the spirit of life."

Elder Quirinus began to explain. "'In the beginning was the Word, and the Word was with God, and the Word was God.'"

Later, he told me, "This will be the beginning of your training in spiritual and natural laws. You see, Raymond, because you are a prophet, you must operate in the spirit realm but never in the flesh or the natural realm."

"I never thought there was a realm of the spirit."

"Things you see are in the natural, but the things unseen are spirit," Elder Quirinus continued.

I asked, "What about germs? Are they spirits?"

"Just because you can't see germs with your naked eye, that doesn't make them spirits."

"Oh. Well, then what about the devil and his demons?"

"The devil is a spirit that operates in the natural," he explained. "God is a spirit, and we must worship him in spirit and in truth."

"Oh, I see."

"No, it's because of what we can't see that we have faith."

Every day for three years, Elder Quirinus and I talked. And when he was finished, I really understood who I was in Christ Jesus. One time, about two years after I had been taught under the Watchmen's training under seven different elders in three years, I was lethargic and overworking my brain, because the prophet's life must be free of rebellion. The chaos of being a warrior was causing confusion: wanting to rise to the occasion of fighting in the physical instead of battling in the spiritual realm.

I asked sharply, "Elder Quirinus, why must I learn these seven spiritual laws?"

Elder Quirinus, carving a staff, said, "It's very simple, Raymond. You are either going to operate in the spirit and rule with God forever, or you are going to let your flesh dominate you and be the natural and bust hell wide open."

"But why would a loving God make hell?" I asked.

"Why do you think?" Elder Quirinus responded.

I began to think long and hard, confusing my thoughts and wondering what I knew to be true. Then the thought came to me. I blurted it out before thinking about it, and the words just came out.

"In Matthew chapter fifteen verse nineteen that reads: 'For out of the heart comes forth evil thoughts, murders, adulteries, whoredom, thefts, false witnessing, evil speaking;' and too in the book of Revelation chapter twenty-one verse eight that reads: 'fearful, and unfaithful, and abominable, and murderers, and whore-mongers, and sorcerers, and idolaters, and all the liars, their part is in the lake that is burning with fire and brimstone, which is a second death.'"

"That is the law of sin and death, Raymond," Elder Quirinus said.

After that fact of the revelation of hell and the lake of fire was given to me, those lessons became very easy, as far as learning who I was in Christ Jesus and the rest of the seven spiritual laws.

"Well, then, if I am not to fight in the physical realm, why must I carry a sword?" I asked.

"As it is written, we exhort you, brethren, to rebuke the disorderly," he answered.

I asked, "What does *rebuke* mean?"

He responded, "Matthew Henry once said, 'And the people should be at peace among themselves, doing all they can to guard against any differences. However, love of peace must not make us wink at sin.' The fearful and sorrowful spirits should be encouraged, and a kind word may do much good. We must bear and forbear."

"So, I am to be kind to the man I am going to kill," I said sarcastically.

"You are to protect those who cannot protect themselves," Elder Quirinus said. "And if that means you must stand in the defense of the defenseless, then that is why you are here."

"Then am I a minister of reconciliation or a minister of justice?" I asked.

"Both," Elder Quirinus said.

I often wondered how the Watchmen ever came about. So one day when I was in my favorite spot in the garden, I asked Elder Quirinus. He told me, "Well, I was trained by this old prophet who was dying when I met him in the city of Bolivia in Columbia. He told me many stories about the Watchmen—how God was going to rise up seven prophets, and they were going to work as the prophets of the seven churches around the world. The Watchmen Intercessory Council was started by a man named Captain Raymond Jabez."

I asked, "What kind of name is Jabez?"

"It is Swiss," Elder Quirinus responded.

"Were the Swiss ranking officers equal to ours?"

"No," Elder Quirinus spoke sharply. "Now do you want to hear this story?"

"Sorry," I replied.

"Okay, then listen."

"The story of why the task befell this captain of a small Swiss militia, and how he came to be the founder of this prophetic intercessory group, which was unknown to historians, goes something like this. The man named Captain Raymond Jabez became for many in the organization known as the first to don the title of Watchman and all that it stood for. On an early evening in the spring of 1435, thirteen Waldensian Bible missionaries were running from Roman Catholic mercenaries assigned to murder them.

"As the mercenary army approached the captain of the Swiss Army Raymond Jabez a small band of Christian made up of Swiss army, Raymond Jabez, and his wife, a local Anglican priest, and two other men that were volunteers of the Swiss Army. The Swiss Army were risking their lives to hide these monks that were the Waldensian Bible missionaries in their village, while Captain Jabez took his volunteers and formed a blockade while the others took the missionaries and hid them. During the whole summer and into the winter, the Waldensian missionaries taught from the bishop's Bible, and gave them the true teachings from the Word of God.

"Before the Waldensian missionaries left for France and Germany, they anointed these brave souls as Watchmen of his Lord Christ's word. The king of Switzerland soon found out about what the captain did, and ordered the captain to be brought before him to explain his action.

"Once Captain Jabez told King Ladislaus the whole story of the Waldensian missionaries, and why the king's army stood up against Roman Catholic mercenaries' army, he and all his men were knighted and became the order of the Knights of J.A.D.E (Jehovah's Anointed Deacons of Evangelism). The mission of the Watchmen and the Knights of J.A.D.E has been to protect the ministers of the gospel, serve the body of Christ, and minister to and teach the lost by keeping the ways of biblical truth. Unfortunately, under a new king who was in league with the pope, the

Watchmen had to go underground to protect their identities and families.

"Captain Raymond Jabez and his wife, along with many of the Watchmen who didn't go underground, were martyred. The Watchmen were labeled heretics and were killed off by the Roman Catholic mercenaries' armies under the guise of the crusades. However, the loyal order of the Knights of J.A.D.E's mission later was to protect the Watchmen, so that they could do their ministry."

We have not been a secret organization, but men and women of prayer not of war, and we keep and build the body of Christ—not a literal building of bricks and mortar. "You will protect this body as we have prayed over them. If we bring them all together, then you will be their guardian," Elder Quirinus said to me.

I thought about the history of these brave men and women who gave their lives to prayer. And I wonder if I could ever live up to the challenge of this noble task. The Vicar family would be more of a challenge than all the Roman Catholic mercenaries and enemies of the Watchmen had ever seen. God Almighty would give me a mission to protect the very ones who would destroy, the ones I was to protect: the family of the nightmare of my childhood.

The master Lord Charlimas DePaul Vicar and the Black Knight known as Sir Louis El-Deon Ignatius tried to wipe off the bloodstained gloves of many of the disciples. The Waldensian Bible missionaries were the rebirth of the Watchmen, but through operations these spiritual laws were the force of love. I would be tested to keep the prophecy of the book of Revelation alive.

Sincerely, your servant,
Raymond Moore

CHAPTER 8

♣ ♣ ♣

A Tree Called Vicar

July 4, 2057

Dear Abba,

Some days later I was relaxing with Elder Quirinus in the prayer garden again. In addition, many people were always in the place to go in that warehouse. I could always look at the sky and lie on the grass like when I was a kid. As the clouds would roll by, I would remember things that sometimes I wished I could forget. But then again, they were like pictures, and strangely, the things I saw made no sense.

Moreover, I was feeling a little sleepy, and I drifted into a deep slumber and went into a dreamlike state. I saw an ocean of the clearest blue, as if I had gone to the Virgin Islands. Then suddenly from a distance, a silver cross ring came from the horizon and hovered in front of me. I watched the cloud, which began to form into the picture of a man's face. An angel flew from that cloud and threw a closed red rose down to me.

As the rose began to float slowly to the ground, the ring

grew larger. The closed red rose was floating at first, and then it began to tumble off the ring. The ring that had been floating on the horizon fell into the sea, and then it came back out again, rising toward the tumbling red rose, which began to bloom. When the two met, the rose fit inside the ring. The two visions of the rose petals began to blossom into two women's faces.

The faces' outward appearances came from the petals of the rose. One petal's face was that of a redhead, and she had crystal-like blue eyes. Then the other petal formed a face of darker purple that shaded down into a woman with brunette hair and green eyes. The redheaded woman had tears rolling down the stem of the rose. When the teardrops dropped off, they would turn into diamonds and splash into the water.

Then the splashing of the water in the dream began to bubble and boil like a kettle on a hot stove. Suddenly the monster of my nightmares arose out of the water and it was Republicus, the Leviathan that had seven heads. As he drew near me, I could see one of the heads of the leviathan, called Bogus Chrio Nāgîd, that would draw and call all dreamers and slothful people into thick dense fog.

"This is Camelot," echoed the bottomless voice from the fog.

Because the poor, the dreamer, and the slothful would believe his lies, they would work effortlessly for the dragon. It drove them into an insane frenzy to steal anything and murder for the dragon as it whispered from the fog. As I peered into the fog, I saw the resemblance of a family at the dinner table with the television on. They were like the Cleaver family but worse. All of them behind their serving trays were eating whatever the television served them.

"Mom, this partially pasteurized, hydrogenated monosodium benzoate with beta-carotene and vitamin A

palmitate acid is good," the little boy said. "Can I have some more?"

"Not until you finish your potassium sorbate disodium red dye one," she said as the television spooned out another helping of what the child wanted. "Make sure you eat all your corn with yellow dye twelve, so that you'll grow puny and deformed like your dad."

"Wow, honey, you sure can cook a mean mechanically separated chicken," the husband said. "And these sodium erythorbate flavorings covered in sodium nitrite and garlic powder just makes the dish so filling."

The wife asked, "Would you like dessert, dear?"

"What are we having?" her husband asked.

"Sugar," she said with a big smile.

The husband asked, "Can I have it with a little corn syrup on top?"

Then the family would look at the television and turn into blank, expressionless, zombie-like people, and they would be like the walking dead as they entered the clouds to do the dragon's bidding. Trying to keep from being fed to the monster from the deep, these Caucasian-looking zombies would go to the cities, villages, and into far-away lands to enslave first the Native Americans, and then African-American men and women that were used as pawns to do the dragon's binding. The children of these cities would hide from the great leviathan so it would not eat them, and would be terrorized as they helplessly watched their parents being devoured. Nothing could stop the beast called *Bogus Chrio Nāgîd* that would draw all dreamers from every generation into the fog. Then the dragon said something that was weird sounding.

Then I woke up, and although I looked puzzled, I didn't tell anyone about the dream that was troubling me. Elder Zarepath, a woman with brown eyes and reddish-blond hair, came up to me. I began thinking she was the woman who had been crying. As she came closer to me, her eyes didn't look like those of the woman in the dream. The eyes in the dream were blue, but Elder Zarepath's eyes were a haunting brown. Because of my disappointment, I turned away from rolling my eyes downward.

"With your pardon, sir …" I jumped and stared at her, unsure where I was. She spoke again. "With your pardon, sir," she said. "Didn't mean to clutter the view of your thinking."

"Where is Elder Quirinus?" I asked. "I am sorry …"

"Sorry. For they who are without Christ, that statement would be true," Elder Zarepath said as she sat on a stump across from me. She continued, "But maybe you were expecting I was someone else, and I might not be a very beautiful woman who looked like a rose …"

"Oh, no, you are attractive …" I stopped myself and then said, "Wait a minute. How did you know that?" Elder Zarepath started laughing at me and turned, playing as though she were pouting.

"We are a prophetic group of men and women, Raymond," she said. "So, who is the girl?"

"I don't know," I said, disappointed.

"Exactly: you don't know," Elder Zarepath said, glaring. "You are the first person to admit they don't know."

"Huh? Now I am confused," I said.

Elder Zarepath said, "Another true statement of mankind."

"What are you talking about?" I asked.

"Which is a true statement," she said. "Is there power in the word or do words have power?"

"I've never thought about it," I said sharply.

Elder Zarepath asked, "Then is there anything you do think about?"

"You've asked a lot of questions," I barked back.

"My name means to ask by coming to me and to me by asking," she said.

I asked, "What is your name?"

"Imani."

"And that means 'to ask by coming and by coming asking'?" I asked in confusion.

"No," she responded.

Stunned, I said, "What? I thought you said …"

"My name means 'faith,'" Elder Zarepath said as she sat down. "And faith comes by hearing and understanding the Word of God."

I began to get irritated with her riddle-like form of speech. I couldn't understand why I was still sitting there. I listened to her as she spoke that day, and by the end of the day I was eating every word she said. She wasn't speaking in a straightforward fashion, but the more riddles she said that day, the more questions I asked. Even though the stream babbled nearby and there were birds singing their songs, she sang a song to me sweeter than any words any person has ever penned on any album.

Elder Imani Zarepath was not entrapping me in the snare of useless laws or meaningless parables from some dead religious scrolls; she turned those words to life, and now they are alive in the law of faith. Nevertheless, how did this woman learn about the law of faith? Up till now she had appeared to be a simple-looking woman who from all appearances was playing dumb, but as I talked with her, I found that Elder Zarepath was sagacious and that her character was truly of the spirit of faith. She used her wisdom in her own right but had in the beginning of her search for truth connected with people who never listened to the voice of the Lord.

But one day Elder Zarepath told me a story that had stopped her from being a blind follower of the blind, and it almost made her one of the faithful martyr counted under the Brazen Altar of the Holy Temple of the Almighty. She was but twenty-one years old when she found herself in the tribal islands of Indonesia doing missionary work with her husband, Todd. He was a strong, tall, dark-haired man from New Zealand who had graduated at the top of his class in missionary and foreign evangelism studies. He had a boat that carried him and his other partners into the dangerous regions of the Muslim territories of some of the western islands to smuggle Bible and supplies to the friendly tribal islands that were needy.

This particular time Imani decided to go with her husband and set up a base camp with their nine-month-old baby named Roger on what was thought to be neutral territory. They used an old, abandoned Japanese barracks that at one time had housed the Imperial Army of Japan and had been deserted since World War II.

"How did you become so knowledgeable about faith?" I asked.

"I was so blind back then," she said, smiling. "I guess everybody thinks that is how you are to follow God."

"But I thought that *was* the way you are to follow God," I responded.

"What like General Cluster at Little Bighorn? Just race right off and do it?"

"I guess that would be foolish," I replied.

"I was so foolish back then, but I missed Todd so much and needed to be with him …

"Todd, my fair and strong husband, stood at the wheel of our ship the USS *Constantine*. To me back then, he could do no wrong. I trusted him because he was smart and so strong.

I would just melt in his arms some nights as we lay in bed together. Todd and I thought we would be safe in setting up the base camp there at the old abandoned Japanese barracks with his partners. As our party came ashore, everything was deathly quiet as we pulled up to the dock in the hidden lagoon.

"'Todd, can you get the baby?' I said, getting off the ship. "I'll bring the supplies later."

"'Sure, honey,' Todd said as he reached for the smiling baby while Bryan dropped the anchor and Terry tied the ship's first rope to the dock. 'Hey, Roger my boy.' Roger started grinning as I handed him to his dad.

"Just then Bryan jumped on the newly built deck that the boys had done six months earlier as he tied the other side of the boat. 'Man, this place gets creepier every time I come ashore.'

"'What's-a matter? Yeah, big chicken, you're afraid the ghost of some dead Jap soldier is going to jump out and get you,' Terry said, laughing as he helped me with the supplies.

"The ship was not really that large, and it had two big diesel engines. But then, it was a larger, powerful PT-397 boat refurbished after the war by Todd's dad when he was working with the Navy Seals in the Vietnam War. Besides, the boat was given to Todd's dad after the war. Then Todd had inherited the boat, which made a prefect wedding present when I married him at eighteen. I was now twenty-one and Roger was nine months.

"I thought I needed to help Todd by being by his side delivering Bibles. My part in doing my husband's ministry was to help feed the hungry men that Todd, Terry, and Bryan brought to the camp to clear it and get it ready.

"The feeling Bryan had of being watched always hovered over us, but we thought it was natives wanting food, or the wild animals in the area. However, I couldn't reason away my fear or do the same thing Terry did by laughing my fears away.

"I would drive myself crazy, as if anybody wasn't crazy to go to an island near hostile Muslim tribes no more than a hundred miles away. The business of the day of setting up camp would move those fears away, and the beauty of tropical sunsets would bring those phobias to a silence. The calm ocean breezes would make for a quiet night's sleep. I moved on with my day-to-day chores.

"The next day we had a quick breakfast of wild rice, papayas, and coconut milk, and my husband was off to smuggle Bibles with Terry and Bryan. I stayed at the base camp to staff the short-wave radio in case there was a storm or they got into trouble with the Muslims. Then I could call the Indonesian Navy to help, because they knew about us being in the area.

"The sky was clear and calm that day when Todd and the boys left, and I had Roger in the crib. He played with his feet and blanket, but most of the time he played with his favorite rattle. I would forever keep that memory of looking into my baby's eyes, because he looked so much like his father. Whenever Todd was gone, I would feel his love for me, but I needed his warmth; then I would look into the eyes that looked so much like his father's, the soft hazel eyes that made me think of him. Whenever Todd was gone, I could look at our son and feel that somehow Todd was looking back at me.

"Somehow in my innermost being I knew I should check the lagoon inlets on the other side of the island, but I was letting my false sense of security take control. Besides, the thought that God was on my side gave me security.

"Roger was busy with his rattle, and I was amusing him. I could not see what was going on behind me. High bursts of static were coming from the radio, as if a storm was coming our way. This particular day it was like the popping sound of popcorn. One time I thought I faintly heard Todd's voice, but I couldn't make it out because the baby threw the rattle under the desk and started to scream.

"I said, sighing, 'Oh now, Roger, I am a little tired of this game now …'"

"Then suddenly someone grabbed me from behind, and I bumped my head under the desk. Suddenly, a hive of bees was loose in my head as I was whirled around, and I knew I was going unconscious. I heard Todd's voice along with shooting in the background, and then the man who grabbed me began speaking in Arabic to another man.

"Todd yelled, 'Imani, get out of there. They are coming onto the island for you.'

"Then the noise of shooting overtook the radio speaker; I heard broken Arabic and broken Thai being spoken in an authoritative tone. Suddenly the radio went dead. I tried to fight the attackers off, but my arms were pinned down. I could hear my clothing being ripped off me. I looked for my baby and heard Roger screaming and crying for me, and when I turned, I saw him being taken away.

"I felt something warm in the back of my head, and I thought my brain was turning into jelly and coming out, because I couldn't feel my lower body anymore. I knew there was a man on top of me, but I couldn't feel him enter me. I saw he was laughing and he looked warped. I started seeing the room spin out of control, and then I blacked out.

"When I awoke from my sleep, I was looking at a little girl lying in a grassy field. As I looked around, I wasn't a twenty-one-year-old black woman any more. I was standing beside the body of a young Caucasian girl dressed in tattered clothing. I couldn't see anything until I felt myself leaving her body, but then I saw she had painful bumps all over her arm. I walked over in the direction of two men in the field.

"'Where is that damn girl?' the first man asked, looking around.

"'She almost certainly is daydreaming again,' the other man said.

"'She has been that way since her mother died,' the first man said, sighing as he made a sign of the cross. 'Bless her heart.'

"'I miss my sister,' the other man said. Then he asked, 'Do we look for her?'

"'She looks so much like her mother,' the first man said. 'She would come out here to the wheat field and look at the road.'

"'Well, brother-in-law, it is getting late. We should call her,' the other man said.

"The father cupped his hands around his mouth and began to yell, 'Mary, Mary, where are you?'

"As they looked for the little girl, I turned away from them. I knew that they were the little girl's father and uncle. As I looked at her, I could see that her body was quickly becoming rancid in the hot midday sun. She seemed to have died from the bubonic plague. I know it wasn't that I was this little girl and myself, because I knew there was an explanation. Then I remembered a prophet friend who told me about some of the visions I would be having. He called them prophetic windows, which allow people to see their past lives.

"Just then, a man caught my eye. I was watching a man in full battle armor riding a horse at breakneck speed toward a country manor in England. At the same time, the little girl's father found her in the field. The dust of the road rose from the horse's hooves plodding down the old Roman cobblestone pathway. The man had a message to give to Lord Charlimas DePaul Vicar the master of the Synod of Clement. The man went and got a blanket to put the girl in, and the uncle dug a hole for the body, which lay flat in the warm sun. The feeling of rising upward, forward, and toward the man overcame me.

"The people beside me never quit working as I sped toward the man, flying faster and faster alongside the rider and his horse. I started to giggle as I twirled in midair. At the same time, I realized I was dead. However, it seemed as if I was an angelic seraphim, flying like a flaming phoenix faster and faster, and I raced with the rider to reach his destination. We went through meadows and hillside cottages as the local villagers watched the man, some moving their children in fear, thinking it was a pale rider of death with bad news.

"Dashing day and night, the rider came closer to the familiar areas, but it was a long trip ever still, and the soldier wouldn't stop until at last a distant manor with dim lighted lamps was in view. The night drew its blanket over the scenery of a northern England castle was warm and inviting, and the castle there would be his resting place from the hours of darkness.

Some oats and water for his horse were going to be his first duty, and some ale and hot mutton for him. It would be a fine feast and a night's rest, he thought. The soft bed and a warm bosom to lie beside would have to wait while the messenger rapidly rode onward.

The hooves of the galloping horse clomped on the cobblestone courtyard. The mist from the roadside had rose as the horse tried breathing more easily and resting from its long journey. The knight had a noble crest on his shield allowed his noble steed to rest and drink the cool water from the trough. The knight beckoned two squires to take the dismounting soldier of fortune to the master of the shire. He walked through the castle's cold corridors toward the shire's entrance.

It was now 1565, and Lord Charlimas DePaul Vicar and Lady Roseland Andante Rothschild were being wed in a chapel, but the two were shaping history after the birth of the child of Lord Charlemagne DePaul Vicar. Because something strange happened before the baby was born, the Lady Roseland Andante Rothschild was shrieking in a devastating call from her sleep, which made her water suddenly break.

She saw in that moment of the dream Cardinal Besant with a shepherd's staff, holding a large royal jewel sphere. As he began coming toward Lady Roseland, Cardinal Besant opened the sphere, and a baby was quietly resting in silky linens. Cardinal Besant grimaced at the child in the jewel sphere while grabbing it by the ankles. Cardinal Besant turned with the lifeless baby in his hand. The cardinal held a large flake under the baby's nose, and as he dripped three drops of blood on the baby's head, the woman drank from the goblet.

Suddenly the wicked woman pulled out her breast and began feeding the infant. The more he drank from the woman's breast, the more the baby shriveled up, until he died. Then Cardinal Besant said prophetically while looking at the child, 'Your blood will pool in thy veins; a mystery must find its abortive strains.'

"'No, no, no,' Lady Roseland yelled. 'You will not, you bastard, you will not have my son. No.'

"'Your blood will pool in thy veins,' Cardinal Besant said in a monotone. 'Inscrutabilities must find its abortive word of three times ten strains.' Suddenly the apparition burst into flames, with the royal ball becoming fiery brands that fell into a pit of hell. The baby began to sink into a molten lava grave that screamed of hellish torments. Moreover, while Lady Roseland watched in horror, the apparition of the cardinal burst into a flaming cloaked skeleton, which took his bishop's staff from his left hand. It suddenly turned into a wheat reaper's staff that cut into her belly, and the water broke.

"The baby came into the world unharmed, or so it seemed to the naked eye. After the wedding, the child was christened Lord Charlemagne DePaul Vicar II, and he grew to become a bishop of the church. Then, all children leave the nest, so did; Bishop Charlemagne DePaul Vicar II moved to France and was placed over the cathedral of Notre Dame until now.

"The rider I saw walked through the castle's cold corridors toward the shire's entrance. Going up the winding stairs toward a lighted room, the weary traveler would soon find rest. Coming in with news from a hard ride, he was coming to see his master, Lord Charlimas DePaul Vicar. He was now much older, and the time was thirty years later.

"Moreover, he was in France, coming to see his father for his birthday. As the knight began to climb the top steps of the cold corridors, many things could be said about his master, Lord Charlimas DePaul Vicar. The knight had wiped many bloodstains off these gloves for his master. He would help clean the memory of who Lord Vicar was while his son was a bishop, but many years earlier at the Synod of Clement, Lord Vicar had spoken of needing a fresh start in a new land.

"Britain at the time was the only place to cover the tracks of his sin-stained hands in hypocrites. Many a tear and much blood had to fall to cover the tracks of the former bishop of the Synod of Clement. Lord Charlimas DePaul Vicar sent a small band of mercenaries to England to make room for the timely arrival of the Vicar family. While he sailed across the English Channel, he had to make the needed preparations to make his castle a home.

"Meanwhile, the people unknowingly never considered that they wouldn't be a problem that needed a solution as residents. They would be looked at as trespassers, to be removed and wiped clean, as if one would wipe blood off a sword.

"The first knight said, 'Look at them.'

"'Like suckling pigs left for the slaughter,' the second knight said.

"'Then let us be the butcher of these hogs,' the third knight said, laughing. 'Hee haw.'

"The Black Knights of the Diocesans of the Order of Christ on the lone hillside marched forward in a line for their tempest of murder. The horses formed a line of twenty men that morning, the vapor from their breath rushing forth as they moved into position. Then they rushed down into the village.

"They began lighting tar-pitched bundles of straw as torches, dragging them through the fields of wheat. Screaming women and crying children of the village tried to run, but none escaped the massacre of the shire that day. Not even a crying baby was spared, for they were all lambs of the slaughter. Meanwhile, in another part of the world, the Crusades were moving toward an end. However, many soldiers and knights were out of jobs and became mercenaries for whoever would pay their price in gold.

"The Spanish Inquisition was beginning her terror, and many of the Waldensian Bible missionaries were running from Roman Catholic mercenaries assigned to murder them. The mercenary army approached a group consisting of Raymond Jabez, the captain of the Swiss army, his wife, and a small band of thirty soldiers with some Lutheran Christians, the two local clerics, and two other men hid the Waldensian Bible missionaries. Meanwhile, a sergeant and a private saw a company of Roman Catholic mercenaries coming toward them.

"'So, what do we have here?' said a Swiss army sergeant.

"'Should we go get Captain Jabez?' the private asked.

"'You tell the others to stand at the ready,' said the Swiss army sergeant.

"'Yes, sir,' the private said.

"'And tell them to keep it quiet until I give the signal.'

"The private crept off into the bushes unobserved by the Roman Catholic mercenaries while the Swiss army sergeant stalled them at the roadblock. 'We bid you good day,' the squire of the Knights Templar said. 'Give us the road of passage in the name of his Eminence Clement VII.'

"'Then let me be thy guide, my lord,' the Swiss army sergeant said respectfully, and then he continued, when he saw the private coming up the road, to act like a guide to the camp. 'By your leave, sir. For it is just beyond that bend, my lord.'"

"The knight sternly exclaimed, 'Granted.'

"As the Roman Catholic mercenaries and the renegade Knight Templar moved forward to advance on the spot where the Waldensian Bible missionaries were in their village, Captain Jabez and his small band of volunteers prepared an ambush, to the surprise of the Roman Catholic mercenaries and the renegade knight. They killed all the Roman Catholic mercenaries but left the renegade Knight Templar alive but very naked and humbly tied to his horse.

"The knight shouted, 'I will come back for my revenge, Captain Jabez.'

"'You better hope your horse remembers where His Eminence is,' Captain Jabez said jestingly.

"'Maybe you should have ridden a carrier pigeon instead,' the Swiss army sergeant yelled. The men in the militia roared with laughter as they saw the scantily clothed knight tied to the horse.

"'Hee haw,' the private yelled as he slapped the horse's flank. 'Get out here!'

"Risking their lives to hide Waldensian Bible missionaries in their village, Captain Jabez took his volunteers and formed a blockade while the others took the missionaries and hid them. The Spanish Inquisition was beginning her terror, and the terrorists moved closer than ever out of the Dark Ages, so they had to hide in the light of the interpretations of life and dawn of enlightenment.

"We would parallel our universe to rise upon the occasion to protect the innocent. The league grew into what might be the Order of the Knights of Jehovah's Anointed Deacons of Evangelism. Our symbol was a jade cross. This is where we gained the name in later years as the Knights of JAD.E to be forbidding antagonists. The Knights Templar, the War Council of the Druid Celebrant, and finally the Sect of the Clover Red Dragons know because of the tattoo the menacing men wore on their right arm. These men were known as the Dregs.

"The Black Knights of the Diocesans of the Order of Christ lasted only as far as steel being tempered in the fire, and only one rose to be the leader of those twenty men and know about the murder they committed. The horses made a line of twenty men who had murdered that morning at the new home of Lord Charlimas DePaul Vicar at the Synod of Clement and who, along with the bloodstained armor, removed their helmets. One lone rider kept his helmet on and raised his hand, lowering it as he watched the nineteen assassinated by crossbow from the woods, and burning and burying their bodies with the rest that day.

"'My lord, they are all dead,' the archer said, bowing.

"'Good,' the lone Black Knight said. 'Make sure there is nothing left, and crush their bones and feed it to the villages for bread as a warning.'

"As the masked man watched, some of his soldiers began burning the bodies and stacking them in front of the burning village. Donning his priestly robe, he came up on the other side, watching the other soldiers driving other villagers toward a field and church near Saint Clement of England. The lone priest began to ride back to the Synod of Clement to Lord Vicar.

"Making the sign of the cross, the priest gleefully said, 'May the Lord bless you in the city and in the field, my children.'

"These destitute children of God moaned, although they had no idea of their fate as lowly serfs. The new villagers of Saint Clement had too much fear to fight back as they went into the village of the former village of Saint Clement as the priest watched from afar. This was the same rider who did all of the Lord Vicar's dirty work from that time on, but he wasn't considered the Black Knight of Clement. He never revealed his identity until after the deed was completed.

"If you were wondering about the Black Knight of Clement, our history would have to go back to the beginning of the Spanish Inquisition. The priest who would one day become the archbishop of Spain, Louis El Deon Ignatius, was called by some in later years the Black Pope. For now, the Black Knight of Clement would rise to power by the edge of his sword.

"As Sir Louis El-Deon Ignatius began toward the doors, passing the great Danes, he stood in the great hall of his master, Lord Charlimas DePaul Vicar. The Black Knight this time didn't have to worry about the smeared bloodstains on his gloves.

"Many times Sir Louis El-Deon Ignatius would have to be alive for centuries to come, and God Almighty kept him alive as a curse to wipe bloodstains off his gloves. For he would drink the cup of iniquity of the innocent blood for a thousand years and create the blood cult of parasites to do his bidding.

"The Synod of Clement came to be small things for Lord Vicar overpowers the peasants of the village as he came into his own. Sir Louis El-Deon Ignatius was secretly becoming a man of great power and substance. He could not bloody his hands while he was the priest of the village of Clement, but he became a masked bandit known as the Black Bandit of Saint Clement.

"Once an unaware local lord or friar came into the Commonwealth of Saint Clement and went through the dark forest of Saint Clement. The lone bandit came to call on the foolish rider and his small band of soldiers.

"The bishop called, 'Captain?'

"'Yes, Your Grace.'

"'How long to the shire?'

"'Well, if we take the left path, it will take two more days,' the captain responded.

"'And what about that path?' the bishop asked, pointing at the road on the right of the fork.

"'That one will be about two hours,' the captain continued. 'But there are rumors of bandits on this road.'

"'Well, rumors are like mouths …'

"'Yes, sir, to the right driver."

"The coachmen and guards went farther into the deep, dark forest, which had an eerie sound of silence that made even the horse edgy. Then from the trees came an arrow, hitting the captain in the chest and knocking him off his horse as it dragged him back down the path. The coachman slapped the horse and drove forward as the bishop screamed like a girl at the rough ride ahead. A black flash of a caped man knocked the driver off to the ground, and the bandit drove off into a cove from a steep cliff.

"'Whoa, horse,' yelled the bandit.

"The bishop happily asked, 'Driver, are we at the end of the line?'

"'Yes, Your Grace,' the bandit said as he pointed his sword at his throat.

"'You scoundrel, I am a man of the cloth,' the bishop barked in anger. 'How dare you.'

"'Then maybe you would prefer to meet your maker now," the bandit said as he looked over the cliff and kicked a rock over the edge. "It's a long way down, Your Grace."

"He shouted, 'You wouldn't dare.'

"'Since you don't have wings,' the bandit said, yanking the bishop out of the coach, 'I would get moving, my fat friend.'

"As the bishop limped on up the road, the bandit drove on the road and saw the captain of the guard standing in the middle of the road on horseback with his sword drawn. The bandit stopped the coach two horse lengths from the captain, and they stared at each other for a moment.

"'Have you been waiting long?'

"'Long enough,' the captain said.

"'I suppose you want this?' the bandit responded.

"'It would be nice.'

"Well." Reaching into the chest, the bandit threw two bags of gold, one at a time, at the captain. When the captain caught them, he continued, "You are lucky I am a good shot with my crossbow."

"'Well, I am lucky that I doubled my mallet and armor,' the captain said, grinning.

"'You've earned your keep, my old friend,' the bandit said.

"'Thank you again, my lord,' the captain responded. 'Until we meet again, sir.'

"Then the bandit revealed his identity as Sir Louis El-Deon Ignatius, the Black Knight of Saint Clement. Lord Charlimas DePaul Vicar had to have a mercenary such as the Black Knight to do his bidding.

"Nevertheless, how did Lord Vicar truly retain the service of Sir Louis El-Deon Ignatius? Lord Vicar was once the bishop of the Synod of Clement and keeping the balance of being a humble servant of God and trying collecting pew taxes from fifty shires in a peaceable manner.

"Moreover, when the bishop of the Synod of Clement first came to the region, he sent his priest to collect his tithe from the lords of the area. However, when the mogul barons beat the priest and stripped him bare, he decided to go and do it himself against the advisement of his priest.

"When Bishop Dominican came to the first twenty shires, he was badly beaten while running into the forest. In the distance, a shadowy figure of a horse and his rider stood watching. Then when the bishop fled into the forest, running tired and wounded, he looked up and thought he saw a ghost following him.

"As Bishop Dominican lay against a tree to tend his wounds, in wrenching pain, he met the then young Spaniard, the Black Knight Sir Louis El-Deon Ignatius. The Black Knight of Spain had just come from a jousting match in Paris. He was courting a fair lady at one of the shires and saw the good bishop, and when Bishop Dominican had just fallen asleep, he woke with a lance tipping his bishop's coronet into his naked lap.

"Bishop Dominican asked roughly, 'Are you here for your bundle, too?'

"'If I were a rogue,' bellowed back Sir Louis El-Deon Ignatius, 'then yes, Your Grace.'

"'Then be done with me if you are of those barbaric baron rogues,' snapped Bishop Dominican.

"'What would you do to my lords, Your Grace?' Sir Louis El-Deon Ignatius asked.

"'And if I could be the man I was,' Bishop Dominican exclaimed, grinning, 'I would be like David, who took the foreskins of the Philistines, or Samson when he stripped the Philistine lords of their clothing and then burned their fields with foxtail firebrands.'

"'Your anger is ferocious, but as you wish,' Sir Louis El-Deon Ignatius replied calmly.

"Bishop Dominican stood in marvel of the young knight as he began to ride away, and the bishop walked back to the monastery. Then Sir Louis El-Deon Ignatius arose and went, taking fifty men, and slaughtered all of the one hundred men, taking their foreskins and burning their fields with fire, because the shires robbed the bishop and his priest of their dues. Sir Louis El-Deon Ignatius brought their foreskins, and then gave them in full tally of the tax to the bishop.[5]

"He threw the bag of foreskins and money that was owed to the monastery at the bishop's feet. The bishop came to depend on Lord Louis El-Deon Ignatius with a grateful smile, and wanted to reward him. 'What can I do for my lord Ignatius to repay your valiant deed?' the bishop asked gleefully.

"Sir Ignatius replied, 'Whenever you need me, I will be in your debt.'

"'Why are you in my debt?' Bishop Dominican asked, marveling.

"'Because you are a true patron of the church,' Sir Ignatius said.

"The bishop of the Synod of Clement, casting doubt on his sincerity, asked, 'And how much will this debt cost me?'

'In time, Your Grace,' Lord Ignatius said vaguely. 'In time we will, yes, we will fill in those blanks.'

"While Lord Charlimas DePaul Vicar was a man of substance, he could not bloody his hands when he donned the robe and collar of the Anglican clergy. Now Lord Charlimas DePaul Vicar and Lord Louis El-Deon Ignatius had moved back to the Synod of Clement in northern England, and they had to keep secret the moving of the mother church's rise of the new theocracy.

"In Scotland and in shires of northern counties of England he removed the name of the old monastery and had his castle. Now standing before his partner both Lord's Charlimas DePaul Vicar and Sir Louis El-Deon Ignatius came to gather for a different reason. Unexpectedly, Lord Louis El-Deon Ignatius had to tell his lord something that he knew would hurt both his wife and Lord Charlimas DePaul Vicar.

"After the wedding, and the birth of the child, who was christened Charlemagne DePaul Vicar II, he was going to become the bishop of Brussels, a political chess move of his father. The young Bishop Vicar II, who was the prize of his mother's looks and caught the eyes of any of the fair ladies of France, was finally turning thirty years old.

"Bishop Charlemagne DePaul Vicar II could have been a fine prince or duke who could have married into royalty. Instead he wanted to please his father, and was going to be the youngest bishop of France's Notre Dame Cathedral.

"Providing his father had his way, Charlemagne DePaul Vicar II could soon be the next papal leader over the mother church in Rome. He was greeted at the large doors of the great halls and manors all across France, and Lord Louis

El-Deon Ignatius was always guarding Bishop Charlemagne DePaul Vicar II. Many times Lord Ignatius would come bearing news of the bishop's affairs, and he never needed an introduction to the couple but was always given a warm welcome at the estate.

"Coming in with news from a hard ride, Lord Louis El-Deon Ignatius was approaching the door of his longtime friends' sitting room. Lord Charlimas DePaul Vicar was with his wife, Lady Roseland Andante Rothschild, and both were much older. 'My lord,' Sir Louis El-Deon Ignatius said in a sad voice, 'My lady.'

"Lord Charlimas DePaul Vicar said, smirking, 'Why the long face? You had spoiled wine?'

"Now standing before his partner, Lord Charlimas DePaul Vicar, he had to tell his lord something that he knew would hurt both him and his wife. "Your face does read so obvious," Lady Roseland Andante Rothschild said while doing petit point. "It's as if you had something of tragic poison to say."

"Then she looked at his face again and stopped what she was doing. Lord Charlimas DePaul Vicar stood up and walked over to Lord Ignatius, trying to hide his tears. Sir Louis El-Deon Ignatius forced himself to be the bearer of the news he had to tell.

"'Unexpectedly,' Lord Louis El-Deon Ignatius said, 'Bishop Charlemagne DePaul Vicar II, your son, is dead.' Hearing the news, Lady Roseland Andante Rothschild flung herself onto her husband with a scream of disbelief.

"'My prince is gone,' Lady Roseland Andante Rothschild sobbed. 'No, not my little prince.' Coming over to her, Lord Charlimas DePaul Vicar put his arms around her, a blank look on his face. All Sir Ignatius could do was watch with tears in his eyes. Many months later in the quiet of the spring sun, the villagers were working in the fields, never having to feel the wrath of soldiers raiding Vicar Manor. Peace was finally in this part of the country.

"This was not a time of joy for this man, because this was not the grave of a person who had finished running the race of life to its full, and the tombstone read as such: *Here lies the body of God's young soldier. My beloved only son: Bishop Charlemagne DePaul Vicar II. Born September 14, 1535. Died April 6, 1565. For God so loved the world that he gave his only begotten Son, that whosoever believeth in him shall not perish, but have everlasting life. John 3:16.*

"'Why must my son die of noble birth,' Lord Vicar yelled, shaking his fist. 'Take my cursed life?'

"Meanwhile, in the domicile of Vicar Manor, Lady Roseland Vicar tossed and turned in bed. She began to sweat from her brow as her closed eyes fluttered frantically.

"'Your blood will pool in thy vein,' Cardinal Medici said in a monotone.

"'Mysteries must find its abortive strain.'

"Suddenly the flash of apparition burst into flames. "No, no, no!" Lady Roseland yelled, 'Stop! You can't have my son, you can't have him, No, no.' She had to see the horror of the same apparition flashing of the cardinal burst into a flaming skeleton.

"'Stop, not my son, no,' she screamed in torment.

"Then all fell quiet as the sweating woman raised herself in the large bed and looked around for someone. Meanwhile, Lord Vicar looked up toward the window from which the scream came. Knowing it was his wife, he lowered his head, because in his soul he knew he was the cause of these family tragedies. He would carry the grief of his sin to his grave and lose another jewel in his crown. Many years later, his wife died from the black plague too.

"Bishop Charlemagne DePaul Vicar II died suddenly of an unknown plague before his thirtieth birthday, and Lady Roseland Andante Vicar died as well. Lord Charlimas DePaul Vicar and Lord Louis El-Deon Ignatius were now in northern England alone, and the Vicar's kept the moving of the mother church from coming to power in England. Lord Vicar hoped his son would rise to power by came the next pope. When Bishop Vicar II had died of an unknown disease, yet the hope of another Vicar would be on the rising of their theocracy by their grandson the Reverend Samuel Charlimas Vicar. Because his father, Bishop Charlemagne DePaul Vicar II, was a man with an appetite for the ladies of court much like his father. Rather than being a fatherless child, he secretly married a baron's daughter while taking care of her by writing her from the estate of Vicar Manor.

"So that the Reverend Samuel Charlimas Vicar could continue to be the clarion call to keep the church growing, Sir Louis El-Deon Ignatius stood before his partner to help Lord Charlimas DePaul Vicar pay his debt to their old friend Pope Clement VII for the curse he now realized had come true.

"Lord Vicar called on his friend to do one more task, so Sir Louis El-Deon Ignatius, who was now the archbishop of Spain and thought to be the fabled but feared Black Pope of the Society of Jesuits, was coming one last time, not to do his master's bidding, but as a friend.

"'What is thy bidding, my lord?' Archbishop Ignatius asked.

"'It is you that I should be calling lord, Your Grace,' Lord Vicar exclaimed while coughing.

"Nonsense, old friend. I have made a pledge to you," Archbishop Ignatius said.

"'I need the thorns in my side removed,' Lord Vicar said.

'All of them that threaten my line. Then I will release you from your pledge and reward you with this devil's brew.'

"The archbishop asked, 'What is it?'

"'Take this and mix this blood with your wine,' responded Lord Vicar, 'and the Count of Transylvania will be in your blood and you will be of the undead.'

"'How did you get this?' asked Archbishop Ignatius.

"'I was in his region as a young priest. They had slain Count Vladimir Dracula and I saw him on the battlefield dying, so before he died, I gave him his last rites. He told me these words before he died: "On a red full moon, take my blood and drink it. You will be as the undead, my boy."'

"'This is my gift to you, my old friend …'

"When Archbishop Ignatius heard the plea of his old friend, a rider was sent forth to poison the elderly Pope Clement VII. The poisoning was so shrewd that it makes me quiver. The messenger had a letter addressed to the pope from the dying Charlemagne DePaul Vicar asking to be forgiven of his many sins. The letter went something like this:

"My dear graceful Clement, the seventh of the fifty-seventh papal dynasty,

"Your Grace, I have sinned before my Father in heaven and your holy church. My last wish is to be taken from my plight of purgatory and forgiven of my many sins and given my last rite of burial.

"Yours truly,

"Lord Charlemagne DePaul Vicar

"When his eminence read the letter, he stroked his chin and the corner of his lips, which caused the poison to go into his skin and made them dry. Consequently, he licked them and unknowingly swallowed the poison. He laughed at the request, and then he was laughing so hard, he clutched his heart and died on his throne with the letter in his hand. They had to break the finger of the vicar of the mother church to get the letter out of his hand—the same finger that had cast such a wicked curse on the Vicar family.

"As great King Solomon once said, 'When the whirlwind passes, the wicked is no more; but the righteous is an everlasting foundation.'

"In the intervening time, Lord Vicar began to laugh on his deathbed, and then he coughed his final breath. 'My sons will come to power,' he said as he gasped for air. 'Even though it's my final hour, a Vicar will be the next pope—if not the emperor of this world.'

"I could see the man dying, and the end of what I saw as a terrible dream or vision, and then I turned away from him. I watched the closing of these events in what seemed like history. I was no longer a spirit being, but I was myself. I turned, and saw my body being dumped into the sea, and I heard a voice behind me softly calling my name.

"'Imani … Imani … Imani … turn around.'

"It was the Lord Jesus Christ and all his angels lined up in a row, and it was he who called my name. 'Imani, it was me who called your name.' He continued, 'I could call you home, but then who would I have to do my work in your home of Australia?'

"'Do I have to go back to where I was?' I asked the Lord.

"'You will have no memory of what happened," the Lord said, 'until I bring the grief and pain of what you lost back to you.'

"'Will I get my son back?' I asked.

"'That will be up to you,' the Lord said. 'But there is someone who wants to say something to you.'

"Then from behind the Lord came Todd, my friend, my husband, and lover, and he spoke to me as only Todd could have done. I felt like my heart could jump out of my chest and land in his arms, because here was everything that was important in my life. I had known no other man but Todd, and I had his baby, who was now gone from me as well.

"'Todd,' I cried.

"'Imani, babe, we can't stay here for long,' he said softly.

"'What do you mean?' I asked. 'We've got all eternity ...'

"'I can't explain. Lord, please show her,' Todd said, turning away from me as the Lord showed me Roger down in the bow of the ship alone and crying. My heart broke for him. Then Todd turned to me. "He needs you, Imani, he needs you." Then Todd went up into heaven, leaving me to make that choice by myself. I didn't understand then, but it was Todd's time to be with God, but my time had not come yet. He faded from my sight, going through the gates of heaven.

"I was thinking about what I should do when the Lord came to me as I looked back at my body floating in the water. I heard people of my native tongue shouting at my body as it floated lifeless and empty above the water. "Hey, there's a woman overboard." I was taken out of the water and started coughing up the seawater in my lungs. I couldn't think anymore, and for some reason I couldn't remember how I had gotten in the water or why I was naked.

"I was labeled the mermaid lost at sea, but I had no memory of who I was or how I had gotten into the predicament of being in the water. The authorities knew I had been raped and left for dead, but how I got that way was the mystery of my life for years. I didn't even know my own name. I would be a mystery that led me to meet and marry my husband, Hauschka Makoto, who is a Watchman of extraordinary abilities and gifts. We always work together."

When Elder Zarepath finished her story, I was almost

breathless with wanting to know how she had gotten her memory back and how she had met the next elder who would train me, but mostly how she had become the elder to learn the law of faith. As we walked, she wouldn't reveal her story or even go back, because we had to go to chapel that night. I was invited to her house that night, and then maybe I could pry the end of the story out of her. Then I asked her one more question.

"Who gave you your name, Imani?"

She just looked at me and smiled, saying, "You should know that answer …"

From that point on, I knew I had met my younger sister and that God had reunited us. I wanted to talk with her more, but she never gave me too much time. I wanted to know what had happened to her and how she had come here to the Watchman's tabernacle, Had she ever found her son? But time would bring us together again for a reunion.

CHAPTER 9

♟ ♟ ♟

The Birth of a Legacy

July 16, 2057

Dear Abba,

I can remember the day when my father, Richard Anthony Moore, was dying in his bed. I came home from the White House for my vacation because he was dying. The cabdriver took me back to 4388 Colony Square Parkway in my old neighborhood in Norfolk, Virginia. His nurse let me in, and I went in to his room after I had fixed him a good lunch.

We began to talk about my crazy ways when we lived in Port Norfolk, and the times he had to bail me out of a lot of butt whippings. He began to flash back, and the subject came up when I told my dad that I was taking care of the president's nephew, Natal Apollyon Vicar. When he told me he knew the father of Rebecca Carolina Vicar's son, I was all ears.

In a smoky local hotel and casino named Sierra Tahoe Hotel in downtown Incline Village, Nevada, the late spring weather was hot in that small town. It was the late sixties, and many of the people were playing the penny and nickel slot machines. Some were standing around milking the bar for every drop of liquor they could get from the bartender.

A couple stood out in the crowd, and several drunk patrons stood watching the man in an army uniform dancing in the misty smell of cigarette smoke and liquored perfume that swelled the atmosphere. The jukebox blasted Curtis Pennington singing "When a Man Loves a Woman" before a live audience. All the jealous and prejudiced stares were peering at the dancing to the music. The couple began to sway back and forth to the old tune.

"We were back in the sixties," my dad exclaimed. "No colored boy in his right mind would make the moves on a white girl." My dad started telling me about this couple.

Many people were dancing, and my dad, Staff Sergeant Richard Moore of Third Battalion, Fourth Army Division of Fort Douglas, Nevada, was in Bravo Company and in charge of Second Platoon. Where I was over the entire soldiers in Second Platoon, and Walt Parson was dancing with the pretty little brunette. We were not that close in those days, but you know how you get when you are about to meet your maker going into combat. I guess it was time to confess my sin, and I was the one to be his priest that day.

"You just didn't date a woman of another race in the in the town of Incline Village, Nevada," Richard told me.

While the couple was dancing away, it seemed that some of the locals didn't care in those days, but others good ole' boys of the town tried to make it a problem. Nevertheless, Walt was my father's friend. Walt Parson was his buddy in the Army, and he was going to protect my friend. "I tried to keep Big Walt in check from the neck up," my dad said.

"That fool is going to get us killed if not lynched," one black soldier said as he sipped his beer.

Gulping down his whiskey another black soldier said, "We're in the west. They don't lynch here …"

"No, they just shoot you outright," Staff Sergeant Moore barked. "Shut up, the both of you."

I guess his friend Walt was going to let his other head do the talking that night. The way my dad told it as he flashed back, he wasn't going to let anybody so much as step his way. "I'd be on them like a chicken on a June bug," he said, laughing.

The two looking around after coming back to reality tried to leave the dance floor. Rebecca unintentionally bumped into a white man. The man was a stud of a specimen: tall, blond wavy hair, and steel-blue eyes. He grabbed Rebecca's dainty hand and tried to pull her closer to her.

"Come on, honey," the man insisted, "let's do some real dancing instead of that nigger jitterbugging." Walt just calmly moved between them and grabbed the young buck by breaking the foolish white boy's hold on Rebecca.

"Excuse me, sir," Walt calmly interrupted. "I believe the lady is with me."

"Hey, boy, when I want a nigger's advice, I'll get a whip and a chair," the foolish man said, moving toward Walt.

Meanwhile, my dad told me the tension was getting thick enough to cut with a knife. He and a couple of the boys who were with Walt Parson began to move out from their back-row seats, and if you looked at Walt, you knew he was not a person to be taken lightly. At six feet two inches, he was a powerhouse, and Staff Sergeant Moore and the other men made their way closer to the bar where the action was about to take place.

The three were outnumbered by the locals, who had started laughing at what the tall, blond redneck had said. Walt spun around with a bar stool and broke it right across the man's frame. Blood gushed out of the man's mouth as he sailed across the bar into the bartender.

Walt just smiled at the men. "You mean this chair?"

The two studs were outnumbered when the men could only look in shock and dread as the hail of fists rained down on their foolish racial parade. Walt grabbed Rebecca, who had her mouth open in shock, and they ran out of the bar as my dad and his partners in crime fought off the onslaught of attacks from the mob and then ran out of the bar.

The two left for a hotel later that night to hide from the MPs who had started looking for the rioters. They knew they couldn't get a room together, so Rebecca got one. She was nervously trying to put the key in the door when Walt came up from behind, surprising her.

"I'll help you with that," Walt said, romantically calm.

"Oh my God," she cried softly as she hit his shoulder. "You scared me to death."

He flung open the door, picked her up, carried her over the threshold, and then turned her around. Walt used her feet to close the door with a slam. Rebecca leaned closer to his ear and held him tight as he carried her to the bed.

"I hope you are able to do this for me again when it counts," she said softly.

Walt put her down by sliding her small, shapely frame down in front of his tall body. Her chestnut-brown eyes peered into his for that answer every woman needed to hear. Rebecca began thinking, *Will this last just for tonight or will this be the last night I am ever alone?* Rebecca had experienced that too many times with men of her own race.

Reassuringly Walt said to her, "I'm here as long as you need me."

They smiled at each other, and then she leaned toward the large framed man, pushing him to sit on the bed at the headboard. As he tried to pull her to him, she moved his arms from around her.

Then she got up from the bed, walked around the corner of the bed, and sat down with her back to him. Rebecca began to move her long brown hair over her right shoulder, and slowly unzipped her dress. Then she pulled it off with her back toward Walt while he sat back on the bed. Watching the show, he gazed at Rebecca as she elegantly removed her glasses and slip, and then the lights were turned off.

Only the blinking of the florescent light showed the silhouette of her frame. The shadow of them making love ended as they lay together in the room. They both knew that more had to come of this love affair.

"I want you to see me for more than what you see here," she said softly. "And I want to ask you this one question."

"Okay," Walt said reassuringly, and he leaned toward her.

"What is it you see in me?" Rebecca inquired.

"I see this as a sign of your love for me," Walt said, stopping his approach toward her. Then he continued, "I've never had a woman search my heart this way."

"How is it that you can't see my heart?" Rebecca questioned.

"Because when I look into your eyes it's that," —he paused—"you are mystique, and at the same time since we first met two months ago as friends in Incline Village. I didn't know whether to would like me the first time we met, and our chemistry together is great."

"Why do you think I'm mystique?" she asked.

"There is something about you that is unknown, it's in your eyes," he said.

"Really," Rebecca responded. "Will you bear your soul to me?"

"If God is not bringing you and me together"—Walt came closer to her—"then I hope I die never loving again."

Rebecca smiled and leaned toward him, kissing his lips while her hair fell, covering her face like a veil. They both fell back on the bed, and Rebecca moved between his legs as she began stripping off his shirt. She kissed his chest and rubbed her nose against his chest hairs. They began to make love to each other, and this was the beginning of their courtship toward a relationship and marriage. I knew my father's story was from the point of view of a sinner. I wondered why he was telling about these two people as he continued.

As Rebecca lay in Walt's arms later that night, the streetlight shimmered over their nude bodies. They looked at each other, knowing that she was carrying the life of someone who would change the spectrum of their lives forever.

They were in love, and both of them being so young brought together a love that they hoped would bear all things, believe all things, and endure all things. The time passed as things do. As it is written, to everything there is a season, and a time to every purpose under heaven: a time to be born, and a time to die; a time to plant, and a time to pluck up that which is planted.

When Walt found out that Rebecca was pregnant with his baby, and he went to her place to ask her if she was really pregnant without a hitch. My dad remembered the day well. They were at the barracks that rainy day in November, and it was supposed to snow up in the mountains that weekend. Walt showed up at her house to get the news from her. He knocked at the door, and She opened the door to see Walt standing there.

"Are you pregnant, is it true?" he asked.

"Yes."

"I'm going to make my wife Rebecca, the child will lack for nothing," he said.

Walt picked her up and swung her around, and kisses her as the door shut. My dad said that after Walt got the call, he ran back to him. Staff Sergeant Richard Moore was sitting behind his desk in the Quonset hut while the rain rattled on the roof. Walt ran around like a chicken with its head cut off.

"What's a dazed and crazed thing got stirring you about?" Sergeant Richard Moore yelled.

"I got to go get married, Sarge," Walt shouted, showing him the ring.

"Get out of here and take care of your business, boy," Staff Sergeant Moore said, laughing.

Then both of them were standing at an altar in front of the priest at Saint Michael of the Archangel Catholic Church at Stead Air Force Base, and the baby came seven months later. Walt and Rebecca tried for many years to have a baby, but Rebecca had one miscarriage after another.

Six years later, on January 30, 1968, the men of Bravo Company under Staff Sergeant Richard Moore with the help of Corporal Walt Charles Vicar were in the Vietnam War before the Vietnamese New Year's celebration of Tet and the Tet Offensive was about to take place. In the early morning, the men of Bravo Company Second Platoon were coming back from night patrols. Corporal Walt Vicar was in charge of Third Squad, which was in the rear. Corporal Bill Johnson, a farm boy from Montana who was in charge of the heavy weapons of second squadron, and Sergeant Richard Moore were covering the front with the main body of the assault and auto machine gunners.

"Hey, Corporal Dicey," Sergeant Moore whispered sharply, "you get those AMGs' asses in gear and quit bunching together."

"Sure thing, Sergeant," Corporal Dicey responded.

As the assault and auto machine gunners were moving

back toward Corporal Walt Vicar, Third Squad Corporal Johnson of Second Squadron got hit by sniper fire and fell down with three shots to the chest. The Montana farm boy lay motionless, and then three other riflemen followed his lead when they came over to help.

"Hit the deck, you clown," Staff Sergeant Moore screamed. "Walt, give 'em cover fire on our flank." However, Charlie hit two of the M-60s before they could move. Walt knew that if someone did take the M-60 spot quick, they would be overrun. Suddenly he jumped up, and he was seen hit by the fire of swarming bullets that came at him like angry bees.

Diving over the other dead soldier as though playing leapfrog, he picked up one of the M-60s from a dead man and began to ward off the advancing Viet Cong offensive. As Walt charged single-handedly with the M-60, I tried to warn him to get out of there.

"Hey, you dumb-ass Negro, we don't need a black hero," my dad yelled at Walt.

Nevertheless, Walt got his squad around to set up a perimeter as a counterattack against the ambush that we were suddenly being pulled into. Along with running out of ammo, he continued fighting them with his pistol and even with an AK-47 he took from a dead member of the Viet Cong.

When it was over, Walt was facedown. I ran over to him. He said he was shot up pretty bad, but this was my best friend, my dad told me, and if this was going to be his last time seeing him, he told me he needed to do something for him.

"Rich, Rich," he gasped.

"You damn fool, I told you to keep your ass down," Sergeant Moore cried. "Medic, get your ass over here."

"Listen, man," he said as he grabbed me, getting serious.

"Okay, I'm listening." My dad started crying as he looked his dying friend in the face.

"Man, will you do this for me?" Walt asked.

"Okay, what, Walt?" my dad asked.

"When I am dead, Rich, take some of my blood and keep it for my son." He repeated it twice as he handed my dad a capsule encased in a thick cassette.

"What the hell is this?" Moore asked.

"Listen, man, I don't have time." Walt began to choke as he pleaded, "Have one of the corpsman transfer it from my vein."

"Okay," Richard said.

Walt said, looking into my eyes, "It must be blue with no oxygen."

Then, pulling my ear to his lips, he whispered something in my ear. When I heard it, I called over the corpsman. As he heard me and what I asked him to do, I got the craziest look.

"Just do it, damn it," he said to the medic.

"I have to make a vacuum, so take this capsule," the corpsman said. "Now, when I say go, take his capillary as I tie it off and put it in the container, got it?"

With the skill of a surgeon, the medic somehow made an airtight seal, and I saw Walt's blue blood in that small vial. When the medic was finished, I put it in the steel cassette, and then my dad's flashback of those days was gone as he stared out the window. Little did I know what the blood was going to be used for in the future.

I kept the blood frozen in dry ice until I got it back to Rebecca. She gave it to a scientist who was doing experiments in cloning and DNA alteration. Ten years later Natal Apollyon Vicar was introduced to the European world as the first successful human clone.

When they brought Natal's father back, he had died at thirty years old, and my father told me that he was questioning what Walt had told him. Coming home from the war, he never thought that I would be a part of the group that would have to protect his best friend's son.

Corporal Walter Charles Vicar was awarded the Medal of Honor for bravery and self-sacrifice above and beyond the call of duty. Nevertheless, my dad couldn't get that old war story out of his head that his friend had told him, and as I watched my dad slip into eternity, I couldn't believe he had held that story all those years.

I first met Natal Apollyon Vicar when he was ten years old after the death of his mother, Rebecca, and his uncle, who was president. He was the son of a Medal of Honor recipient, but his father was as hush-hush as Jefferson's black children were.

Natal was soon sent to a military academy in Portsmouth, Virginia, to keep the family secret. The president had other children to deal with, in addition to his half-breed nephew. I would hear that argument, like a dripping faucet in my mind, from the first lady.

"He's your own flesh and blood, damn it," the first lady said sharply to her husband.

"He might have my sister's flesh, but he's not blood," the president replied. "But I have to take care of her abomination."

Many doors would slam, not so much to help him deal with his feelings as to keep the staff and servants from leaking their words to the press. The Secret Service kept every argument under their radar of silence.

The young Vicar didn't cry from the dreadful beatings and tongue lashings he got almost daily while he was at the academy. For the many years that he suffered, Natal could never grow or heal from those inner wounds from the prejudice that came from being a half-breed child.

He remembered the prejudice that came from being a half-breed; being a melting-pot child, the brown-haired, green-eyed boy used his hidden charm in years to come to build and feed that necessary monster of his own design.

One time when he was about twelve, he didn't come for home spring break. I made my way down to the academy and walked into his room. The room was very stately and well furnished with medals, trophies, and plaques of his many achievements and letters of appreciation.

One lonely bed with a cover of the school's colors was neatly made in the corner. A shelf kept his color guard dress cover, and a parade saber hung over them. Although the room was neat and tidy, it seemed very cold and calculated, as if some wife with an excessive compulsive behavior dysfunction was cleaning it. The spirits of bondage seemed to try to grip me to see if it was clean, and I had to operate in the law of kindness just to keep my sanity.

"Well, my little conqueror seems to have done very well here," I said, looking around.

"It would seem you are the only one to notice," Natal said sharply.

"I didn't come here to defend him but to comfort you," I said, and then, "You aren't coming home, dear child."

"What is there to come home to?" he responded in a depressing tone.

I asked, "What are you working on?"

"It's my finals term paper," Natal said softly. "I have to give a purpose for my mission in life."

"You aren't even a freshman in high school," I said, and began to ponder.

"What else is there to do when you have nowhere to go?" he said.

"Some friends of mine used to tell me a long time ago,

'Put the vision in writing and make it clear on stones, so that the reader may go quickly …'"

"Why on stones?" he questioned.

"Well," I explained sympathetically, "the stone means the tablets of your heart."

"Why does the vision go quickly after I read it?" Natal asked while sitting up straight.

In detail, I began to explain to him as he nodded. "It is intended for the vision to be completed for a fixed time."

"What does a vision have to do with a purpose?" he asked.

"For one thing, every person has a purpose," I said. "But only God can give a vision, and when you ask God for your purpose, he shows you a vision, and it is moving quickly to the end to make you complete."

"Will this vision God gives me ever not comes true?" Natal asked.

"It will not be false, even if it is slow in coming," I explained, "because waiting for it gives experience, and experience, hope, but hope that achieves shame isn't from God. If our hearts are full of the love of God through the Holy Spirit, which is given to us … it will bring true peace and not shame."

Then he asked me with tears in his eyes, "Will my dream come true?"

"If you trust in God as your Father, it will certainly come true." I put my arms around him and said, "If you ask Jesus as your Lord and savior, it will not be kept back."

He asked, "Can I have this Jesus?"

I said reassuringly, "Yes, as it is written, you are my friends if you do what I give you orders to do."

Then Natal Apollyon Vicar said something that came straight out of the Bible, and it was as if the whole earth stood still to see what he was going to say. I never would have believed it and never understood that this boy was going to be saved. Until now, the Watchmen would have called me a liar. It was poetic when he made the statement that seemed to seal his faith; nevertheless, he just came right out with it.

He asked, "What must I do to be saved?"

I mean, what choice did I have? I couldn't just ignore what he'd said, so I had to lead him through the steps of salvation. I was a believer in Christ, never doubting for a moment that he was sincere.

When it was all said and done, I was responsible for bringing Natal to a full knowledge of the truth of who Christ Jesus was, and I was going to take him into the knowledge of becoming an obedient Christian in action. I was going to help him, if not make him; understand who he was in Christ. Even if it cost me my life.

My purpose was his discipleship, and I needed him to work the spiritual principles that I had been taught by getting him to know who he really was in Christ. I took him back to the White House to his aunt and uncle. I then packed up his things and took him to my summer place out in Camp David, where a lot of the White House staff stayed when there was no room at the White House. I was one of twelve chief stewards for the Oval Office.

The White House had more than 620 on-call housecleaners, butlers, chefs, nannies, and chief stewards. We had to be ready to serve at a moment's notice. I had to ask the president if I could take on the responsibility of mentoring Natal. I ran it by the first lady before I went into the lion's den.

That particular day, the president had just returned from golfing with Mr. Hope. The president asked the main kitchen staff if they could bring him a cold drink. I had to show the first lady the menu and wine list for the dinner as well before he took his shower so he could go meet the secretary of state about some important meeting with the Soviet leaders. I knew this was my chance to make my move as far as the news about Natal's future. The president was in his stateroom with the first lady. As I carried the tray into the president, the first lady gave me a smile when I passed by her.

"Here you are, Mr. President," I said, handing him his drink. "Madam, here is the menu and wine list for the Soviet diplomats and their wives."

"Thank you, Ray," the first lady said, smiling. "Honey, have you heard anything from Natal since he's been on spring break?"

"I haven't really thought about it, baby," the president responded while drinking his iced tea. He had a dubious look on his face. However, never willing to show it to me, he grabbed the paper from his desk and, picking up his glasses, began reading.

"Well, I was thinking that instead of the boy hanging around here all summer and every break," the first lady said, continuing her pitch, "maybe he ..."

"Well, now that's a deep subject. Let's talk about that," the president said.

"He could stay with Raymond at Camp David," she said with a smirk.

"My mother was right about you. You always lay your case out like a lawyer," the president said. "And I suppose you've already approved of this, Ray?"

"Well, sir, he does need some family guidance," I replied.

"If you weren't an ex-Marine, and if *you* weren't my wife," the president said sharply, "I'd send you both to Russia to deal with Brezhnev."

That was the beginning of my disciplining Natal, and we had many great times together. He even got baptized in the stream right down from the ranch in the area. Once I took Natal to the church in town, and we went to the Antioch Assemblies of God. Natal was complaining about his head hurting, so he went up and got prayer. When the elders came around him, they anointed his head with oil. He didn't have the headaches anymore.

CHAPTER 10

The Testimonial of Truth

Things began to make sense to Natal, and life seemed to make sense for once, like I told some of you a while back while I was lying down. I saw this fully white-haired man standing in front of me in my dreams …

"Ahh," I screamed, and then I shouted, "Who are you?"

"Do not be afraid." The man spoke softly. "I am one of the twenty-four elders here to give you a message, Watchman Moore."

"I was told that to be a Watchman, you have to have died."

"It is written in the book of his law as the apostle of the Gentiles wrote, 'Beginning from the baptism of John, unto the day that he was received up from us, of these must one become a witness with us of his resurrection. … And they prayed, and said, Thou, Lord, who knows the hearts of all men …' so the Christ has chosen you as one of his Watchmen," the elder said.

I asked, "When did this happen?"

"Remember when thou died in the land of Afghanistan?" he asked.

"Yes."

"Have you seen the Lord Christ in a vision?" the elder asked.

"Yes."

"Then behold Watchmen stand upon your watch, and the Lord will set you upon thy tower, and will look forth to see thee moreover what he will speak with you, and what the Anointed one shall answer concerning your complaint," the elderly man said.

"But I have some questions …"

Suddenly a host of angels surrounded the man, and then came Christ the Lord, and he moved on me to bow down with great fear. Moreover, the Lord, touching me like before when I was in his presence, came and picked me upright.

I cried unto him, falling down again and saying, "My lord and my God."

"Get up, my friend," the Lord Jesus Christ said to me. "Write the vision, and make it plain upon tablets, that he may run that reads it. This chronicle is designed for the vision that is yet for the appointed time, and it has toward the end, and shall not lie: though it tarry, wait for it, because it will surely come. It will not delay."

I started to question, "I ask you, my lord, who is this man to you?"

"He is one of my elders and was a Watchman like you," the Lord said. "Hear him."

"Forgive me, my master and king." I began to tremble as I said, "Your word has commanded me to test every spirit whether it be of God."

Suddenly I remembered Elder Makoto, the Japanese elder who was formerly a Bushido grand master converted to Christ, who had spoken to me back in Orlando in the warehouse, and I was praying about the very thing that I had seen in a vision. I was standing by the brook where I love to pray, and I had an open vision about the dream I had in the past …

Suddenly I saw in the distance a silver cross ring, which came from the horizon and hovered in front of me. I watched the clouds begin to form into the picture of a man's face. An angel flew from that cloud and threw a closed red rose down to me.

As the rose began to float slowly to the ground, the ring grew larger. The closed red rose was floating at first, and then it began to tumble. The ring that had been floating on the horizon fell into the sea, and then it came back out again, rising toward the tumbling red rose, which began to bloom. When the two met, the rose fit inside the ring and two of the rose petals began to blossom into two women's faces. The rose that had two faces came closer to speak, and I was puzzled about the dream because it spoke differently.

"Do not listen to these men who are here," the rose said to me.

What the rose said began to trouble me, and I was questioning what the vision was saying. Meanwhile, Elder Makoto came toward me as if he was going to pray silently to himself. I did not greet him as was my custom, and I turned away with a distrustful manner. Then he said to me, "What does it mean in the scripture? For the word of God is living, and active, and sharper than any two-edged sword, and piercing even to the dividing of soul and spirit, of both joints and marrow, and quick to discern the thoughts and intents of the heart."

"I think …"

"Do not think," Elder Makoto said sharply. "You either know or you don't."

"I don't know, Elder," I said humbly. "Teach me his ways of wisdom that I may understand."

Then a cloud formed in front of me, and I closed my

eyes, and the cloud turned into a screen, and I looked at what appeared to be a scroll that unrolled in front of me. Along with the other Watchmen, Elder Makoto taught me in this method, teaching by writing in the mind of my soul the spiritual laws and principles of the Lord Jesus Christ. For the next three years they used my imagination by putting pictures in my mind and began to write the principles of the spiritual laws and natural laws on the tablets of my soul.

"For the word of God is living …"

I responded, "As Christ said to his disciples, 'My words, our spirit and life, the flesh profits nothing and is void of understanding.'"

Then Elder Makoto asked, "Then what does it mean when the word reads, 'Active, and sharper than any two-edged sword.' Does this mean it is a physical weapon?"

"No."

He asked, "Then what?"

"Our weapons of warfare are not carnal," I said.

"And?"

"Worldly … material or physical," I replied.

"So why did the Knights of J.A.D.E use worldly weapons?" he asked again.

"Because they thought they could protect God's people better than the angel of the Lord," I said. "Because of their unbelief. That is why they failed."

"Why would the word of God want to be piercing?" Elder Makoto asked. "For that matter, the word of God begins to the dividing of soul and spirit?"

I responded, "Well, because when man fell in the garden, Satan dominated us by tricking us into being a soulish being and not a spiritual being."

"Can the word heal and change the soulish human back to a spiritual being?" Elder Makoto asked.

"Yes," I said.

"How?"

"By simply putting your hope and trust in something," I replied.

Elder Makoto responded, "Something?"

"I mean someone other than yourself."

"So you mean to tell me that this word of the Almighty can even heal?" he asked in a scoffing tone.

"To the joints and marrow of a human's bone," I said, continuing joyfully. "The word of the Almighty is quick to discern the thoughts and intents of the heart."

He turned and began to walk slowly away from me as he asked me these last questions: "So what does the scripture mean?" Then he said, "Hereby know ye the Spirit of God: every spirit that confess that Jesus Christ is come in the flesh is of God: And every spirit that confess not Jesus is not of God: and this is the spirit of the Antichrist, whereof ye have heard that it cometh; and now it is in the world already ... ' What does this mean?"

"God sends only a vision that line up with the word," I said. "For the testimony of Jesus is the spirit of prophecy."

"Very good," Makoto said.

"So is this vision of God or not?" I asked.

"Don't ask me. Ask the vision," he said sharply.

"Oh, I forgot."

Remembering the major point that I had forgotten, I was taught to recall the vision by the principle as it is written. He said, "Casting down imaginations, and every high thing that is exalted against the knowledge of God, and bringing every thought into captivity to the obedience of Christ; and being in readiness to avenge all disobedience, when your obedience shall be made full." This process taught me to ask the vision where it came from. I should have asked that about every open vision I saw. Moreover, despite the fact that the vision came by a spirit or unknown creature, if what it said did not line up or obey the Holy Scripture, then I knew it was a spirit of error or the spirit of the Antichrist.

So I asked in a demanding tone, "Who is the Lord Jesus Christ?"

"Very good, my friend. You are wise unto the scripture," the man said as he slowly appeared while I knelt at his feet, and then I fell into a deep sleep. "He is the one that came in the flesh, and He is the one that sits by my God the Father."

Christ Jesus then said, "You are not unwise to question me or this fellow laborer of the truth, for my words are spirit and life."

"I had to make sure, my lord," I said, and then the Lord Christ and the host of angels left me with the man.

"It is intended for the vision to be for the fixed time, Watchman," the man said in a rumbling, hollow voice. "In the midst of the week he shall cause the sacrifices and the oblations to cease, and for the overspreading of abominations, that day shall not come, except there comes a falling away first, and that man of sin will be revealed, which is the son of perdition."

I asked, "Who is he, the son of perdition?"

"This will be the sign of his coming," the Watchman continued, "He shall also set his face to enter with the strength of his whole kingdom, and upright ones with him; thus shall he do: and he shall give him the daughter of women, corrupting her law of liberty and kindness. But she shall not stand on his side, neither be for him, for you must remember the legs of iron and clay. They are his feet, part of iron and part of clay."

"Remember his feet and legs of iron and clay?" I asked, bewildered. "What can I do with this mystery?"

"This is what his kingdom will be like, and after this, he shall turn his face to the isles and shall take many." He was still speaking in prophetic riddles. "A prince for his own behalf shall cause the reproach offered by him to cease."

"Does this mean that Natal will have children to expand his empire?" I asked.

"That will be to come, but without his own prince of reproach, he shall cause it to turn upon him," the Watchman said. "Then he shall turn his face toward the fort of his own land: but he shall stumble and fall, and not be found."

"Are you saying this boy will die?" I asked. "Is he the son of perdition?"

"No, but then another shall stand up in his estate, a raiser of taxes in the glory of the kingdom, but within a few days he shall be destroyed, neither in anger nor in battle."

"So there will be three Antichrists?" I asked.

"The spirit of the Antichrist has already been on the earth for six thousand millenniums, which is according to history that the United States of America could become a necessary monsters with avoiding the purpose of freedom, and now the New Roman empire is ruling the world shall bring up a vile person, to whom they shall not give the honor of the kingdom," the Watchman's voice proclaimed. "But he shall come in peaceably, and obtain the kingdom by flattering. And with the arms of a flood shall they be overflowed from before him, and shall be broken; yes, also the prince of the covenant."

I asked, "Why can I just destroy this one, which will bring the kingdom of God here sooner?"

"Because this one must fulfill the testimony of Christ," the Watchman's voice said. "For the vile one to come, the Vicar bloodline must finish its curse, and I beheld another beast coming up out of the earth, and he had two horns like a lamb, and he spoke as a dragon."

Then I asked, "Who is this beast that looks like a goat?"

"The Black Knight of the bishop of the Synod of Clement will help the son of perdition enter in peaceably even upon the fattest places of the province." He continued to proclaim, "He shall do that which his fathers have not done, nor his fathers' fathers. The son of perdition shall scatter among them the prey, and spoil, and riches: yes, and he shall forecast his devices against the strong holds, even for a time."

I woke up thinking about all that I had heard and seen, and then wondering why I had spent all those years killing other men and terrorist factions for this country, only to find out that my nation was the left leg in the line of the Antichrist bloodline. My mind felt numb, and I wondered, *Why me? How could I be given the burden of coming to protect this son of perdition, and could I die for this son of Satan?* I began to think, *Could I dare protect a lie, and who is this Black Knight?*

I fell asleep again and began my dreaming of the dragon of my consciousness. "It is but a dream or a vision," one elder of the cities said, and then they all yelled at me.

Another one said, "He is a bad bit of undigested pork."

All the while, the mockers spoke; it was the shadowy voices long passed away that were the last echo I heard as the beast destroyed them all to the last. "Save us from the beast." Moreover, while I ran from it and watched the viper before me conquering those same cities while hiding behind a cloud of fire, lightning and hail would sweep away all those cities that mocked me and other pilgrims who went through the door of fidelity. We the Watchmen of that city of Mount Zion warned by the spirit of prophecy of the winds of war caused by its venomous scorpion's tail.

CHAPTER 11

🏭 🏭 🏭

The Seed of Division

September 11, 2057

Dear Abba,

My visions were coming ever so clear as the Watchmen began to take me under their wings of protection, and this protection began to come at a great price. My insight into the spirit realm started to become clearer. I was able to see the wonder of the other prophets who could see into another person's past life through a process called prophetic windows. I learned this procedure, which one of the elders told me was the force of love that was moved by the spirit of prophecy.

She was a younger prophetess about thirty years old and very beautiful to look at. I would see her singing in the worship service as the other Watchmen served the homeless and poor of the area.

The story of how Elder Juniper came to the Watchmen was amazing if not a miracle. She was from Great Britain and practicing to become a nun in the place of origin of this tale about the Vicar family when she came upon the convent site where the Synod of Clement had been built. Sister Susan Ann Juniper was raised Roman Catholic and was from Ireland, which had seen many bloody civil wars with England, and she had lost her family in those battles. Instead of joining the Irish Republican Army and becoming a rebel with a cause, she decided to be a woman of peace and love.

One night as she was doing her evening prayers in Latin at the chapel, and saying the rosary for the fortieth time, she saw a shadow of what looked like a man ...

Sister Juniper whispered, "*Áve María, grátia pléna, Dóminus técum. Benedícta tu in muliéribus, et benedíctus frúctus véntris túi, Iésus. Sáncta María, Máter Déi, óra pro nóbis peccatóribus, nunc et in hóra mórtis nóstrae. Pater noster, qui es in caelis, sanctificetur nomen tuum, adveniat regnum tuum, fiat voluntas tua, sicut in caelo, et in terra. Panem nostrum supersubstantialem da nobis hodie; et dimitte nobis debita nostra, sicut et nos dimittimus debitoribus nostris; et ne inducas nos in tentationem; sed libera nos a Malo ...(Hail, Mary, full of grace, the Lord is with thee: Blessed art thou among women, and blessed is the fruit of thy womb, Jesus. Holy Mary, Mother of God, pray for us sinners now, and at the hour of our death.)*"

Suddenly another voice whispered, "Susan Juniper ..."

"Amen." She kissed her rosary and made the sign of the cross before asking, "Who is there?"

"Sister Susan Juniper," the voice whispered again.

"I hear your voice. Who are you?" she asked fearfully.

"Come this way if you want to learn the truth about the convent that you pray upon," the voice said.

"Come where?"

Then I saw an angel standing before me, and I fell on my face. The angel set me on my feet. Its wing filled the entry room, and I could barely see my way. When the angel took its hand and pressed it against the stone walls of my room, and then I saw a tunnel filled with cobwebs. The tunnel had stairs that led down a curved stairway.

"Follow me," the angel said.

I grabbed a lantern from my desk and followed the angel. The two of us walked through this long tunnel until I saw a pile of little skulls and what looked like broken remains of baby skeletons. In horror, I turned to the angel and asked, "Whose children are these?"

I remembered that before the rebuilding of this convent more than two hundred years earlier, there was this convent and beside it a monastery of the Synod of Clement that had been destroyed. I knew the historical root of the Synod of Clement, but I didn't know about the killing of babies.

However, the angel didn't stop walking from there, and I kept walking because that wasn't the only thing he wanted to show me. We came to a room that was right under the old monastery.

"Whose room is this?" I asked.

"Who was the sixth bishop of this monastery during Pope Leo X?"

"Bishop Adrian Dominican!" I said. "I don't believe it."

Then the angel put his hand over my eyes, and in a moment, I saw with my own eyes and heard with my own ears the sound of giggles, groaning, and moaning from behind the wooden door, which was bound by ropes of hemp. A lascivious setting of passion would give our eyes a festive span over the fireplace that warmed the room, past the tablecloth setting of two wineglasses and a basket of fruit on the table.

You could see the silhouette of a man and woman under the covers of the feathered, stuffed, pillowed mattress with a cover of royal purple and gold tapestry. The young, beautiful woman rose from her bed. Her tight breast was red from her lover's bed of fornication.

"Come, my love, let us go another round," the man's muffled voice said while pulling her back under the covers.

"Stop, my lord, I must protest," whined the young mother superior known as Angelina as she tried to pull herself back out from under the covers. "For alas, I must be about my devout duties."

As she tried to clothe herself in her black robe to cover her nakedness, he grabbed her again and pulled her back to the bed for one more round of making love. "You devil lover of my fiddle," she said, giggling poetically. "Stop pulling the strings of my tart fruit to your lips."

"Aha, but I must play you, my beloved," he said, grinning.

"Don't strum me again, for I must leave with haste," she said, and then moaned.

Grinning, the man whispered in her ear, "Then if I am a fiddler, let me strum you again until dawn."

Then I awoke from my sleep. I wondered if it was a dream, but when I looked and saw the stone wall opened, I knew it was forbiddingly real. I quickly ran away from the convent and found myself among the Watchmen of this temple.

"How is it that you didn't think it was a demon?" I asked.

"When I was at the London airport, I met a Christian named Alberto who gave me a chick magazine known as the *Crusader*, and I read the eyewitness account about children in a Spanish monastery that was found guilty of infanticides," she said. "Then I knew that this ex-Jesuit priest's story was based on truth."

"How did you know it was not just propaganda?" I asked.

"Raymond, don't fight with your soul and spirit," she said softly, "but see it with the insight by the Holy Spirit."

"I am not that good at getting deep," I replied. "And besides, there are some things I don't like about myself."

"You are experiencing what is called the dark night of the soul," Elder Juniper responded.

"What is that?" I asked.

"It is when a child of God's character is being formed into the spirit of knowledge, and the fear and reverence of the Lord Jesus begins to take over the personality of the soul," she said.

"When will this depression end?"

"When you go through the walk of fire," she replied.

"Fire?" I yelled. "I ain't walking on anyone's hot coals of fire."

Elder Juniper began to laugh. "It is when you are fasting and the Holy Spirit begins to deal with the inner conflict of your soul, my boy."

"What do I do about my inner conflict now?"

"Breathe, Raymond," she suggested softly. "Relax your mind and just breathe."

So I breathed in through my nose and out through my mouth to calm my mind, will, and emotions, and I was suddenly able to transform myself. The being of Lord Charlimas DePaul Vicar was with me, but mind you, I wasn't channeling some familiar spirit but looking back into the past to see why Lord Vicar was so important to the Watchmen and me. I saw him in hell being tormented by demons.

I said to Lord Vicar, "Speak to me and tell Vicar why you are being tormented."

Lord Vicar moaned in pain. "Why do you care about the damned?"

"I know your great-grandson, and I could help him," I said.

"I will tell you my story if you only promise to let him fulfill his destiny."

"God has granted me the ability to protect him," I said. "Now tell, please."

"All right, as you wish …"

From that moment on, I was watching the chronicle of one of the damned in hell. I have to ask my reader to hear his story. I could not remember my aged life in which I began. Until the day I gasp my last laugh on my deathbed with my final, chain-smoking breaths. You begin to see the realms of the spirit world as your eyes roll back into your head. Seemingly, I never saw myself as a bad person. Until I stood at hell's gate with my angelic companion, I felt the sweat of my soul and the terrible stench of burning, rotten flesh mixed with sulfur.

The angel that took me there was four times the height of an average person, and given that I wasn't that tall anyway, he seemed huge. To my dwarf size, he was gigantic in stature. I pleaded my case and asked, to a certain extent, very loud prodigious pains that it must have worked. I heard the Lord say to the angel with such a loud voice that I thought the whole earth and the universe heard him, "Bring up this son of man here to me."

I saw the Lord sitting upon a throne, and in the midst of the seven candlesticks one like the Son of God, clothed with a garment down to the foot, and girt about the side with a golden girdle. His head and his hairs were white like wool, as white as snow, and his eyes were as a flame of fire, far above the ground and distinguished, and his procession of luminosity filled the temple.

Above his throne stood fiery-like spirits that could only have been the seraphim. Each one had six wings; with two, they covered their faces, with two, they covered their feet, and with two they flew.

Moreover, one roared to another, and said all day long, "Holy, holy, holy is the Lord of hosts: the whole earth is full of his glory." The pillars of the door enthused at the voice of him that cried, and the house was filled with seething, blowing billows of vapor, which had lightning and other illumination coming from them.

"Wretched man am I," I screamed. "I am unraveled."

Mockingly the Lord said, "Son, remember that you in thy lifetime received your good things, and now you are to receive your torments."

"But Lord, I was your patron," I said, pleading my case. "I led a good life for you, did I not?"

"For I was hungry, and ye gave me no food," the Lord roared back to me. "I was thirsty, and ye gave me no drink."

"Well, my Lord, I needed all that strength to rule thy people," I said, grinning in fear, and trembling.

"Wretchedness to you that is full." The Lord continued, "Intended for you for eternity shall you suffer hunger, and despair to laugh now."

I ask in a proud tone, "My Lord, could I have been that bad?"

"You shall mourn and weep in the place of Hades's flames."

"Oh Lord, my God, I am a man of unclean lips,"

The Lord called me closer and said, "How is it that I hear this of thee? Give an account of your stewardship."

"How can I give an account for my stewardship?" I cried, saying, "I dwell in the midst of a people of unclean lips, for my eyes have seen the king, the Lord of hosts."

The Lord asked, "Do you think you were a good person?"

"Well," I said sheepishly.

"That's a deep subject." He laughed and continued, "Let's talk about that."

"Hmm, Lord, according to your word, only you are good … But yes, I was a good person."

He asked, "Did you ever lie?"

Lord Vicar said, "Define for me what exactly a lie is."

Then suddenly a big cloud formed, and I was seen giving the young nun I had burned at the stake a letter falsely accusing her of being a witch, and then the young nun gave the note unknowingly to Mother Superior Anna. The next day the same beautiful nun was condemned to burn at the stake for being a witch, and then the clouded screen went black …

"Do the words *Thou shall not bear false witness against thy neighbor* ring a bell?" the Lord asked.

"Well, my Lord …"

"Well, you say that's a deep subject, so let's talk about it. How about this one: whosoever hates his brother is a murderer," the Lord said, "and you know that no murderer has eternal life abiding in him."

"Well …" Lord Vicar said.

"Is that all you have to say?" the Lord exclaimed, and then continued, "Okay, I give you one more chance. If you have three sins total, you're out of here."

"Okay, now I know that I couldn't be that bad of a priest of God," I said smugly.

"You have heard it said, thou shall not commit adultery, but I say unto you, that every one that looks on a woman to lust after her hath committed adultery with her already in his heart."

Then the Lord Jesus added, "And if thy right eye causes thee to stumble, pluck it out, and cast it from thee: for it is profitable for thee that one of thy members should perish, and not thy whole body be cast into hell."

"You didn't expect me to go around blind, did you?" I asked.

The Lord Christ Jesus called, "Roll the tape."

Suddenly, the cloud formed in front of me, and I was a friar looking through a peephole from the floorboards of the tunnel between the monastery and the convent. It was the first night I saw the young nun I had convicted of divination. I was shown with the same nun as we two quietly faded into the shadows with a kiss of secrecy.

I saw my thoughts speaking louder than any town crier of a castle courtyard of our surreptitious deeds while I walked as a Judas Iscariot. However, I would for a handful of coins either prove my love to her or we would both burn under this hypocrisy. Thus, with that I gave her a kiss on the cheek while in the background I was acting pious under my authority as a bishop and watched her burned at the stake.

"Do you have anything else to say?" he asked.

"No," I said in a disappointed tone.

"So, by your own words, thoughts, and deeds you are a lying, thieving, adulterer at heart." The Lord pointed at me in judgment and said calmly, "If you cannot show this court proof of your innocence, then you are …"

"Guilty," I said in a low voice.

Suddenly the sea of golden glass opened and a lake of flames engulfed my soul. I began to cry out with everything in me for mercy. I knew the life that I lived, and how I couldn't measure up. For as the prophet Daniel spoke to King Belshazzar of Babylon, I saw the holy finger of God write on the palace walls of heaven this inscription: MENE, MENE, TEKEL, and UPHARSIN, which means, "God hath numbered my kingdom, and finished it. I have been weighed in the balances, and I am found accountable."

As King Belshazzar of Babylon's kingdom was divided, so was I going to be divided by the demons of the fires of hell, but this was promised of a warranty against my soul. Because this was the reason for my travels, and I was damned to the eternal punishments, why not make the most of this adventure?

This is why my angelic companion is here at my side and

why I hopelessly know my end as I weave this final tale that I spin. I can remember not too much, but the fact that I wrote that letter is very fresh in my mind. As the cerebellums did send down the message of the electrons, to the nerves to make my hand write every stroke of that cursed pen, it seemed that with each letter I could see the demon stoke the flame more and more.

My dear Holy Father Clement, the second of the fifty-seventh papal dynasty,

Your Grace, I have sinned before my Father in heaven and your holy church. My last wish is to be taken from my plight of purgatory and forgiven of my many sins and given my last rite of burial.

Yours Truly,

Lord Charlemagne DePaul Vicar.

As I walked through my walls, suddenly I found myself at the speed of light in the Sistine Chapel. At the same time, my old friend the Spaniard Sir Louis El-Deon Ignatius stood in front of old Pope Clement VII for the curse he spoke over my son, the Bishop Charlemagne DePaul Vicar II. Before I could think, the words shot out of my mouth like arrows.

"You jealous bastard," I said.

When I realized I was in front of a holy angel of the Lord, I smiled sheepishly. Then I whispered to myself, "If I am going to hell for my sins, why should I care?" I knew he couldn't hear me.

"You selfish, jealous bastard," I shouted. "If I were still alive, I'd kick you right in the groin—and poison you, too!"

The angel only shook his head in disbelief, but he still didn't say a word. He only stood there with its arms still folded. Then looking to the heavens the immortal messenger of God looked forward, knowing prophetically my next mistake to come was like a town crier who shouts continually.

I began to croak, "Yes, you fool, rub your old, dry lips."

When His Eminence read the letter, he stroked his chin and the corner of his lips, which caused the poison to go into his skin and made the lips dry. Thus he would lick them.

"That's right, you damn old fossil, lick those chapped lips," I barked. "I'll be seeing you in the abyss soon enough."

As I watched, Pope Clement VII clutched his heart and died on his throne with the letter still clutched in his hand. I was asking only to be forgiven, since I had granted forgiveness to many people on their deathbeds.

"I forgave many who needed forgiveness," I said.

A voice echoed, "As soon as the coin in the coffin rings, a soul from purgatory springs."[6]

"Never mind …"

My untimely death was never missed, because sadly, I was the worst papal leader of my short-lived life. I still laugh at that statement; of course, the angel standing by my side doesn't think any of this is amusing. It is just awaiting my delivery to that final destination.

Historically they have me recorded as being Pope Leo X's successor, and even Cardinals Medici and Antebellum were quoted as saying, "Cardinal Adrian Dominican was the candidate of the Holy Ghost, for we certainly did not pick him." At the same time, the marriage of Count Charlimas DePaul Vicar and Lady Roseland Andante Rothschild were joined to cradle like their newborn baby, which was being rocked by two nuns, twelve priests, and a company of the Knights Templar.

Now, being dead has its advantages, but I never for a moment thought it would happen like this. My life flashed before my eyes. I was standing before my body in the intervening time, and I watched myself begin to laugh on my deathbed and with a final breath.

I saw myself gasping for air speak, which was very frightening at first. However, when the body is at rest, it looks extremely peaceful. "My sons will come to power," I said as I gasped for air "Even though it is my final hour, one of my sons of the lineage of the Vicar will be the next pope, if not the emperor of this world." The shadow of light encompassed my body and the opening of the door of the time past time of the Vicar family.

I was between my Anna's thighs, and the long legs of that gorgeous woman bring me in reverence of her beauty. As I was planting the seed of my loins into her body, I was foolish in thinking that we priests should not marry. I was not pure in my thinking, nor was my walk then peaceable, because I never saw anything in all my many studies about letting men walk in the law of liberty. These thoughts ate at me like the worms around a corpse.

As I heard about Martin Luther great explodes by the great Satan, which was the name given to the Rome Catholic that was called mother church, when he was speaking to many of his followers in a field in the region near Bavaria. The angel that was with me brought me through time again to hear what my enemies were barking from their tongues about me.

"I say therefore to the unmarried and widows, it is good for them if they remain even as Paul. But if they cannot contain, let them marry," Luther said while walking and talking to his followers. "For it is better to marry than to burn."

He sauntered toward me and passed right through me, not knowing I was standing there. Turning the spirit back through me again, he bellowed as he raged. He had the most furious stare on his face, and came and took up his child from his wife's arms. He turned his back away from me.

He asked, "Does it mean we burn at the stake or suffer lashings if we marry those we passionately love?"

"As it is written in the scriptures, speaking lies in hypocrisy, having their conscience seared with a hot iron, forbidding to marry," Luther continued loudly. "For they command us to abstain from meats, which God hath created to be received with thanksgiving by them who believe and know the truth. They make the law of God of no effect because of the traditions of man."

I was not gentle when I spoke against him and many of my enemies. I condemned many hordes around while I did the very same thing with Anna before we got married. I did not treat mankind with mercy, but I tracked those who crossed me with death or imprisonment. I had my Knights Templar destroy many villages in flames because I had the lust of the flesh for many women, including Anna.

The lust of the eye was when I was both an abbot in England at the shire of York and the bishop of the Synod in Clement. Bearing good fruits on my tree of bitterness, as the roots formed alliances with local rulers and while pope with kings, I wasn't without partiality. I was blind with the pride of being the bishop and papal king of the Holy Roman Empire.

"Rome was great under Caesar, but greater by far under Pope Innocent III," one of my many paid priests said. "The first was only a mortal man, but the second is a god."

The pride swells in your head when your enemies and friends of my extended hands made the poor use entreaties, but I would answer roughly. I couldn't see far off, for I was blind by power because I had forgotten that I was purged of my sins. My words kept coming back to haunt me. As I was speaking at the Synod of Clement, I spoke, pretending words that were nothing more than a sound that clanged like a cymbal.

"For I would that all men were as I myself. However, every man hath his proper gift from God, one after this manner, and another after that," I continued piercingly. "Since priests are supposed to be God's temple, vessels of the Lord, and the sanctuaries of the Holy Spirit, it offends their dignity to lie in the conjugal bed and live in impurity."

We would play our piloted course of hypocrisy like two pious, privileged chess pieces like a queen and bishop that would secretly pass each other. As two ships, we would battle in the day the same as opposing armies on the field of battle. One time I failed to see the monks in the diocese's priest to come to noon prayer. When it was that, my lady just wanted to see more of me and nothing else.

"Mother Superior, you seem to think that prayer is open and not personal," I snapped at her.

"Your Grace, we must all become the house of prayer for the Lord," she snarled.

"And for pretenses of making a long prayer," I began to quote, "Therefore ye shall receive the greater damnation."

"What are you saying, my lord?" The mother superior grinned. "That my sisters are devouring widows' and widowers' homes now?"

"No," I said, frowning.

The spring-like weather smelled of roses and fresh dew as we stood in the garden. The men and woman of the monastery and the convent were there, and I knew that I enraged her. Turning her back, she stood with her fellow sisters and me with my fellow priest and monks.

"Woe to you, monks and priest," she bellowed. "Hypocrites, for ye devour widows' houses. And from the looks of you and your clergy, you have been eating a great deal."

She walked by me, smiling, and patted my stomach, and they all laughed at us walking out the gate along with me smiling. Then the other priest was outraged that the mother superior would say such a thing to the bishop. I just smiled quickly at our cat-and-mouse game.

Not a soul in the monastery could ever guess that the Anna and I were in a game of furtive concealed pretense in the monastery and convent of the Synod of Clement. We laughed all that night while we made love, but we were not married and were deep in the sin of fornication.

"I tell you before, as I have told you in time past, that they who do such things shall not inherit the kingdom of God," the Lord yelled from the heavens.

As I heard this truth, I cringed as those words began to echo in my soul. Sinning has its pleasure for the moment. It's like a great big meal that fills you up until you get up from the table; then the pain of overindulging hits you hard.

"What will be the fate of my sons?" I asked.

"The bishop had a son in secret," the voice of the Lord said.

"And what became of his seed?" I inquired.

The angel took his finger, which glowed brighter and brighter. It shone like brimstone. The orange sapphire glowed like a coal taken from a hot blacksmith's smelting pit. He took that finger and poked a hole in the darkness that was before us, and began to swirl it around and around until the darkness and the lighted orange sapphire finger were mixed as though a baker had mixed the ingredients of a cake.

And the light was shining in the darkness, and the darkness could not figure out nor was the darkness in my heart able to be understood what was going to happen in the plan of God all along. Little did I know or understand that I was traveling back to the future. Little did I know that I was being transformed into another creature as a host of hell to change by doing his master's bidding.

When we stepped through the porthole of time, we went

into a thick darkness you could feel and then moved into a shadow of darkness that was flexible and flashing on and off.

I could hear the voices of two people talking and giggling and the familiar sound of people making love to each other. Only the blinking of the florescent light was showing the silhouette of the woman's frame, and a dark-skinned man leaned back intently, watching her every move as I watched her remove her bra and panties.

The beauty of that woman was very compelling but made me feel uncomfortable with the angel. Even though she could not see us, I was unnerved by watching what I considered a private and personal act of two humans.

Then the angel began to speak for the first time since I was in his presence. He started his spoken sentence to my empty soul in the form of a rebuke. As the woman was bearing her nudity to the man, she slowly turned to him, allowing her long hair to come back around to cover her nakedness.

"We see this type of thing only when they are not in matrimony," the angel said sternly.

"You mean that when we humans are sinning, you watch?" I said in disgust.

"We record every act of adultery, fornication, and even masturbation in silence," the angel continued. "All acts of sin must be recorded, and trust me, we get no pleasure from watching your sinful acts."

"Can we go?" I asked abruptly.

"No," he replied.

"Then who are these people to me?" I sharply asked.

"You will see," the angel replied.

The woman smiled, leaning toward the black man kissing her with hair falling, covering her face like a veil. They both fell back on the bed, and the woman moved between his legs and began stripping off his shirt. She kissed his chest and rubbed her nose against his chest hairs. They began to make love to each other, and this was the beginning of their courtship in the night.

"Really," Rebecca responded. "Will you bare your soul to me?"

"Yes."

"You will," she said.

"If God is not bringing you and me together"—the man came closer to her—"then I hope I die never loving again."

When they had continued making love, the angel motioned toward the door, and I was forced to move with him. He opened the door, and on the other side there seemed to be a war, because there were explosions and screams of anguish.

"Hit the deck, you clown," the staff sergeant screamed. "Walt, give 'em cover fire on our flank."

"What is this?" I asked.

"Just watch," the angel said.

The Vietnamese soldiers shot two rounds toward two other men holding large sniper rifles before they could move. The young black man whom I saw earlier having sex with the woman in the hotel ran over and took a loaded weapon. Running quickly, the man ran over, suddenly jumping up, and even though he was seen hit by the fire of swarming bullets that came at him like angry hornets, he bravely fought back.

"Hey, you dumb-ass Negro, we don't need a black hero," the sergeant screamed.

Diving over the other dead soldiers as though playing leapfrog, he took the AK-47 and began warding off the advancing Vietnamese soldiers who were shooting at the black man. They returned with rapid fire.

"Hey, you dumb-ass Negro, we don't need a black hero," the staff sergeant screamed.

Nevertheless, I watched the gallant man move his squad around to set up a perimeter as a counterattack against the ambush that we were suddenly being pulled into. Even though the gallant warrior ran out of arrows, he took out a smaller pistol and used it until it was empty, and then he used even another pistol he took from one of the dead Vietnamese soldiers lying like strewn dolls in a kid's playroom.

When it was over, the black brave warrior was facedown. Another black soldier who was the sergeant ran over to him. The sergeant turned over the warrior and saw that he was shot up pretty bad, but this must have been his best friend, which called for a physician.

"Who is he, angel?" I asked.

"This is your grandson of some five hundred years," the angel said sternly. "His name is Walter Charles Vicar but he changed it to Parson."

The physician ran to the aid of the gallant man, but the sergeant's best friend was dying, and tried to see what was to come of him. Then because this was prophesied which was in danger of being destroyed. I was only wishing and hoping that I would not go to hell, and all of my hope and dreams be dashed to pieces.

"Rich, Richard!" he yelled, beginning to gasp.

"You damn fool! I told you to keep your ass down," Richard cried. "Medic, get your ass over here."

"Listen, man," he said as he grabbed Richard.

"Okay, I'm listening." The man started crying as he looked into the face of his dying friend.

"Man, will you do this for me?" asked Walt.

"Okay, Walt, what?" Richard asked.

"When I am dead, Rich, take some of my blood and keep

it for my son." He repeated his request and handed Richard a capsule encased in a thick cassette.

"What the hell is this?" Richard asked.

"Listen, man, I don't have time." Walt was starting to choke as he pleaded. "Have one of the corpsman transfer it from my vein."

"Okay," Richard agreed.

I began to look more puzzled as I looked at the man who was my grandson of forty generation. Then I wondered to myself, *Who was that young woman he was having sex with in a hotel?* but before I could finish, we were in a delivery room watching her give birth. She was pushing out a baby with sweat pouring from her brow. Physician and midwives were helping this woman bring forth her baby.

"Who is she, angel?" I asked as I pulled on his robe.

"She is Rebecca Dawn Vicar, your great-great-great-granddaughter of forty generation," the angel responded with a smile.

If you don't believe a spirit could faint, well, I just proved that theory wrong, because I did. I suddenly saw this vision of a woman arrayed in purple and scarlet and decked with gold and precious stones and pearls, with a golden cup in her hand full of abominations and filthiness from her lewdness.

When I awoke to my sense, the angel was standing over me. I could only wonder what it was I had seen. I realize that darkness is the absence of light, and evil is the absence of good. I saw all of that in the vision I had witnessed. I just played the hypocrite on the wrong side.

I asked, "What was that vision I saw?"

"You know, don't you?" he responded.

Then I saw a young little boy sitting in a hallway that was lavishly designed in a white mansion. The boy was crying as if he were mourning the death of a loved one, and then he sat on a hallway couch. As the boy was sitting crying, I saw a man walk over to him and begin to comfort him.

I asked, "Who is this child, my Lord?"

The Lord said mockingly, "You don't remember, do you?"

"I need to know if he is the fulfillment of my word."

The child began to walk to the car with the president and the crowd of people accompanied Natal to bury the boy's mother. They went to Saint Paul's Cathedral in Washington, DC, and the boy walked into the foyer of the large church where the holy host of the Eucharist was presented. I walked over to it and stood there.

Natal was still showing expressions of grief for his mother, and while all the other friends and relatives proceeded to the front of the cathedral, the angel turned his back to me and was busy watching the funeral.

I moved over to where the holy host of the Eucharist was set up. I started to concentrate my focus, began to try, and touched it. It lighted up and flung itself to the floor. The boy walked over and picked up the Eucharist, and then looked both ways before putting it in his mouth. His eyes glowed with a strange red glow, and he stumbled back as if he were off balance. I walked over to the angel and tapped him on his shoulder.

"I have seen enough here," I barked. "I am ready to leave."

"Very well— as you wish." The angel smiled as he looked at the boy. "Are you ready to receive your judgment?"

"Yes," I said.

"Then come this way, Lord Vicar," the angel said.

"For your sins of idolatry, witchcraft, hatred, variance, emulations, wrath, strife, seditions, heresies, envying, murders, drunkenness, and reveling, which I told you before"—the Lord spoke as the words echoed in my soul—"as I have told you in time past, they who do such things shall not inherit the kingdom of God. You must depart into this form into utter darkness."

In the intervening time, I found myself back in my body as an old man. I began to laugh on his deathbed and with his final breath. "My sons will come to power," I said as I gasped for the last dying bits of air. "Even though it's my final hour as a Vicar, I will see the next pope, if not the emperor of this world."

At last, the games were afoot, and yes, this too must pass. Knowing that I must go to where only the Lord of Darkness must one day find himself, I bid you farewell. On behalf of all who are holy teachers, preachers, rabbis, priests, and prophets, this may be the end of my tale. My screaming will begin soon, but yours, my cleric of the cloth, will engulf you if you ignore my doom.

CHAPTER 12

♟♟♟

The Red Moon Rising

As two stones began to part with the illumination of volcanic lava glowing off the walls of the cave, two figures came forward from the entrance. The two creatures came out of the cave that has smoldering steam and the stench of burning flesh and sulfurous screams of torment. Coming up and around the jagged path of deep cavern, the grinding sound of rocks being pulled across the cave opening echoed from the bottomless abyss. Suddenly, two smoke screened gray figures materialized from the primeval hillside necropolis.

The two animate figures came from the deepest part of the cubicles of hell. You could see that they were not human, but one of them was taller and had the face of a shadowed skull. It was cloaked in a midnight black of night, and darkness covered the first creature from head to toe. The shorter creature was in the form of a man but gray and translucent. They both had the stench of the underworld. As the entrance of hell closed, the fading shriek of voices was muffled under the grinding of the rocks being pulled back across the gravesite.

"You understand the scarcity of this case, and you must be successful," the death angel said morbidly.

The spirit of Lord Vicar asked, "What happens if I fail?"

"Does the white throne judgment have meaning for you?" The angel of death smiled. "It might be a thousand years before you leave again."

I began walking toward them, but it was more like a light speed bolt as I moved faster and faster. The light at the end of this long tunnel was coming up toward another point of light until I was at the door of Saint Paul's Cathedral in Washington DC. The people I saw in my time of judgment were going into the cathedral, and the boy walked into the vestibule where the holy host of the Eucharist was presented.

I walked over and toward the child, knowing he couldn't see me as I stood there. Natal was still showing expressions of grief for his mother while all the other friends and relatives proceeded to the front of the basilica. I moved over to where the Holy Eucharist was set up, and started to concentrate my focus. I began to try, and touched it. It lighted up and hurled itself to the floor. The boy walked over and picked up the Eucharist.

"Eat it, and you will become a god," I whispered.

Then he looked both ways before putting it in his mouth. The Eucharist turned dark right before Natal ate it, and then his spirit was transformed and I was lying dormant inside the brown-haired boy's slender body. The boy's green eyes changed, glowing with a strange crimson luminosity, the kind of radiance you would see when a lunar eclipse occurred.

As Natal moved away from the Holy Eucharist arrangement, he began to stumble back to the bench in the foyer. He started to get sick to his stomach as sweat slowly streamed down his head. Suddenly, he started to convulse while falling toward the ground, gasping for air.

Meanwhile, one of the Secret Service men entered the foyer and came over to Natal when he saw him stumbling. Catching him, thinking Natal had fainted, the Secret Service man was helping Natal.

"Mr. Vicar, are you okay?" the Secret Serviceman asked in a concerned voice.

When Natal shook his head, the Secret Serviceman spoke into his wrist communicator, "Unit six, do you have a nurse available?"

A woman who was a White House attendant looked out into the foyer and gave the sign for the agent to keep it down; when she saw the boy fainting, she ran over and held his head.

The agent said in a whisper, "Be advised that Bright Star [meaning Natal Vicar] needs assistance and I will need an escort at this time."

That was the very moment I came into his life, as if a Christian has a guardian angel. Consequently, I became his guardian as well. I am not the narrator of this tale. But then again, I, the former Marine scout sniper Raymond Moore, will be enduring to voice this anecdote, because I want you all to know who I am.

As far as this story, I do not want any confusion about the tale I am weaving, and some of you may think that I am the apparition of Bishop Adrian Dominican. I could be, but I have done this before, when the Witch of Endor called me forth as the prophet Samuel. If you are even more unconvinced, you will see how I did this diabolical switch against this young chap.

When Raymond Moore first met the boy Natal Apollyon Vicar, I did everything in my power to keep them apart. The boy was just ten years old after the supposed death of his mother, Rebecca. Then his uncle, the president of the United

States of America, felt pressured, even though his father was a recipient of the Medal of Honor.

This wasn't truly the reason the president felt a sense of duty. He just didn't want to be put in the Lincoln Bedroom, if you know what I mean.

The first lady said sharply, "He's your own blood, damn it."

"I never cared what my whorish sister did in the past because it was her life," the president replied, "But I feel that a line must be drawn in the sand when I have to take care of her abomination."

"It is bad enough to see you use your executive powers to sweep the existence of your sister under the rug of the White House, but you will not do that to this child," she said scornfully.

The president snapped back, "If she hadn't gotten foolishly hooked on those pills in the first place …"

"Well, Mister Self-Righteous," she responded.

"Okay, fine; we don't have to go there."

"Well, if you don't want to sleep in the Lincoln Bedroom again," she said, smiling as she left the room, "just accept him. I don't need a unanimous vote from Congress to get the fact of where you will be sleeping to become law."

Natal would move in and out of the White House several more times, but for now, my new young protégé was to be groomed at a military academy in Portsmouth, Virginia. Consequently, the truth about Natal Vicar's background was set aside far from journalists' inquisitive eyes and web search engines, even though the fledgling Natal Vicar was followed by my dark henchmen of the illicit sinister lords who were a phantom of shadows from the nadir of Hades. Only on special occasions would he feel he was being watched, and it wasn't just at the White House under the prying eyes of the

Secret Service agents. I can safely say it was all of heaven as well as me.

Nonetheless, Natal hostilities after taking the Eucharist were becoming evil in his actions toward that Christian Raymond Moore. Mr. Moore had gotten the boy to have his first Christ-like relationship of becoming saved or experience in religion. I had to work hard at keeping him from understanding that he was raised in the Lord. It was as the scripture said in Matthew chapter twelve verse forty-three that reads: "When the unclean spirit is gone out of a man, he walks through dry places, seeking rest, and he finds none. Then he said, I will return into my house from whence I came out; and when he is come, he fined it empty, swept, and garnished."

Then Natal Apollyon Vicar said something that came straight out of the Bible, and it was as if the whole earth stood still to see what he was going to say. I never would have believed it and never understood that this boy was going to be saved. It was so poetic when he made the statement that it seemed to seal his faith; nevertheless, he just came right out with it.

Natal asked, "What must I do to be saved?"

I mean, what choice did I have? I just ignored what he said; I had to suppress my feelings of revolting against leading Natal to Christ Jesus. I was unprejudiced by putting the doubt of salvation constantly in his mind.

Sincerely at Ease,

Lucifer

CHAPTER 13

🏭🏭🏭

First Journal Entry

Date and time unknown

Dear Abba,

I bought this journal at the store down the street from work on the spur of the moment, and I couldn't avoid the urge to mind dump into something when I looked into Natal's eyes. I thought I was looking into a hollow soul. I had this vision a couple of nights ago, and this is what I saw: a woman draped in two flags. One was an old American standard with the circled thirteen stars, and the other was the British battle standard. The woman was giving birth to eggs, but the eggs turned black like granite.

    Steaming mists of caustic vapor that gave the aroma of rotten sulfur caused me to gag. The gigantic granite-colored eggs formed a very strange-looking feminine creature, but it was really a malefactor of past kings and presidents and has worsened by the ages. As the spectral vision continued, the hankered repeated the historical mistakes by way of the arachnid that spun a trap of her history of mythical anecdote of origin.

The British flag shrouded the thing, and the ensign unfurled into thirteen stripes with fifty snakes coming from edges of the flag. The head of the malefactor reminded me of the demoniac in Homer's tale of the Odyssey but was nothing compared to this dappled being.

The dragon called Republicus ate the reprobate and started its rage again. I looked at Natal and got a spine-chilling, appalling feeling, like when I read this poem:

> *The evil that I think in heart,*
> *it's darker than any night I've walked in.*
> *Deeper than any pit I have sinned,*
> *my mind looks from the hole of the copulation;*
> *I want out of my sin of justification.*
> *None but I am deliverer's in sanctification.*
> *Damn this Hole.*
> *Praise the Day I am whole.*
> *Then it came; the empty soul.*

The picture and the poem were from an artist named Michael R. Jones. I hope it is not the one I knew in the Marines, because he was a weird fellow. Always looking at me like he knew me.

Sincerely,
Raymond Moore

I heard something like a voice from the deepest part of my soul or spirit. I heard it speak as if I could hear it in my inner soul, and it came from Natal. The thing said, "I only acted like I was gone, and I will bring in seven other spirits of the Antichrist, whoredom, lying, fear, bondage, and divination. They will enter in and dwell there: and the last state of this boy will be worse than the first.

"So now that I have played the religious game with Raymond Moore and the Watchmen, I am only going to say that when I came to possess the lad, the purpose was a divine one. And when Lord Vicar prophesied that his sons would rule the world, he did not realize that something was sealing this covenant with an allusive satanic presence, only to open a window of opportunity for me to walk through. For as it is written in John chapter ten verse one, 'But climb up some other way, the same is a thief and a robber.'

"My robbery will take more than this boy's soul, for it will be the path that will fulfill my destiny in eons to come. For I was the serpent in Eden, the garden of God, watching every move of the parents of humanity, and I will sit also upon the mount of the congregation, in the sides of the north in the Vatican and in the sanctuary of that amount."

When I opened my eyes, I was in Natal's bedroom in the White House. Then my enemy whom I will take pleasure in destroying came in—that man who was trusting in the blood of the anointed one.

He stood over me like a mother hen, and I had to play it cool and reserved as he cared for me. I had to wait in the shadows of this boy's soul, like a cobra waiting for my chance to strike. This was the labor of demons, and I began to make my plot to destroy this man who was his caretaker.

Thinking that I was still king of this world, I began moving in the boy as he slept in his dreams, by showing how to take command of his fears of hell and also his fears of right and wrong. I would show him how to resolve the allusion of power nevertheless; mendacious wonders as the

Bible writes are only the start of an enigmatic plot to a moral modification movement.

In Natal are hidden hypnotic entreaties to change the thinking of those who believe in God. The Watchmen are the only ones who stand in my way. I will destroy them all once the boy is disciplined. However, my discipleship means he would need to learn his enemies by becoming the enemy.

When I heard that, I made sure I didn't speak a word out loud, but kept my thoughts clear and focused. I saw this shadowy figure watching Natal, which made me nervous as a young child. Then I noticed there was another shadowy figure looking at me.

As Natal was getting older and had gone into combat, the figures were always with him. I never got used to them being around, and Natal wasn't about to let that shadowy figure turn the corner at the White House every time they felt like it.

"What in the name of God is that?" Raymond Moore asked.

Natal answered, "What are you talking about?"

I knew he could see them because his eyes didn't scan the area in confusion, but looked right at them instead. This wasn't a little boy I was dealing with but a combat veteran who knew about the terror of war.

If this shadowy figure was some dead president, or the roast beef he had had at his uncle's table that night that was one thing. Then again, how many times have you seen a side of beef walk like a full-grown man?

"Natal, are you all right?" I asked.

I heard a sound in, of all places, the White House that sounded like someone had actually was crazy enough to break into the president's house, but you know the times we live in. Nothing surprises me anymore. I picked up the house phone to call security and the Secret Service to protect the president. Their Natal was running down the hall after this sinister apparition.

"Natal," I said softly as I released the war that had gotten ahold of the boy. "Natal, hey boy, come here."

With a boyish look of surprise that always made me love and want to father him, he turned to me and briefly came back to his senses. However, he was acting like me when I came back from wartime—jumpy and uneasy in motion.

"Did you see that figure going down the hall?" He turned around with a starry-eyed, spooked look on his face as he pointed. "Down there." Now I was spooked, as the figure even appeared to me in the form of a shadowy short figure. I knew I could not dare deny what I was seeing. Because on the battlefield you see all kind of things that will play tricks on the mind, I slowly walked over toward Natal to save him. I foolishly thought, *Who in the hell is going to save me?*

Then like a scene from a comedy routine in the old movies, Natal turned again, saying, his eyes big as softballs, "Now, tell me you didn't see that." As the apparition moved quickly down the hall of the presidential common area, I turn and grabbed at the sinister phantasm. About to get the shock of its celestial existence, pouncing like a cat going for a mouse, I reached for the phantom of the White House.

What was I thinking? I landed on the floor with a clunk and heard the ghostly essence giggle as it moved into a wall while I watched. When it finally dawned on Natal and me what had just happened, I rushed him back into his room. I forgot that Natal wasn't even a little boy anymore and went on.

I said, "What the hell was that?"

Putting my hand over my mouth, I tried to correct myself, "I mean, heck." Natal just kept looking out the small crack of the door, trembling in his urine-stained pajamas, but in the front was vomit. I didn't ask him about the obvious. "Why did you get sick?"

"I don't know. I just did," he responded sharply, "and then when I saw Caspar, I peed on myself."

When the phantom was gone and hours had passed on that cold, full moonlit night, I drew Natal a bath and he went back to bed. Yes, even at his age I would tuck the lad in bed, and although my small friend was fearful only while he was awake, I stayed with him until he fell asleep. It seems even little soldiers have the same fears of things going bump in the night.

The next morning the White House was busy with activity as usual, as if nothing had happened. None of the security cameras had seen anything, and I shrugged off the whole night as a nightmare from hell. As I walked into the employees' dining hall, the clang of plates and chatter made everything seem normal, but in the depth of my soul, I knew what I had seen.

"How's it going, Ray?" Agent Summers asked cheerfully. "How are you?"

"I am okay," I said, shrugging.

Agent Summers was a heavyset black man with an ex–Marine Recon background. I knew him while I was in Desert Storm in the Persian Gulf back in the early nineties. Back then, he was Captain Dave Summers—very trim and much younger, with a lot more hair than he had on his now bald head. Now the shaven and rather overweight Agent Summers was only forty and I was only five years his senior, but in the White House I was nothing more than butler and personal houseman to the president of the United States.

Agent Summers walked toward me smiling, with coffee in hand. "Ray, my brother, so what's the deal with you?"

"Is that a rhetorical question, sir?" I came back, smirking. "Or are you checking my pulse?"

"Cool, my Bro Ham," he said. "Not feeling very well, huh?"

Bro Ham was my nickname, which was Agent Summers's cute way of saying Abraham. He was trying to be funny—his way of coming back with his dry wit. Agent Summers was dead on when he came back at me. I wasn't feeling very well, what with being up all night fighting demons with Natal and then cleaning him up as well.

I wasn't going to be very sociable either, and as far as I was concerned, I didn't need to be. I just calmly walked out of the room as the entire staff looked at me. He remembered me when I worked for the Marines, and Agent Summers was first lieutenant over my platoon. I couldn't even look back on those days; I guess that's why he couldn't understand why I had taken the job of chief executive butler of White House Affairs.

I never needed to worry about shedding blood unless I was helping the chief with dinner. Then I made sure I had plenty of Band-Aids. Little did I know that in my later years I would have to shed blood. I had thought that a Christian would be delivered from the shedding of blood, and I would be a believer in the cleansing blood of Christ. I was hiding from my friends the Watchmen, and on the morrow my perspective would change back to a sense of duty.

The next day there was haze over the District of Columbia area, which gave the sky a pinkish tint. It was almost as if the clouds were going to rain but because there was no water in the air, they just floated by. The president and first lady were gone to a European summit, so Natal and I played chess upstairs until he got sick and I took him to bed.

The correlation between the sky outside and Natal

getting sick never dawned me until the moon began to rise, and it was a red moon rising. There he was again, head in the toilet, but this time he was coughing up blood. The bowl was as red as a new candy-red Mustang, and as I looked out the window, I saw the moon rising, and the celestial body was the exact same color as the blood coming up out of the boy. I shouted for the intervention to get a doctor and then started praying over him. Then Agent Summers was running down the hallway.

"Summers," I screamed, "get a doctor over here."

When one of the younger agents came in and saw the blood, he got sick and vomited on the floor. Then he ran out. "Pansy-ass kid—must have been in the air force," I muttered. "Summers, I need some help in here."

"What the hell, bro?" Agent Summers barked. "Here some towels. Ray, you just keep praying over the kid, man."

Another agent came in with his radio. "An ambulance is coming up the front way."

"Don't just stand there. He's coughing up his shoes," Agent Summers yelled at the other agents.

Agent Summers grabbed the kid, who was swimming in sweat and convulsing in his own blood now. I kept looking at the blood-red moon that was rising. The world didn't know that Satan himself was entering this boy's body. Natal would have been influenced by the lord of darkness. At that moment, I never thought to see, nor did I believe that Natal Vicar was becoming the fulfillment of the prophecy. The moon darkened into a deep crimson red, and then it eclipsed. Natal threw up even more. The night of the crimson red moon rising was the beginning of the fall of America, and he was the horsemen that was the white horseman's rider of the Apocalypse. However, the red crimson moon was a symbol. Even though he wasn't the first of many Antichrists, he would be the last Antichrist. Besides, I was going to save his life many times after that, but he wouldn't save mine when it counted.

Ten years had passed, and Natal had no memory of that bloody moon; nevertheless, it never faded from my memory, as it did the president's. Now Natal would be graduating from the military academy and then going to West Point. Consequently, Caesar Natal Vicar got his military and political training, and soon after that, I didn't see him anymore. We had good and bad times together, but that's a story for another chapter, and I miss that little boy I met in the hallway of the church; he was innocent.

As Natal Vicar became older, he had more fainting spells because they found a blood disease that aged him rapidly. Moreover, we had to take him to a specialist who said he was aging rapidly, so they put him in a cryogenic chamber every ten years to stop him from aging.

The time he spent in the cryogenic chamber added ten years to his life, so while everyone else grew old, he stayed younger. I was his consistent guardian and caretaker. I wasn't put into a chamber, but I was the only one who knew the whereabouts of the president's nephew, and I became the guardian over his life and watched over him. I would watch over Natal while he was in the cryogenic chamber until a cure was found some thirty years later.

CHAPTER 14

🏯🏯🏯

A Tree in the Midst
of the Garden

September 25, 2057

Dear Abba,

Waking from the chamber after thirty years was like being born again for Natal, but only the body was like new. Old friends he knew would die off, and presidents would come and go. I found out that before President Vicar left office, he passed an executive order making me provisional guardian over Natal, and that he would live in the White House in a secret room away from the press's eavesdropping eyes and without the knowledge of the public. It was as if he was a king over the White House before his court but this king would gain power from another prince.

Natal wasn't tutored by the finest scholars, and was an eternal monarch over the United States of America. When he finally reached eighteen, he was given a cure for his sickness and allowed to leave the White House. When Natal was twenty, he was sent to Officers Candidates School in Annapolis, Maryland and joined the Marine Corps instead of going to West Point.

The marching orders of the military was never a slow process, but Lieutenant Natal A. Vicar moved up the ranks and became a captain. The familiar cry of war always brings back fond memories to me. Even if it is from the letter of an old friend I never got tired of getting them. Meanwhile, Captain Natal A. Vicar was the company commander of Alpha Company, First Battalion Third Marine Regiment; the Third Amphibious Brigade Third Marine Division of the Third Marine Expeditionary Force was over in Afghanistan for the fifth time.

Captain Vicar was fighting against those who had devastated the World Trade Center, and these wars were made for soldiers to fight. They never seem to end. The captain was now an upright American and not the sickly little boy I knew.

He stood majestically leaning forward in motion. He was hard-nosed but respected by his troops. These were the letters I would get at the White House, but they were addressed only to me, since I was the only father he had ever had in his whole life.

Many of Natal's letters moved me to tears because they reminded me of my time in the military. I would even have flashbacks of those days of the battlefield and skirmishes of hell.

The battle-hardened Captain Vicar commanded his men with the leadership that earned him awards and meritorious recommendations for medals. He earned a Silver Star, a Navy Cross, a Bronze Star, and the Medal of Honor. These medals were given for his gallantry in two raids and three battles against the Taliban and Al-Qaeda insurgents. I felt very proud to be at the awards ceremony that would make any father honored. Nevertheless, his uncle, former President Richard Vicar, was hard-hearted: no matter how great Natal had become on the battlefield, he was too busy playing golf or signing the books he wrote.

The Richard Vicar silently had a prejudges for Rebecca's half breed child, this prejudges came from him only, but even that silence would be broken after today, because he would be modeled into the stuff that would be honored as a hero as he stepped into his destiny. My little boy was about to go into the battle known as Afghanistan's Bunker Hill.

The hill was called simply 237, but on the map it was labeled TLZ (Technical Landing Zone) Zulu Hill 237. It was directly above the Taliban's' camp, and if the Marines could land undetected, they would be able to rain holy hell on the Taliban below. The battle would later be called the battle of Zulu Hill, and it made many boys into men that day. Captain Vicar was forever changed by the terror of the day's single battle.

As the Sikorsky CH-53E Super Stallion whizzed by the scenery of the country, Captain Vicar and his men tried to distract themselves while going toward the sure death that might await them very soon. Many of the men were younger than their captain, and it was as if he was more than just a leader; he was their baby sitter as well. As the laughter got louder and louder, it almost had a nervous tone as the men of Alpha Company came into view of the embarkation zone of the front lines …

"Hey, Captain," Private Smith said. "You remember that belly dancer that came over to you?"

"How could I forget? She had your money stuck in her waist," Captain Vicar said, laughing.

"Yeah, she really liked those men in uniform," Smith replied, grinning.

"No, Smith," Sergeant Grant barked out as he slapped Smith's head forward and laughed. "She like those railroad tracks."

"No shit," Private Smith said. "Then I think I'll be a captain one day, so the girls will love me."

"In your dreams, Smith," Lance Corporal Johnson said jokingly. "What a waste of sperm."

Captain Vicar looked up from the map, knowing where this was going. He shook his head, pulled out the compass, and kept reading the map while the two jarheads went back and forth at each other. This kind of thing happened often but never broke out in a fistfight; it was like a sparring match of words between two brothers.

"Drop dead, Johnson. You ain't had pussy since pussy had you," Smith replied sharply.

Meanwhile, Captain Vicar looked at Grant, knowing where this was going, and Sergeant Grant nodded in a reassuring wink that he would have to handle the problem. As Captain Vicar tried to keep his mind on reading the map, the chopper made its sweep up the hill of the TLZ. You would think that the stomach-jumping motion of the aircraft would shut the mouth of these men, but they were battle-hard Marine veterans.

"Okay, you two, shut it," Sergeant Grant barked. "Or when we get back, I'll have a tank trap for the both of you."

"Hey, Sarge, we were only joking."

"Okay, you jar nuts, let's check to make sure our weapons are ready to debark," Sergeant Grant called.

The platoon yelled in unison, "Ready."

Sergeant Grant yelled, "Lock and load."

"Uh-raah." They did a final weapons check, clicking off the safeties, and then they all started turning their rifle muzzles toward the deck of the helicopter. In the distance the captain saw the other five helicopters getting ready to land. The men waited for their next order as they stood in the ready to debark into the hellhole.

"Debark," Sergeant Grant yelled.

The moment of endearment those memories evoke can be interrupted when you are a soldier on call to give your life, and one can cry a sigh of relief when you are old and gray, lying in your bed. I still have those moments of faded nightmares, and dream of buddies long gone. Natal in many of his letters wrote these same nightmares, and this one would kick off bad from the start.

The Taliban saw them coming in low and were tipped off from the jump. They started lobbing Russian 82 mm mortars and rifle-propelled rockets at the helicopter. One of the fragments from the rockets exploded in the air, hit the pilot, and knocked the lateral control out. The craft began to spin out of control and slammed into the ground, causing the blade to fly out of control toward the encroaching enemy.

The men came out of the craft like a swarm of hornets struck by a bear, and with the platoon scared and scattered like an anthill on fire, they began firing sporadically. As the bomb burst in the air and the men of Vicars Company ran for cover, Captain Vicar was pinned down with his radioman Corporal Skyloskie, trying to call in artillery cover fire from the hail of bullets being fired from the encroaching Taliban raiders. Captain Vicar did everything he could to lead his men out of the slaughter that was ahead of him, but he was struck by a stray bullet, immobilized under a fruit tree, and knocked unconscious.

Dear Raymond,

If you are reading this letter, dear friend, then I am either dead or very near death's door. I am writing this letter to you, my dear friend and father, because you are the only man that has ever given a damn about my well-being. My uncle never cared or wanted to care about me.

My life was never easy with my mother. She had to work night and day to keep a roof over our head, and I felt like any kid in that situation would feel. A burden I would often feel like a dragging weight to my mother; because, she had to take care of me without my dad. Even when I would asked question about life and God. One time when I was at the kitchen table struggling with my math homework, she tried to explain to me that God was her guide, but I will talk about that memory later …

Try to picture me at nine years old, with reddish-blond hair and greenish eyes. I never combed my blond mop top. There I sat with my elbow on the table, mulling over my multiplication table. Trying to study long division was not my cup of tea. What was I thinking at that age? No red-blooded American boy thought about what nine times three equals.

And who cared? If you wanted to get the nine multiplication table, you could line up all numbers from top to bottom from one to ten and then flip the number from bottom to top. You would get the answer to both nine times three, which is twenty-seven, and the answer to nine times eight, which is seventy-two. My life at nine years old was hard enough, and if I needed to know anything in this world, I could ask my mom. She was the world to me, and at my tender age, I needed nothing more than her love …

"You know, Nat." She smiled at me while doing the dishes. "The problems you're doing will never solve themselves if you just stare at them."

"I know, but it's so hard," I whined.

As she rinsed the last dish, she tried her best to make this something I would always remember. She had a way about her to remind me to work hard. My mom would try to get me to understand the meaning of life and my purpose in life. She came over to me and gently caressed my hair, and sat down beside me to give me help with my math problem. I can remember as if it were yesterday that I stood there with my elbows propping my two-pound head up to keep me from falling asleep.

My mom had a way of making me warm and secure in myself. However, the circumstances of life came at me, and she tried to deal with my young problem head-on. She had to, because she was the only parent I had after my dad died in Vietnam.

As I lay there unable to get up by my own power, I felt a force of darkness overcome me. Lying there, my life began to flash before me, which started making me think that I was dead under that fruit tree in Afghanistan. More pictures of my life began to flash back to the very day I began to feel this way—that I was no longer in my body—when suddenly I heard a familiar voice.

"Come on, Nat, you know you're not really trying," she said calmly but with a stern tone.

"Okay," I whined.

"So, what's really bugging you?" she asked.

I sighed and asked, "What do these stupid multiplication tables have to do with my life?"

"You sometime amaze me with your questions." She got up from the table, went into the living room, and brought back her favorite book in the world, which was the Bible that had been given to her by her mother when she finished her catechism at eight years old. The book was worn from having been read so often, and the once white leather Bible was now a dirty off-white gray. You couldn't even tell what it was by the title of the book because the words *Holy Bible* were worn completely off from constant reading.

"Come here, baby." She spoke to me softly. "Nat, life isn't what you make it." She hugged and pulled me close. "Life is always the choices we make—some good, some bad, and, yes, sometimes ugly."

"Why, Mama?" I asked.

"Nat, baby, it's because the Bible says so," she said softly. "Read this for Mama and see it for yourself."

"'I call heaven and earth to record this day a … gain … st …'" Reading out loud, I stumbled over the words.

"The word is *against*," she said.

"'Against you,'" I read. "'That I have set before you life and death, blessing and cursing, there … fore …'"

"That word is *therefore*," she said in an encouraging tone. "Keep reading. You're doing fine."

"'Therefore, ch-ch-oo-se,'" I said as I stumbled untrustingly over the word.

"Yes, that is very good," she said in an encouraging tone.

"'Therefore choose life,'" I continued reading. "'That both thou and thy seed may live.'"

"That was very good, Nat," she said.

"Mama, who's the seed they're talking about?" I asked.

"That's you, baby," she responded.

"Oh, so we have to choose whether we are going to be blessed?" I asked. "But what does God want from us?"

"Something like that, but really God made us a promise. What it really means is that our life might be in God's hand," she responded. "The word of God is saying that you can make any of a number of choices. But no matter what, God wants the best for us, which is life."

Then suddenly I faded away from my mom's view. She was a good sport about making the best of everything, and God was her strength and guidance. Even when things didn't make sense, her Catholic faith gave her a means when all hell seemed to come at her. It was as if some unknown force was trying her and testing her, and as a little boy, I was unknowingly angry with it sometimes. When she would trust God in spite of what was thrown at her …

"Nat," she called. "Come on, honey, I've got to get you ready for school now or I will miss my bus."

I never liked school because of the many color pits and booby traps I had to walk through as a child, and some of those booby traps I'm still walking through today. I had to cross the unjust prejudges of being a half-breed at an early age, and I slumped at the breakfast table, never trying to go to school this or any other day.

I would try to play sick or sometimes strike up an argument to get my mom to let me stay at home. She never would bite at the bait with which I tried to manipulate her, simply because I wasn't old enough to have the skills I now have. I couldn't charm her or whine enough to get out of going to school. I went all 150 days and sometimes more during summer programs that would help me with math and science. However, like most kids my age I suffered from a short-term memory, and we went through this epic battle every day …

"I don't feel good, Mom," I said, sighing sadly.

"Let me see." My mom felt my head and said, "Nope, no fever."

"I really feel sick, Mom," I said with a sad face.

"Are we playing this again?" she said, smiling.

"Oh, man," I grumbled.

"Now take that hot water bottle from under your shirt," she said sternly. "Put it back in the bathroom, and come and sit yourself down and eat, Natal Apollyon Parson, before I get sick of this game you are trying to pull for the one thousand eightieth time."

"Mom, what's hy-po-cri-ti-cal?" I asked, trying to get off the subject.

"Maybe you can look it up along with your other spelling words tonight," she snapped back, "Don't you have a spelling test this Friday?"

"Yes, Mama, I did the ones that Miss Graham gave us in class Monday. But why do I have to be the smart one in the class? Everybody else is stupid, but I have to make the grade."

"Because, Mr. Parson, you don't live with them," she said sharply. "You are just whining too much about nothing."

"I don't whine. I just need a break from this junk at school, Mom."

"I promise you this," she replied. "If someone wants the added burden of feeding and clothing you and making sure you make something out of yourself, then that will be the day, Mister Smarty."

"I just don't like it when the kids at school pick on me."

"Well, Natal, this is no picnic for me either."

"I just wish Daddy was here," I cried. "He'd take care of those kids that pick on me."

"Natal," she spoke softly, "even if your father was here, he'd tell you the same thing."

"What's that?" I asked as I looked up and into my mom's green eyes.

"You've got to take the good with the bad, the bitter with the sweet. Life on this earth is always going to have those four things coming at you, no matter if you're the president of the Unites States or a street sweeper in front of the White House."

"I need help now," I whined, "not when I am in the White House."

"Then take care of it now," she said, getting up and taking my bowl to the sink. "Take care of that problem or it will take care of you."

Those words ring in my ear to this very day, but they didn't help me that day when I got my butt handed to me for being a half-breed black boy in an all-white school. Even though I was smart, it never changed what the kids called me. Besides, they say sticks and stones may break your bones but names will never hurt you. They've never been at my school, because it hurt worse than a punch in the face. The worst was them coming after me: the memory went down in the core of my soul. I had to deal with the name for that day until I had to learn some stupid secret that gave me the rite of passage to be a part of humanity. Today the word only meant one thing. I was only a lowly, friendless scum.

"Hey, red nigger boy," *the oversize white boy yelled.*

His name was Todd Harold, and his name fit him well, because not only did he have the biggest mouth in Gary Elementary School but he had one hell of a right hook to back up that big mouth. As the pool of blood formed in the front of my mouth, I began to look from the ground at the criminal who had assaulted my body, and I could only do one thing about the overpowering hit I had taken.

"Come on, you big baby," *Todd was yelling down at me.* "Get up, you ugly red bone."

"Get the hell away from me or …" *I sobbed, waving my hand at him.*

"Or what? You'll get your white mama to whip my ass?" *Todd said as he started balling his fist and coming closer.*

I could only curl myself into a fetal position and pray that my pain would be gone when I opened my eyes. As I heard the dragging of Todd's feet come closer and closer, his taunting word got louder and louder. Then I felt a blow to my back and head. *The more I tried to cover myself, the worse the beating got, and the abusive blows from his fist beat me to near unconsciousness. I began to lose my sense of where I was, and my hurting minds of my soul as I felt the pain of being a half-breed and the prejudges of not being consider white of black.*

The scenes of what an abused person goes through entered the will of my soul. The psychological impact of each stroke of his hand made me think a sick thought of him being an artist and I was his church of marble.

It was as if he was trying to sculpt by chipping away the little boy with his fist to make me into a man with each blow on my body. I wasn't ready for manhood that day as I fell out cold again to the taunts and jerking of the crowd that encircled me. I decided to finally fight back, and fight back I did by kicking Todd Harold between his legs.

Down and out for the count that white boy went, and I just kept kicking him until the teacher pulled me from him. Todd had to go to the hospital from the beating he got that day. I kind of blacked out from the rage I felt when he hit me a couple of times, but it just came over my body and soul. I went to a place where I was in a smell of sulfur and the smell of dead bodies, like when you smell a dead animal. I saw shadows of demon spirits coming toward me. Then in a flash, I was somewhere else, and it smelled like a hospital with ammonia and bleach and a person talking over a loudspeaker.

I awoke to the smell I knew, so familiar since the time of my birth. I tried to get closer to that smell because I began to feel safe and warm. I knew in my heart it was all a bad dream, because the way I was feeling was as if I was in my own mother's womb. Then reality woke me up to what was real, and I felt the push of my mother's hand on my body ...

"Natal," she said in a weak voice. "Be careful that you don't pull out Mommy's tubes."

I was sitting in my mom's hospital bed. I was in a hospital, and my mother was very sick. I awoke to a room full of all the relatives who hated me because my mom and dad weren't together. I looked at their faces, and they were looking at me as if I was the reason for her death. Somehow in this state of being my spirit was causing me to see into their ugly souls. I could feel their emotions and see right into their evil hearts of fear and bigotry.

I seemed to be the only one in the room who had love and compassion for my mother's pain, because I seemed to feel this deep sense of sorrow and remorse. The only woman in my life who had ever cared for me and seemed to be the only person who would ever know me in this life was about to leave me.

As the tears began to fill my eyes, I felt her gentle touch for what would probably be the last time. She looked as though she was in pain, and yet she was not afraid. I couldn't understand this memory; nor could I understand her faith in God.

I was only ten years old, and in the mind of a ten-year-old, death meant only one thing. I would never see her again, and if you don't care about God as an adult, then talking to a young boy about God and life after death made no sense to my young mind.

"Mommy, why do you have to leave me alone now?" I asked in a whining voice.

She looked at me with those warm green eyes of endearment, and even though she was in pain, she could always speak to me in an encouraging word, and my mother did her best. Soon the warmth of my mother candle would be gone, and I would be living with my uncle, who had just been elected president of the United States of America …

"Mama, Mama, wake up," I screamed.

Then as I relived that experience, I heard a scream much as I heard my voice echoing in a long cavern. As I turned to see where the scream was coming from, I heard my voice again, saying louder the word I said to myself at my mother's grave.

"If God is so almighty," I said in a whisper, "then why couldn't he save my mother? I hate you, and one day I'll get even."

The thing I said even though it was to myself was shouted louder than the words of a rooftop preacher in a Sunday morning sermon. I forgot I said I hated God, but I never forgot my promise. So, with this, Raymond, I say goodbye …

The letter I wrote to the only man who cared never got mailed, but that's what I wrote. Suddenly, I saw my body again and the battle that was happening two feet from the fruit tree I was lying under. I saw a shadow from behind me, and there was screaming and moaning.

As I turned to see who was screaming, I found myself in front of a huge stone entrance that was opening. I could smell the rodent stench of bodies' decaying flesh mixed with sulfur. The smell was unbearable, and I tried to avoid it.

I tried to run away, but suddenly I was swarmed by dark, hideous creatures from the underworld that at first glance looked like they would attack me any minute, but to my surprise they all bowed down to me. A figure came to me in the form of a man from out of the shadows. At first he appeared old and much wrinkled, but when he came closer, he looked like a young man of great power.

His hair was slicked back into a ponytail, and as he spoke, all I could see was darkness and creatures forming that would curse and blaspheme as he drew closer to me. I realized that I was now in the very power of the underworld. This was the chief of the demons himself, Satan, and he was speaking to me. Nevertheless, he didn't refer to himself as Satan; instead, he said, "My name is Count Charlimas DePaul Vicar."

"Okay, Count, what can I do for you?" I said, grinning.

"Well, my boy, if you haven't noticed, you are dead," Count Charlimas DePaul Vicar said jokingly.

"Yes, I know. That thought did cross my mind," I replied.

"Did you know that because of your lack of faith you are now down here?" he said.

"So what's your point?" I barked.

"Well, these demons are very hungry for human flesh," Count Charlimas DePaul Vicar replied. "And with just a snap of my finger, they'll be on you, dragging your worthless soul down to hell."

I was afraid at first, but then I thought to myself foolishly that these demons had all bowed down to me. I realized that this wasn't Satan, but a principality that was the spirit of the Antichrist. His mission was to take me straight to the prince of darkness himself. All I had to do was play along to make a deal with Satan, and that is what the devil had in mind for my life anyway.

All he wanted was my agreement on the situation. If I had known that this was the same spirit that used to torment me as a little boy, I would have just played along and gotten what I want—that is, power. I knew that power was the name of the game, and every man in history, from the kings of Babylon to Greece's Alexander the Great to the emperors of Rome, all wanted power, and that is my goal: to get power. Then Satan was the one to get me this power.

"Well, now that you have managed to scare the hell out of me ..." I barked at him.

"You know I do that to the unfaithful," Satan questionably responded. "But you may be wondering why I brought you down here."

"Yes," I sighed, "that thought did enter my mind."

"You are related by blood to Count Charlimas DePaul Vicar. That would make you his heir, wouldn't it?"

"Okay, so what's your point? So I'm this dead count's heir."

"I will give you all the kingdoms of this earth, if you will bow and pledge oath to me and sign this contract in your blood."

"All I have to do is bow and pledge my oath to you, and then sign my name in blood on some contract? And you will give me all the kingdoms of the earth?"

"Right," Satan said, smiling.

"There is only one problem, my lord," I said.

"Yes? And what, pray tell, might that be?"

"All of my blood is up there on earth," I yelled.

"We can solve that problem right now," Satan said. "We just give you your life back, once you bow to me."

"Then I can have power?" I asked.

"That's right," Satan said with a grin. "So how about it?"

The place was getting hotter by the second, and I was getting pretty annoyed with the smell and endless sweating I was doing. Nothing in this world was on my mind but wanting to get out of that dark and horrid place. I didn't care from that point on what it meant to get out of the place of no return. So, I bowed, and when I rose to my feet, the demons cheered.

"Let me show you," Satan said. "Take my hand, and let me show you."

I took Satan's cold hand, and he flew me back to the hill where my bloody, dead body was being stripped of my clothes by a Taliban soldier. I was facedown and missing one of my arms, and two of my Marines were fighting, trying to get me. They were greatly outnumbered and losing ammo fast if I didn't sign that blood contract.

"Here's the deal," Satan said as he grinned. "Make the blood contract or back to hell you go."

"What will I get if I allow you to do this?" I asked.

"The world at your feet," Satan said with a smile. "I can cause you to come back to life right now, but you must be willing to sign the blood contract and do my bidding."

"If I sign the blood contract," I asked, gritting my teeth, "you promise to keep me alive?"

"Yes, but you must sign the blood oath before your thirtieth birthday."

"That's next year," I shouted.

I began to look at the results of the battle before me. At that moment Lance Corporal Johnson got shot in the face, which knocked his eye out, and as he turned, holding his eyes, he was shot again in the arm, which knocked him backward. Private Smith and Sergeant Grant covered the area while fixing their bayonets to charge the advancing rebels.

I screamed at Satan, "Okay, okay, I'll do it. I'll sign the contract in my blood."

As soon as I made the agreement, I felt myself being grabbed by the devil, and I was reanimated. The Taliban soldier who was trying to take off my bloody pants turned just for a moment to get a knife from his backpack leaving his AK-47 rifle beside me.

I grabbed his rifle and shot the soldier and watched his corpse fall to the ground. I grabbed my web belt from around my waist and made it into a tourniquet on my leg. I began crawling toward the other dead Marines. The tourniquet was stopping the bleeding from my leg. Once I got into a position, I crawled painfully and slowly over to where one of the dead Marines was. It was Lance Corporal Davis from weapons platoon. I was still wracked in pain shooting through my body. I saw an M-60 machine gun and began to fire on the Taliban rebels, who had Sergeant Grant, and Private Smith pinned down the others. Marines were shooting from the cave.

"Hey, the rebels are pulling back, Sarge," Johnson yelled.

The other Marines realized that the Taliban rebels were being shot at, and started returning the fire. "Captain Vicar is alive!" Smith yelled back. Then Sergeant Grant and Smith charge at them, which caused the Taliban soldiers to run toward my crossfire.

It was all but over when Sergeant Grant and Private Smith saw that it was me firing at the Taliban rebels, and they began mopping up the rest of the rebels in the area as I collapsed from the firefight. The next thing I remember is being in a chopper going toward a naval hospital ship in the Indian Ocean.

I was on board ship when I was met by the captain of the USSH *Florence Nightingale*, my friend Major Ellis, and Brigadier General Morgan. I didn't understand all the fuss until they found out that my uncle Richard was the president of the United States. The man never gave me the time of day, but his soldiers were more concerned about the near-death experience I had just gone through.

The Purple Heart, Silver Star, the Bronze Star, and the Medal of Honor were awarded to me for my acts of bravery because I risked my own life while wounded to shield my men from the onslaught of the Taliban rebels. I have been in the hospital now for three months recovering from my injuries and will be coming home soon.

I started to remember the agreement I had made with Satan. I would keep my end of the bargain. The prince of darkness was the one who kept me alive, since God had been willing to let me die like my mother. Therefore, I will serve Satan, and make his kingdom of darkness my own. I saw the paper in my robe pocket—the letter I had written to my friend Raymond Moore. I knew I could trust him, so I finished the letter.

Even if I only see you, Raymond, my old friend, and eat some of your collard greens and sweet potato pie, that will mean more to me than all the medals on my chest. I hope to see you soon.

Sincerely yours,
Natal

CHAPTER 15

🔔🔔🔔

Wolves in Sheep's Clothing

It was an early sunny morning in Orlando when I got an e-mail from President-elect Richard Vicar to come to the White House to take care of Natal, causing me to disappear off the radar. I was waiting on my next assignment when I was approached by two men in tattered street clothes. Two hooded men came up to Jessica and me while we were living together and I was still working for the agency.

"Excuse me, sir," the older one said.

I reached into my back pocket to give them some money, because I knew that most homeless people used this kind of approach to get money. I was a soft touch, and Jessica and I were both homeless when we met, so she didn't mind helping others either.

"Here you go, fellas," I said as Jessica and I sat on the bench.

The other one said, "That won't be necessary, because we didn't come for that."

"Okay, cigarettes." I pulled out a fresh pack. "Do you need a light?"

"No, that's not what we came for either," the older one said softly.

"Well, I guess you are about to run out of options really quick." As I reached into my own underarm holster to pull out my Glock 9 mm, I pushed Jessica behind me.

"We aren't here to do you any harm." The younger one lifted his hands, and my pistol floated out of my hand and into his. As he gave it to his partner, the pistol glowed with a red-hot, fiery heat and then melted. He looked at me with an innocent smile.

"Okay, I must be either dreaming or I'm out of my mind," I said. Jessica pinched me and I said, "Ouch! What the hell did you do that for?"

"Nope, you're not dreaming, because I saw it too," she said fearfully.

"Okay, who or what are you?" I asked

"I am Watchman Maximus Coven, and this is Watchman Samuel Yohash," the older man said.

"Hello," Yohash said.

"Hi," Jessica replied.

I looked at her as she shrank behind me and hit me on the arm as if I was supposed to be polite, or something. I didn't want to get hit again, and I did want to get to the bottom of this close encounter.

"What can I do for you, gentlemen?" I asked.

"We would like to know if you are still interested in becoming a Watchman," Watchman Coven said.

"I didn't know you were hiring," I replied with a frown.

"It is your skills that we are looking at," Watchman Yohash replied.

"And what skills are those?" I asked.

"What my young apprentice means," Coven interrupted,

"is that we would like to finish your training that the other Watchmen have started."

"These skills don't sound much like the spiritual laws I've been taught," I said.

"You seem to know them moderately well," Watchman Coven said.

"Well, with those skills comes a high price, gentlemen," I said.

"We could supply those needs," Coven said, smiling.

"I am sure you could," I said. "But the question is not how much, but who?"

"We will contact you about *who* later," Coven said.

"Then the answer is no," I said abruptly.

"No?" Jessica questioned my decision.

"No, because I'm retiring from the killing business," I said.

When Jessica looked at me in confusion, I knew something wasn't right about their offer. I knew the Watchmen would never ask someone to do murder, and I figured that Maximus Coven had other reasons to hire an assassin. I stood firm on this hint of a lie hiding behind a truth.

"Then I have misjudged you, Raymond Moore," Watchman Maximus Coven said.

"Apparently, you have, Watchman Coven," I said.

"Then we will leave you until we meet again," Watchman Coven said. "Good day, sir."

The two walked away from Jessica and me. We argued all that night about why I had turned them down. I never gave her a good reason why, but I didn't feel right in my spirit about the way Maximus Coven asked me about killing someone. I sent Jessica home and walked around Lake Eola to sort things out.

The last time I had felt this type of tension was when

I was a sniper for the CIA and when I came back from my mission. I was having nightmares of seeing Jessica dead in my arms. I would disregard these prophetic dreams. Maybe I should have talked about them to the Watchmen. Jessica and I were just married and were living in a loft by Lake Eola. I was walking around the lake that night when I heard drums on the northwest side near where Jessica and I had made love—where I had given her the nickname the Black Swan.

I did not pay attention to the drums echoing across the lake because many of the local pagans and beatniks who were naturalists would play, smoke pot, and jam all night long. What I saw that night under the Japanese *kanji*, which is loosely translated as "gazebo," was far from a group of wild pagan hippies hyped up on weed.

When I turned the corner, I saw three hooded people with a naked young woman. Her arms were tied behind her back, and she was being held by two men. I ducked behind a bamboo bush to watch the strange show. To my horror there was a group of people. The young woman was in a trance, and a man with a large single-edged sword on the left side of his head looked like he was about to cut her head off.

The woman name was Lynn who was a local homeless crack addict I knew. I had seen her at the Salvation Army many times, and now she was weaving back and forth her arms were tied and pulled back on both sides. As the hooded people pulled, the sound of the ropes crackled, cutting into her wrists. She was still weaving as if she was stoned out of her mind, and the next thing I knew, the blade flashed forward, cutting off her head. Blood splattered all over the place as the head rolled toward my feet, and I almost screamed when it neared me. Nevertheless, I would have to fight for my life if they found me standing there.

The next thing I saw was even more gruesome. They

took a knife, opened her chest, and took out her heart. Then a van door opened, and three more people with hoods and faces painted like skulls got out. One of them wore a goat's mask and began to walk over to the headless body. The other two men came toward the corpse carrying a black velvet bag. They were given the heart of the dead woman, and then they turned and started looking around.

The man in the goat mask asked, "Where is the head, you fools?"

"My lord, it rolled over there near the shore of the lake by those bushes," one of them replied.

"Then go get it," he barked.

"Oh shit," I whispered.

They were coming right over to where I was, and I hadn't brought my gun with me. Who would think they would have to bring a pistol to a beheading? I just hadn't woken up that morning and expected to see something from a horror show. I could only do one thing, and that was to grab the bag from the person coming over to me and take the head to the police. I knew nobody was going to believe it. Nevertheless, I had to brace myself for the fight of my life. Right when I was thinking that, the hooded man parted the bamboo and saw me standing there.

"Hey, what you are doing in there?" he asked.

"Hoping I could join your party," I said, smiling. Then I punched him backward while snatching the black velvet bag out of his hand, scooped up the head, and started running. I had only twelve blocks to run with an eight-pound head in my hand. I bolted out from the bushes.

"What are you waiting for? Get him!" the man in the goat mask yelled.

It never crossed my mind to run out in the open. The terrain reminded me so much of many of the combat scenes of Panama and El Salvador that I lost my head in the heat of the excitement. I saw them jump into the van and take off toward me, so I began cutting down back alleys.

As with any chase, I had to get away from them and get the woman's head to the police, thus proving that there had been a murder. I need to buy some time, so I cut under Interstate seventy-five to get over to Hughey Avenue and the Orlando Police Department. This life-and-death situation was about my life or theirs, but this was also about the bloodlust of these pagans of Satan who wanted to stay hidden. I could only think of me standing in their way to remain mere phantoms of the night.

I needed something to defend myself, so I picked up a rusty pipe. Under the I–75 freeway, the van pulled to a skidding halt, and my survival instincts kicked into overdrive. Before, when I was Alexander Lynx, I had the agency to back me up, but now Agents Davis and Jones were nowhere to be found. Besides, I had been a scout sniper for the Marine Corps. Back then, I could call for a chopper to airlift me out, but now I was on my own. Like a swarm of angry hornets, they came out of the van with swords gleaming in the moonlight. As they twirled the eight katanas in my direction, I knew only one thing to do: attack the smallest and closest one to me.

I hit him in the back of the legs, grabbing his sword as he went upward and to the ground. Another one swung his sword, barely missing my head, as I flipped another man who charged at me. I grabbed the man, flipping him forward on top of the first man. I grabbed his sword and thrust the sword into the heart of the man that had missed me. When I thrust the sword into his flesh, he gave a muffled groan as he fell to the ground. When I pulled the sword out of the man, I took off his mask and saw that it was Watchman Yohash I had just killed.

Out of the corner of my eye I saw another man holding a sword over his head like a battle-ax, about to hack me in half. I then moved to my right, parried his sword to the left, and swiftly sliced open his stomach with a single motion. Blood gushed out of his bowels.

I turned to repel more attackers, waiting for the rest to come at me. But there were no other attackers. I was left by myself with three dead men as the van spun off toward the highway. There was not even a trace of the injured, and gone with them was the velvet bag with the severed head. There went my evidence, down the highway. I knew there was no point in going back to the scene of the gruesome crime, because they would have cleaned it up.

When I got back home, I saw my door kicked in, and Jessica's bloody body in bed. On the wall of our bedroom in her own blood were the words *You're next*. I looked at the wall and clenched my fist, and shaking and crying, I crawled in beside her. I knew I was too late to save the day this time. I called 911 and waited for the ambulance and the police to come take her body away and clean up the mess. I called several times but the police were to busy, so I sat on the bed waiting for the authorities to come.

I played back the night's events in my mind. "Damn it all to hell!" I yelled, crying.

The next morning, the workers of iniquity who were the Dreg's who had brought about the murder of my sweet Jessica. Two FBI special agents Jerome Clemens and Doug Pinkerton handed me their cards and showed me their badges. They were not your stereotypical flatfoots on a beat, and they and the police detectives with the crime scene investigation unit of the Orlando Police Department arrived on the crime scene at my loft. They were all taking pictures of the scene, of Jessica's body lying on the bloody sheets on the bed. Then they took a picture of the words on the wall, and then I watched as they wheeled Jessica's body out on a gurney.

The feds and police were buzzing around much like they did back in Port Norfolk when my stepfather was murdered. They were doing the same thing that day in Orlando: asking me questions and taking fingerprints. It took all my strength and will to listen to them …

"Mr. Moore, we are sorry for your loss," Agent Clemens said in a respectful tone. "We have to ask you these questions, but I need to know if there is anyone that you could recall that had …"

"Anything against me," I said softly. I knew it was Maximus Coven who had had Jessica killed. "Well, to answer that, you can call this person, Agents Clemens and Pinkerton." I handed Agent Pinkerton, who was the senior officer, a card with Michelle Renée Davis's name on it. "She's with the Central Intelligence Agency. That's all I'm allowed to say."

"Thank you, sir," Agent Pinkerton said. "We will contact you and Agent Davis if we have any questions."

I knew I had just put myself on the short leash the average African-American would normally be on, and that I would be a suspect if I didn't find Jessica's killer. I wanted to do only one thing, and that was to find out who had been wearing the goat mask. As the two agents left, my mind went back to when Jessica was alive and how I had been able to depend on her covering my back. The agents would be woven into my life in years to come in a way that would bring chaos to my already complex life.

I knew I had to make right what justice refused to do, and get my revenge for her murder. I would find out who the Dregs were and why they had put a hit out on Jessica and me.

I would not let the FBI or the police know anything, and I would kill all those bloodthirsty bastards that had done this deed.

I realized that if I was going to find out who was in with Watchman Yohash, I needed to go to the Watchmen's Tabernacle on Orange Blossom Trail. In my spirit, I felt that Watchman Maximus Coven was the man behind the men who had killed Jessica, because I hadn't taken the contract to kill a little boy who was the nephew of President Vicar. Many times I would sleep at the Watchmen's Tabernacle, and I always had to lie on the loading dock to avoid being seen by their closed-circuit television or the police who drove by every four hours.

I was met by two men in hoods who took me down a dark, dingy hallway. It appeared that nobody lived there but that something would jump out and grab you, like in an amusement park's haunted house. We went into a room that was like a loft, and then we went into a closet that I realized was an elevator once the door was closed. I was their guest, and I gathered I would not be leaving. Then we came out of the elevator to the basement floor.

Two guards in purple jumpsuits and armored protective vests greeted us. They were both holding long rods that looked like cattle prods. As we walked down the long hall, I saw paintings of men and women with red-and-black bonnets and dreadlocks coming out of the bonnets. In addition, around their necks were jade-colored crosses with a sword engraved on them. The pictures were numbered sequentially with the day and age of each man and woman. There was the title *Chief Elder* and then the name Naba Zaphah, Raymond Jabez from 1535 until 1540, and then other names with dates. The last picture's label said *Maximus Coven 2004–Present*.

We came into a great hall with a round table with mugs and a warm fire in a stone hearth, which gave the room a medieval character. The last thing I wanted to hear was that we were their welcomed guests, because it made me feel that they might have meant dinner guests of the wrong fashion.

There were twenty-four men and women with the same crosses on their necks and black bonnets, but only one man had the same red-and-black bonnet on his head. However, when I looked for Maximus Coven, I saw that someone else was sitting in the main chair. Watchman Coven wasn't seated with the rest of the council. As I entered the room, all of them were seated around this table, and I was told to sit in the center of the circle of the twenty-four chairs. These twelve men and twelve women had pious looks on their faces, and they seemed very meek in their posture as they waited for me to be seated among them.

"We have been waiting for you some time, Master Moore," the man on my left said softly.

"I didn't know I was being waited on, sir," I said, with a smirk. "Where is Watchman Maximus Coven?"

They all laughed as if I should know the joke they were speaking about. I did not get the joke, and I forgot that I had accepted Jesus as my Lord and savior in a Salvation Army church service three weeks earlier.

"You must have forgotten," the woman on the left said. "We met you at a church service three weeks ago."

"Watchman Coven is no long a member of this body." The man spoke softly.

"I don't remember. I was drunk that night," I exclaimed. "I need to find him to ask him some questions."

"He is gone. Why do you need to see him?" a gray-haired woman asked.

"We remember you because you accepted Jesus that

night," another elder said. "You told us about your wicked past of being an assassin for the CIA, and you said you were sick of killing for the feds that night we accepted you into the body of Christ."

"That was you?" I asked.

"You asked us if we would marry you and Jessica, and we did," the man on my left said.

"So you have been waiting for three years to tell me this?" I said.

They all laughed at me, and I began to feel kind of sheepishly foolish. I could not have even imagined why they had come to me in a million years. However, I came right out and asked what I expected was the real reason.

"So, you are looking for Maximus to kill him?" the older woman asked.

"Yes, and I guess you want me to keep the contract to kill this kid."

"No, not exactly," the older man in the center of the room said. "We want you to protect him, Mr. Moore."

"Okay," I replied.

Then a man in front came over to a screen and asked for the lights to be lowered. Two guards that were present left the room, closing the large oak door behind them. The old man was of great stature, and he started a PowerPoint presentation that made me think I was back with the CIA.

"Mr. Moore, we are nothing but a prophetic intercessory group that has been in existence for more than nine centuries," the man said to me. "But you are a man of war. We can get involved only if the body of Christ is directly endangered."

"So who or—shall I say—*what* is it you want me to do?" I asked.

"First, let me introduce myself," the man said. "My

name is Watchman Zaphah, and I am the three hundred and thirty-second chief elder of the Watchmen Intercessory Council. We need you to use your influence to protect this young boy." They showed me a picture of Natal Vicar as a young boy.

"Is someone trying to kill him?" I asked.

"There are those in the church who would, if they found out who this boy was," Watchman Zaphah said.

"So who is he?" I asked again.

"He is the Antichrist," Watchman Zaphah said.

"Then who is trying to kill him?"

"That would be Maximus Coven," Watchman Zaphah said.

Just then I had a flashback in my subconscious to another part of my childhood nightmare. *I saw the second head of the dragon called Rivalry, whose crown was in the shape of a dome-like crest that came into the shape of battle horns that were jagged and sharp for battles. The horns had worn human skulls and bead-like nodules around the skulls, which represented fourteen of the wars it had fought. Moreover, when this molten-steel-like helmet figure smashed into any metropolis, the monster would totally devastate any populace it encountered with the plagues of war.*

The families of the village became uncaring, learning about this plague of war on television but never coming to the realities of the horror of the being that was moving them. The son of one family was playing a game while the rest of the family watched a program that was on. The mother came in to see the boy playing the video game and walked up to him to reprimand him for his behavior.

"Young man, have you done your homework yet?"

"Aw, Mom,, do I have to learn Mortal Combat tonight?" the boy whined.

"*Mommy, I got an A-plus in my Malibu Barbie game today,*" the little girl said, smiling as she showed her DVD with a big A-plus on it.

Then the mother angrily gave the remote to the child, yelling, "Young man, you turn that channel right now and start on your homework."

The jaded truth is that we are these jagged teeth of blinding stainless steel in the mouth of the dragon and have devoured many of the men of the cities, towns, and villages, and later the women were given as sacrificial offerings by the leaders of the huddled masses. The fiery blast alone of breath of the rumors of war would blaze any hope of coming away unmarred ... Then I came back to myself as I awoke out of the blank stare on my face.

"You mean the Antichrist?" I asked. "The Antichrist of the Bible?"

"Yes," he said. "How did you come to understand about this prophecy of the Bible, Mr. Moore?"

"Well, I had a religious grandmother and a foster mother, but slap me if I am sounding stupid," I said, confused. "But I would think you would want me to kill him."

"Mr. Moore, please understand that we are sworn guardians of the Bible," Watchman Zaphah said, "and prophecy must be fulfilled no matter who it is. Much like Judas Iscariot, the one who betrayed our Lord the Christ, it was fulfilled just as Jesus Christ predicted."

"Well, I thought this Antichrist had protection," I proclaimed. "They're called demons and devil dogs, and Satanists."

"Where did you get that idea?" he asked.

"Talk about creepy," I said, laughing. "What's the kid's name, Damien? Everybody knows that man, from the movie *The Omen.* Are you sure you people are prophets?"

"Well, I hate to be the bearer of the truth, but you can't believe everything you see in the movies," he said.

"Okay, so who is this evil boy?"

"His name is unimportant right now," he said, "because we must teach you the ways of the Watchmen before you start your mission."

"Ways? What ways? Did I even say whether or not I would do this, this thing you are talking about?"

"Okay, we can take you back to your house," Watchman Zaphah said. "But you are the chosen one that the Lord has given this task, and we will wait for you. You are in the Lord's hands now. Plus, you were given an offer to care for the boy?"

"Well, that is true, and you have given me something to think about," I said.

"We will be waiting, Mr. Moore," Watchman Zaphah said.

"Am I my brother's keeper now?" I asked.

"We shall see, won't we?"

"I came here to kill Maximus," I bellowed.

"It was Maximus and Yohash who wanted you to kill this child," Watchman Zaphah said.

"Do you know why?"

The guards opened the door, and as I turned around, they all stood up as I walked toward the door. I was thinking I would never see them again, but how I was wrong. They were offering their protection and training to me so I could be a great warrior for God like them. The thought of what I turned down haunts me even today. I got Jessica killed by being lustful, not covering in marriage, and being stupidly prideful in thinking of myself first and not laying down my life for her. Like the Proverb says, "Pride comes before destruction and a haughty spirit before the fall."[7]

"Of course we do," one of the elders said as I stopped

at the door. "They are the ones who have been killing the homeless."

"Why the homeless, and what's with the beheadings?" I asked.

A woman responded, "Mainly for the sport of blood, but it's part of their ritual, along with eating the heart of their victims."

"Well, I've seen enough of that," I replied. "They are crazy folks."

I walked out the door and then the building. I thought about the things the Watchmen had said the first anniversary of Jessica's death. I kept her picture close to the bed. Over the loft was the living room, and in the kitchen were beer and liquor bottles. On the coffee table were cigarette butts and ashes overflowing the ashtray. Suddenly, there was a knock at the door. I walked over to the door and looked through the peephole. It was Watchman Zaphah and another man. I opened the door. He was wearing a red-and-black bonnet on his head with his dreadlocks up in his bonnet. Dressed in a hoodie and jeans, he came in and looked around the loft. The other man was wearing a jogger suit with a black bonnet.

"What is it, Zaphah?" I asked. "And what's your story?"

"I am Elder Makoto," the other man said.

"Mr. Moore, have you considered our offer?" Watchman Zaphah asked.

"I want to think about this some more, if you don't mind," I said.

Then Watchman Zaphah said something that made me change my mind. "If you need more time to think, we can use your help finding this leader of the Dregs of Society."

Looking puzzled, I asked, "Help you find this leader? Where would I look?"

"You may find that answer in Washington, DC, Mr. Moore," Elder Makoto said as he handed me a paper. "Here is an encrypted password that will allow you to keep in touch with us. It will be a chronicle report that only we can read."

"Will you help us now, Mr. Moore?" Watchman Zaphah asked.

"America is growing darker by the second," Elder Makoto said. "If the Dregs kill the boy and raise up another Dreg leader like Elder Yohash, who was Maximus Coven's apprentice, then we will not be able to stop the onslaught of evil that will overtake the body of Christ, and we are not ready right now."

"I don't understand," I said. "Who are the Dregs, and how did they come to get rooted in America?"

Watchman Zaphah said, "They started long ago during the time of the end of the Roman Empire …

"The Emperor Vespasian in 78 AD was trying to reconquering the Islands of Britannica with the help of General Agricola and the Scottish tribes called Caledonians who were ruled by the Druid priest at Stonehenge, in what is now the lower part of Scotland and the northern country of England. The Druids enslaved the people through fear and intimidation with an army of raiders called the warriors of the Caledonii, better known now as the future men of the Dregs of Society.

"It was during the summer solstice festivals, and the only reason the people gave their young girls was that they were made to fear and believe that if they didn't participate, the moon god's Druid rite festival during the fall solstice by the goddess Anu would send a plague to their crops, and they wouldn't be able to harvest. The Druid priest would have a sacred rite in the Gaelic seasonal festival of the fall solstice, and the result is now Halloween. The villagers gave their young virgin girls as sacrifices to make sure their crops grew, and Satan enslaved the Britannicas through the Druids. The warriors of the Caledonii fought for them rather than submit to the Romans. The Druids needed the young virgin girls from Roman brothels and the slave trade, because the women brought a good price on the slave market. Nevertheless, the people of the Roman Empire would not part with them, because they thought the practice of human sacrifice was barbaric.

"Once in a furious and hard battle that was going in the Roman legion's favor, the Druid priest who learned Latin hatched this plan to capture and kill twenty Roman soldiers and their Centurions, and to hide themselves among the Roman legion, hoping to be undetected. Meanwhile, as the years passed, the Druids would teach Latin to the next twenty, and when those were ready, they would draw the next twenty Roman soldiers until they had infiltrated the legion.

"Soon many of the Roman soldiers were dead and the Druid priests, disguised as the Roman legions, were replaced with another legion of Romans. The Druids were going back to Rome to kill the families of the dead soldiers, and they would free the slaves by marrying them. The Druids would rise as the secret society of Druid worshippers or the Dregs that were hiding among the legions. Then even they grew in the ruins of the Holy Roman Empire and managed to have the Vicar family keep the secret. They kept alive the pagan rituals under the cover of night, under other names, and used patron saints in the form of their gods and festivals, which are present even today.

"The Druids have been doing this for centuries with religions, government agencies, and organizations. The cult you saw the other night was a Druid cult worship group called the Dregs of Society. Moreover, many of the Druid cults are in Washington, DC, today in Congress and even in the Joint Chiefs of Staff. They are in government positions, passing laws to legalize their way of life ...

"If we don't stop them, we will be living in another dark age." Watchman Zaphah finished by saying. "It is even rumored that the president is a descendant of the Black Pope, who was Archbishop Ignatius of the Jesuits."

"I have a lot of thinking to do about this," I said. "I know you need my help, but I can't imagine how allowing one kid to grow up knowing he is the Antichrist is gonna change anything. Plus I am looking for my wife's murderer."

"It will buy us time that we don't otherwise have, Mr. Moore," the female elder said as they watched me turn to leave. "We understand about your vendetta, but Maximus can wait."

"Why is it I feel like I am about to shepherd a wolf in sheep's clothing?" I asked as I left the warehouse.

As I drove back to my loft, I thought about everything the Watchmen had told me. I thought about the image of the woman who had been murdered in the park, her heart cut out by those men. Then I began to think about Jessica, and how she was brutally killed by Maximus Coven and his thugs.

I had promised her I would not take on another job after I took care of the terrorist organization of Mustafa. I began thinking about how many thousands of missing children and people might have a connection to the Dregs. I knew she would be home by now and decided to call her. The place where she was working closed at eight, and it was ten minutes past nine in the evening.

Jessica didn't pick up the phone at home, so I called her cell. Then I remembered that she was dead, and I threw the phone out of the car. My wife, Jessica Swan Moore, was dead. I had come home to see the blood writing on the wall saying, *You're next.*

When Jessica was murdered, I had found her heart in a black velvet bag under the bed and a note in blood. *YOU ARE NEXT.* Jessica was the only woman who had ever loved me and understood my pain. She was the only one trying to rescue me from my own self-destruction.

When Agents Jerome Clemens and Doug Pinkerton and the police came, they did what they normally did: cleaned up the murder scene and asked the same stupid fifty questions. They would call many times to ask about what I knew and see if I had any information. I gave them a dead-end trail, and I would meet the Watchmen.

I would take my revenge later in my travels in life, but for now, the FBI was working on a cold case, and I was on the trail of this Black Pope. I came back to the Watchmen's warehouse and began my training with them, but I was not doing it for the right reason. Nothing mattered to me but revenge. I was going to settle the score with the Dregs until the last of their blood was spilled.

I was knighted as one of their Chief Sergeants of Arms, which meant that I was considered a Knight of J.A.D.E, which carried a great responsibility. However, I carried the title of Minister of Justice, which gave me power to protect and go after all who came against the Watchmen and the body of Christ.

The hypocrisy of the United States was being uncovered as I learned how dark our nation was. Not only did we kill our innocent unborn, but also we were sacrificing our young to satanic gods and giving the blood of the innocent to the beast. The world that I had once thought of as a nation under God was a myth. We were becoming a nation divided between those who believed in legalized murder and a present darkness, and those who were truly good and held life as sacred; the latter were considered evil.

The winds of judgment burn a flame that would destroy this land of liberty. I was going to be protecting the very one who would one day rise to bring judgment to the lands of the new world order. I still think about why I chose that path that day so long ago, and then I remember the oath I took both when I became a Marine and as a Minister of Justice for the Watchmen.

CHAPTER 16

🎗🎗🎗

In Gods We Trust

November 10, 2057

Dear Abba,

It was months after Jessica's funeral that I was lying on my couch staring at her photo in my living room. A stale pizza had left its oily stain on top of its box, beer cans were strewn all over the living room floor, and there were boxes packed up everywhere. I sat up at times, and at other times I paced alone in the night, looking out at Lake Eola. Watching the moon dancing on the water, I began to remember how her murder had left me empty, my love lost.

I remembered the night we danced at the Marine Corps ball. With the fanfare of one hell of a dog-and-pony show, there was enough brass shining in that place to blur the vision of even a blind man. Captains, colonels, and generals were all decked out with their medals. When I was announced and entered the ballroom, I heard the clicking of heels. They all sharply snapped to attention at the sight of that little blue-and-white medal around my neck.

Jessica was breathtaking that night in her blue-and-gold sequined gown and her hair up to show her flawless, elegant, creamy skin. She was Cinderella, and I was her prince as we danced to Duke Ellington.

"Am I doing this right, Ray?" Jessica asked.

"You are fine, sweets," I said softly as we floated across the floor. "Honey, I've got something to ask you."

"We're not going on another mission again, are we?"

"Well, kind of," I said.

"Jeez, can't a girl get a break?" she said.

"This one is a long-term one," I said.

"Where to this time?" she asked, smiling and then giving a frown.

"Guess," I said.

"I hope it's not in Russia."

"Nope."

"Cancun?" she asked.

"Getting cold," I said.

"London." She smiled.

"You're getting warmer."

"New York City," she said, frowning, "We can go shopping in Manhattan."

"Closer than that," I said.

"I give up," she said, sighing impatiently. "Where?"

"A chapel …" I dipped her down, and when I brought her up, I showed her an engagement ring that was on my pinky finger. All she could do as we waltzed under the starry sky was cry on my shoulder. We danced in the cool of the night until dawn.

I began drinking heavily in those months after her death, trying to drown my sorrows in the very bottle I swore

I would never return to. It made my salvation weak rather than trusting in the Lord's power.

I believed in the darkest regions of my mind and emotions that this was my fault because I had opened the door and the enemies of God had taken her away. I tried to blame God by saying he had taken her, but after two years of training with the Watchmen, I knew better than to come to that conclusion.

The voice of Christ came to me and said, "The thief came but to steal, kill, and destroy, but I have come that you might have life and have it more abundantly."

They would only veil the true plan. I began going to every church that allowed me to hide among them. I rested in the church of Laodicea to put the chief bishop of the church outside as he spoke prophetically, and he stood at the door of my heart, asking to be let in, seeking to belong in my worship, and knocking to my closed will. I made Jessica my god, and I trusted in her strength more than I did the realization of God the Father. This is why I drink.

CHAPTER 17

🗼🗼🗼

Let the Weak Speak

"Lo, I have stood at the door, and I knock; if any one may hear my voice, and may open the door, I will come in unto him, and will sup with him, and he with me, and thinking that they are praying to God."

I went to the veteran's hospital at Bethesda, Maryland, to visit Natal, who was recovering from the wounds he had suffered in the war in Afghanistan. I stayed by his side until he regained consciousness. Then I began to read the letter he had sent me the day before he nearly died from his wound. No longer was I dealing with Natal but with an empty vessel that had been filled with the very being of Satan himself.

When I went into the room, I felt the presence of darkness surround me, and I was on alert when I went near him. As the years passed, I had thought that Natal could never do evil in his heart toward me, but now I realized he had the very ruler of hell and death in him. I was the shepherd of the wolf that was in sheep's clothing. He was the first seal of Revelation, the ruler on the white horse that would ride and conquer the world.

I watched him lie in his hospital bed unconscious from his wounds that could have done him in, but the force that kept him alive was of darkness. One could say that it was not love that him alive; I knew it was hatred. Natal would be the rider of the white horse and the conquering king who had no arrows, but he would not be our Lord King who used words to heal. This king would use words to hurt.

My mission was to protect him, and somehow God the Father moved the president to send me on board the *USSH Florence Nightingale*. I met the captain of the ship, Major Taylor, whom I knew as a lieutenant, and Brigadier General Morgan, who was a captain.

We all laughed before we went into Natal because we knew he was banged up bad and we all knew about the hell and had seen many brothers lose limbs that God had given them. All of us knew that it was only fitting to have your reunion outside and keep the man's honor intact. It was like an old family reunion when we were in the first Persian Gulf War. Natal was keeping his bearings but did not like the fuss.

"Why, it's old Staff Sergeant Gatos," General Morgan yelled.

I yelled back gleefully, "Captain America, how are you, sir?"

"Man, you don't look a day older than when you left the Corps," General Morgan said, grabbing me. "Major, you know Raymond Moore?"

"Yes, sir," Major Taylor said seriously. "We served on the same blood-soaked land in Afghanistan. Good to see you again, Mr. Moore."

The nurses were in and out of Natal's room while we remembered the good old days, but they reminded us we couldn't keep him up. He fell back to sleep because of his injuries, so they waited outside. There would be time enough to reminisce back at the White House later. I stood watch over him all that night while Major Taylor and General Morgan waited outside for Natal to recover.

Natal said, holding my hand as he awoke, "Good morning, Uncle Raymond."

I could only smile as I looked into his eyes. As I smiled back into his face, the door opened to the room with other injured men. Major Taylor and General Morgan came in with an oak box. They stood with all their ribbons and battle awards in their dress blues and tan short-sleeve shirts, showing that they were glad Natal was alive and well.

"Well, well, well," Major Taylor said, "it looks as if mother hen is on guard."

"I wouldn't have it any other way, sir," I replied.

"Well, gentlemen, I have a busy schedule," General Morgan replied. "Men to lead and everything, so shall we get this party started?"

As he read the award letters, we all stood at attention. The Purple Heart, Silver Star, and Medal of Honor were all awarded to Natal A. Parson, not Vicar, but that would change. I got these medals for my acts of bravery and gallantry. I risked my own life being wounded to shield my men from the onslaught of the Taliban rebels. Knowing the pain Natal was in and seeing it on his face, I could only sink my emotions and act like a stone-cold mind warrior of the Marines.

However, I was like everybody else when it came to someone hurting: you told old war stories of men who had passed from life to death. The fear of coldness could be felt, and it was so thick, you could cut it with a knife. None of us wanted to stay in the room because it was an evil that made your hair stand on end, and even though no one said anything, I remember that day as the day I looked Satan dead in his eyes.

As I looked into the eyes of the only son I ever knew, my heart burned to hold my little boy; as a former Marine, I knew this warrior needed my strength and nothing less would come from me right now. The general and major said their goodbyes, and then it was back to work for us that day.

As I read and reread the letter, my mind went back to his youth and how I had cared for him. Natal was trying to tell me in his own way that the demon that had haunted him as a child was now in him, and that he was possessed by the very devil himself. It would have sounded crazy if it had not been for what I will tell you later.

I would stare into the cold eyes of the thing in the body of Natal Vicar. I knew there something was different about him. When he looked at me, he would frown or hiss, which went unnoticed by others in the room.

The doctors, nurses, and high-ranking officials were never seeing what I saw, all them blinded by the iniquity of their own hearts. Something came to his attention, and we began a very strange conversation.

I would take breaks and go to a hotel for the night and sometimes go pray in the hospital chapel to stand watch over my mission. Like a Marine guard on post, I stood guard. However, instead of reporting to a duty noncommissioned officer or an officer of the day, I went into the chapel and reported to the captain of my salvation.

"Father God," I cried, "I am getting weak … I can't do this anymore."

"Raymond …" the voice of the Father echoed softly as I saw a light near the cross.

"God my Father, help."

And he said to me, "My grace is sufficient for thee: for my strength is made perfect in weakness."

"But my Lord, he is the devil. How can I save him?"

"For by grace all are saved through faith," God the Father said. "And this faith is not of yourselves."

"But he is just flesh and bones," I pleaded. "He's the only son I ever had and loved."

"Remember the king of Egypt when Moses tested him?" the Father's voice asked.

"Yes."

"My servant came to him eight times to change his heart," the Father said.

I interrupted, "But the Bible said you hardened Pharaoh's heart."

"True," the Father replied. "Nevertheless, Pharaoh chose to listen to the spirit of haughtiness I sent to destroy him with, rather than bowing to my will."

"It is the gift of God," I said.

"Yes, Raymond, I mourned that I judged Egypt, but she would not repent …"

"Why?"

"It is because of my character of the spirit of grace and of supplications," the Father replied, "In the end of days they shall look upon him whom they have pierced, and they shall mourn."

"That is why it can't be of works," I said. "If we did it, man would boast."

"All of mankind is my workmanship," the Father said. "Created in Christ Jesus to good works, which I have before ordained that man should walk in them."

I started walking back as God the Father echoed this last phrase that sent a chill down my backbone. "He's chosen not to walk in them." I came back from the chapel understanding that Natal had chosen to leave God and had rejected the very character of grace and supplications.

However, I would now look at him with pity. As I stared

at him, he started to feel uncomfortable, so Natal picked up a copy of *Rolling Stone* magazine from the nightstand and began to act as if he was reading it. He turned the page slowly at first, and then just a hair bit fast, the move letting me know he was irritated at my staring at him.

Natal said as he tried to read, "Got something on your mind?"

"No, not really," I said, trying to play it off as I thought to myself, *Think fast, rabbit.* Smiling, I continued, "Do you need anything from the PX?"

"No. What got your attention to be staring at me so much?" he asked.

"You've changed," I replied.

"How?"

"You're not the little boy I used to put to bed anymore," I said.

"Things change, old friend. Things change," he said slowly.

"Is it the war or something else?" I asked.

"Something else. Something wonderful …something powerful."

"What is that *something*?" I asked.

"Wait and see, Uncle Raymond. Just wait and see."

I just smiled as I looked away, playing off the fact that he was right. This little boy was gone, but the thing in him was an old friend. I met evil as a nine-year-old boy the night I saw the man who killed my stepfather and raped my mother. It was this same thing that sent the same cold chill down my spine. Because my own parent's choice had been to just go to a church building, it was this choice that judged them. The little boy, now a man, made that same choice.

Natal Apollyon Parson was now an enemy of the Commonwealth of Israel and the kingdom of heaven by choice, and he would hate all who would love God. At that instant, I made up my mind not to kill him but to let him fulfill his destiny. That is the right of every human even if he's the devil himself.

You see, because I am the teller of this tale, and I am the one about to face my own demise, I feel that I must be very frank with you. I have not been honest with you. If it had not been for the training of the Marines, the CIA, and the Watchmen, I would have been like every other deceived fool who believed his lying wonder.

Nevertheless, I watched the nurses take care of Natal, which gave me a lot of time alone with him. Once during the three weeks, after the prep for his fourth surgery to put in the implant he would need for robotic arms and legs, I felt for some reason that I needed to go see how he was doing.

When I got to the floor of the hospital, I realized there were no Secret Service agents, nurses, or orderlies anywhere. I knew something was wrong. All the doors to the other patients' rooms were open, and the patients were gone, although they had been there the day before. I began to think that the president had finally tried to kill his nephew. I went into the closet and got a can of aerosol disinfectant and put it in my back pocket.

I walked down the hall, my heart pounding in my chest. I thought the sound echoed off the walls, and I know my assassin sense heard the noise. This was the same feeling I had gotten the night Jessica was murdered. I found a can of hair spray at a nurses' station and grabbed it before entering Natal's room.

The evil that came upon me overwhelmed me like the darkness that came out of the shadows. Then I saw the killer dressed as a registered nurse with his sword turned downward at Natal's heart. I took one of the spray cans out and with a lighter sprayed a flame upon the would-be assassin, whose wig burst into flames.

He screamed as the flames licked toward the sprinkler, and as the mercury burst to set off the fire alarm, the assassin jumped through the window, leaving the wig behind. I called for help, and security officers came up.

"Stop that man!" I yelled, pointing out the window. However, nobody stopped him. The officers just watched as the blood-soaked flaming man in nurse's clothes jumped into a van as it sped away.

The same federal Special Agents Jerome Clemens and Doug Pinkerton came when they noticed my name crop up on their radar.

"It seems we meet again," Agent Pinkerton said, smiling.

"Yes, gentlemen," I replied.

"Why is it you keep coming up on our radar?" Agent Clemens asked, looking at Doug Pinkerton.

"Maybe you can ask the president," I replied.

"We talked to your friends over at the CIA," Pinkerton said, "and he said you need to call them. It's been a while since they've heard from you."

"Thanks for the message," I said, smirking. "I'll make sure to drop them a line."

Then Agents Jerome Clemens and Doug Pinkerton left the room, the nurses moved Natal to another room, and the local police did their investigative work. I moved Natal away from the limelight of the media after the assassination attempt on his life. I had a friend of mine who worked at the veterans hospital in Reno secretly transfer Natal from public view until I could find out who was plotting against his life.

A dear friend of mine since back in the days of the Marines named De'Angelo Michael Jones was kind of weird, but he would do anything for a person. He was the kind of guy who would get something if you needed it and would lay down his life. Natal's surgeon pieced together a new and functioning limb and spinal cord. The surgery was done for Natal, so he could have walked normally again and been like new. He would need two years of rehabilitation, and even though the Marine Corps asked Natal if he wanted to come back in, he chose to get out.

CHAPTER 18

🏮🏮🏮

The Burden of Love

June 16, 2009

My Dear Nephew,

I have dreamed of this day since you came into our lives some twenty years ago. I have never been so proud of you and your awards of heroism. It is an honor to have you as my nephew that you have served your country well. I have made provision to let you continue to stay at the White House to recover. I hope to see you soon.

Sincerely yours,
Richard Charles Vicar II
President of the United States

"That was a nice letter from your uncle," I said.

"The man never gave me the time of day," Natal snapped, "but let one of his dear soldier boys from the front lines come near death and he's burning a candle at the White House.

"That's not the important thing in life," I said.

"What is important?" he asked.

"Finding love, joy, and peace," I replied, "which comes from God."

"And how do I find that, from your God?"

"Your soul should tell you that."

"I have no soul after the war."

"Then you need to rethink your salvation, Natal."

"It wasn't your God who raised me from the dead," Natal said.

"Then who did?" I asked.

"Can you read my heart, or am I dead to you, too?"

"That's a fine thing to say to me, after all we've been through together."

Seeing the darkness growing in his eyes, I was careful not to upset him. Natal began to turn away from me, and I heard a growl come from him.

"Where was your God or Uncle Richard? Are they here to see me? Hell, no."

"Don't blame God for the horrors of war," I said as I sat on the edge of his bed and put my hand on his artificial limb. "Your uncle does care, Natal."

Natal pulled away with a jerk, like a spoiled child. Then suddenly he spun around with tears in his eyes. "When they found out that I was the nephew of the president of the United States, they began pinning all types of medals on me, which made me prettier than a Christmas tree. I am sick of you defending his lack of faith. I am nothing but his bastard nephew." Then Natal picked up the wooden box with the awards and medals and threw it against the wall. I went over, picked up the medals, and put them in my pocket. Just then the nurse came in. For the rest of that night I had to let

Natal think about what he had said. I was left realizing that the boy I had raised was no longer in that body.

"Your pain can bring you greatness if you would quit feeling sorry for yourself."

I soon began to find myself having a different kind of flashback, but they weren't like the old battles of long ago. These flashbacks were of what the elders had told me what to expect, and who my enemies were in Washington, even in the White House.

Elder Juniper and I were in the prayer garden and I was in silent meditation. The sound of the birds and the fountain gave me the peace to concentrate on a vision that helped me clear my mind of other distractions. It wasn't like I had to focus on my troubles when I first came to the Watchmen; they were waiting for me to come out of them. It was more evident that I needed to see into the troubles that were to come to get ready for the mission I am dealing with now.

"Raymond, focus on the word," she said, "and you will see the truth of what is to come."

I began seeing fifty vipers that were trying to kill this one giant king cobra, and they were trying to bite him in the tail and neck. The snake scales were too thick, and the cobra devoured forty of them in one gulp. That left ten standing, and the fiery vipers hid in the caves.

"What is it you see, Raymond?" she asked.

"I see a large flag with fifty stars and on those stars are also fifty angry vipers that stand against this large cobra that is hiding the truth, men and women. These vipers disapproved of everything that was concerning the faith in Christ Jesus, and they slowly brought to destruction the old order of the Republic of the United States of America."

"That is interesting, Raymond," she said. "Are you sure it isn't Chief Elder Moses, the watchman of the Lord God of

Israel, struggling against the Egyptian temple priest Janis and Jamborees who helped the Pharaoh Ramses try to keep the children of Israel in slavery?"

"No, it is fifty vipers that I see. What does it mean?"

"You are seeing the fall of a nation, and one day this nation will come under the rule of a man much like the king of Egypt."

"I don't understand, Elder Juniper," I said.

"But you will, Raymond," she said. "One day you will."

Little did I realize that the world I was living in would change. The United States of America was responsible for the failures of our school systems, the drugs in the ghettos, and the rampant chaos of gang activity, which led to the twelve-year civil war and the dark times to come. They were looking for a leader who would move them into the twenty-first century, and the election of Governor Richard Allen Vicar was the fulfillment of those prophecies. Governor Vicar, unknown to the Druid councils, was not a blood relative of the Vicar bloodline. As a matter of fact, if the truth were known, it had not been determined where Richard came from, because his birth certificate had never been found. Some say he was of European origin, and others say he was a Russian illegal alien who became an Alaskan citizen, and when Alaska was in desperate need of a miracle because of bankruptcy and bad debt, then-Senator Richard Vicar came to their rescue.

After a hard win in the southern states, Governor Vicar won by a small margin of votes. Senator Kenneth Lincoln, a dumpy, five-foot, two-inch Neanderthal who was loud and obnoxious, and who smoked cigars and drank, protested and demanded a recount of the votes. Some four months later, while at a party for Stephen King's new novel, the senator suddenly grew ill, withdrew his call for a recount, and died months later.

While Natal and I were healing from our wounds from the Dregs, my friend Michael allowed us to come to his hilltop estate in Rattlesnake Hills. Michael was an ex-Marine and was disabled after being shocked from when he was an electrical equipment repairman. He had been discharged after serving six years of reenlistment. I met him while I was detached to Third Recon on Okinawa, a field operation while we were in Pattaya Beach, Thailand.

I saved him from being shot that day, and he never forgot it. I guess it takes all kinds to make friends with someone, and I nearly forgot it until one day. I saw Jones in Orlando. The Department of Veteran Affairs was paying for his way to school, and he was learning how to be a data-entry person. I was homeless, and of course this was before I was Alexander Lynx. At that time, Michael and I were just associates, because I did not trust him—or anybody, for that matter. Volunteering at a program at a local church, Michael tried to get veterans off the street through the Orange Street Outreach Center with Manna Food Distribution. I can remember the first time we met. We were on the rocks in Gator Park and Michael Jones walked up and said, "Here's a sandwich for you, brother."

Raymond Moore snapped back, "Nothing personal, bud, but the only way you be my brother is if you were named De'Angelo or in the Marines."

"Well, then, *semper fi*, devil dog," Michael said as he gave me a Roman handclasp.

Since then Michael had been like a sidekick, or the straight man of the two of us. Wherever I went, he would follow, and because he was a Christian and an ex-Marine, he had the art of acquiring things from old supply buddies from his past military experience with no questions asked. When I was undercover or on an exclusive mission for the

CIA, Michael would get me what I needed when the agency wouldn't. I never asked how he got it, and he never asked me why I needed the supplies or information.

One day, while Michael was praying for Natal and me, God warned him about who his special houseguest was. He didn't ask us to leave, but I could definitely see the prophetic anger coming out. He was not exactly excited about the reality of the circumstances in which God Almighty had placed him.

"I have been praying for you," Michael said as he walked down the stairs as I was watching the news.

"Thanks, my old buddy," I responded.

"You might not be thanking me," Michael said in a mournful tone, "after you hear what I'm going to say."

"Why? Is something wrong?" I asked.

Michael said, "Yes. Do you have any idea who you are caring for?"

"Why?" I said. "Does it matter?"

"This man is the Antichrist!" Michael yelled at me.

I reminded him, "According to the royal law of love, we must care for someone even if he's the devil himself."

Michael started going up the stairs, and then turned. "I don't think those laws apply to the devil's son." After seven years of hiding, Natal came out of the shadows and started working at the Department of Veterans Affair with Michael. Natal slowly started rising through the ranks of the Department of Veterans Affairs regional office, and became well known in the Senate and House of Representatives. Some of his political friends and associates asked him to run for a seat in the United States Senate.

We moved out of Michael's house on Moral Avenue and took up a residence in the hills near the McCarran loop. The estate was Mountain View because it was in the foothills of the Sierras. One day a woman reporter started calling for Natal. As the days passed, she kept being persistent in her calls.

"Vicars residence, how can I help you?" I answered the phone.

"My name is Tiffany Marcos, and I'm a reporter for the *Reno Journal and Gazette*. I need to speak with Mr. Natal Vicar if he's available."

"Well, he's at work right now," I said, "but I can take a message."

"Please tell him that I called," Miss Marcos said in a concerned voice. "I am at (555) 673–1142. Please have him call me as soon as possible."

Natal and I talked about this later, but he never returned her call. Natal was still afraid because of the hit he had on his life; he thought it would be better not to involve himself in the press yet. Three years passed, and while Natal was running for the Senate race in Nevada, he had to meet this reporter at a black-tie dinner. The Republican Party was holding a fund-raiser for him and charging fifty-two dollars a plate. It had the looks and class of a very good dog-and-pony show with all the trimmings.

I was playing Natal's bodyguard that night, and I hated every minute of it. There was a place card for every guest, and I noticed the one right beside Natal's read *Reserved for Ms. Tiffany Ramona Marcos*. I couldn't place it, but I knew I'd heard that name was before, and then it dawned on me that it was the woman who kept calling for three years to talk with Natal. Now she would be sitting right beside him on the very night he was starting his campaign to run for senator. Miss Marcos was going to be able to tell the story about his life and would propel Natal into the spotlight, as the book of Revelation says in chapter 13, verse 1: "And I stood upon the sand of the sea, and I saw out of the sea a beast coming up, having seven heads and ten horns, and upon its horns ten diadems, and upon its heads a name of evil speaking."

The scripture blared and rang in my ears in my head as I remembered some of the friends and associates who had been introduced to Natal that night. Ten of them were prime ministers from countries around the globe. These men and women supported Natal not just with their mouths but also with their money, because they saw his leadership abilities far beyond his being just a senator from some backwater gambling state.

However, the night went well, and was not overshadowed when a woman entered the ballroom over at Harrah's Hotel and Casino. As she entered the room, many of the men were elbowed by their wives. That evening she stole the heart of Natal Apollyon Vicar. The graceful yet elegant Miss Tiffany Marcos was not looking like a reporter from the *Reno Journal and Gazette* that night.

She floated gracefully across the floor toward Natal, who watched every move she made as she greeted him. Natal's dreamlike stare was priceless. I hit him to get him out of his trance.

The master of ceremonies introduced Natal and Tiffany to each other. I could only watch, knowing how the evening would end. I could only pray for protection and not interfere in what I knew was a desirable plan for him to have a beautiful piece of arm candy to show the world he was a man of the world. As Miss Marcos sat down and she and Natal kept talking, the master of ceremonies was announcing the keynote speaker for the event, which was Natal. He was so busy talking to Miss Marcos that he missed his introduction, and I had to poke him to get his attention.

Natal said, gritting his teeth, "What is it?"

"Excuse me, sir, we need to go," I said in a respectful tone.

"Miss Marcos, will you join me for a nightcap?" Natal said.

"Why yes, it would be my pleasure," Tiffany Marcos said with a smile.

Natal and Tiffany came home together. I asked him if he was hungry for some chicken, collard greens, and sweet potato pie. I got an evil smile as he walked out of the room. I laughed out loud and left him alone with his guest for the night.

Natal said softly to her, "I don't usually have sex with a woman on the first date."

Tiffany giggled and said, "So what do you call what we just had? An after-dinner mint?"

"No." Natal began to laugh out loud. "I call that making love, because I love you enough to make a commitment."

"Now, that answer shows promise," Tiffany said, smiling as she lay on his chest, playing with his hairs. "So what is the real story, Mr. Vicar? Who are you?"

As they were both lying there kissing each other, Natal rolled over and told Tiffany his story while they reclined in bed. He wondered if this was the time to be honest with her. She propped herself up on her elbows.

"Well, let's see, I was born and that was it, the end," she said in a choppy tone. Natal rolled on top of Tiffany. She reached under the cover and pulled and pinched his side. He groaned in laughter as she got on top of him and played with his chest. Tiffany noticed his skin tone was different on his legs, which were wrapped around her. She noticed his left arm was different from his right arm.

"I hope you don't mind me asking this," she said in a cautious tone, "but why is your right arm different?"

"Well …" he began.

"Oh, I am sorry. I am so sorry. That was personal. That was personal, and I am being foolishly insensitive."

"No, it's all right. It's really okay," he said as she hid her face in the pillow. "It is a bionic limb—and really, since I am in bed with you, don't you think you can get a little personal with me?"

"How did you get them?" she asked.

"Well, you see …" He began to explain.

"Let's see: I'll tell you my story from start to finish … I will tell you my whole story, okay? I was born to Walter Charles Parson Vicar, who was a third cousin to Angelina Carol Vicar on December 22, 1970, My parents loved each other, and I was only two when my dad died by a sniper's bullet in North Vietnam. My mom never married again, because although I was fair skinned and could pass for white, she did not want me to forget my heritage, nor did she want a foolish white man teaching her son how to hold bigotry in one's heart. My uncle was a hypocrite, because he could have African-Americans work for him but would call one to dine with him to save his own neck."

"Is your mother still alive?" she asked.

"No, she died when I was a small boy. Well, anyway, I was later put in a cryogenics machine for thirty years after they found a cure for my blood disease. When I arrived at my uncle's home at the White House, I was sent to a military academy.

"I went all 150 days and sometimes more during summer school accelerated programs for the gifted that would help me with math and science. Nevertheless, like most kids my age I suffered from a short-term memory, and we went through this epic battle every day …

"'I don't feel good, Mom,' I said, sighing sadly.

"'Let me see.' My mom felt my head and said, 'Nope, no fever.'

"'I really feel sick, Mom,' I said with a sad face.

"'Are we playing this again?' she said, smiling.

"'Oh man,' I grumbled.

"'Now take that hot water bottle from under your shirt,' she said sternly. 'Put it back in the bathroom, and come and sit yourself down and eat, Natal Apollyon Parson, before I get sick of this hypocritical game you are trying to pull for the one thousand eightieth time.'

"'What's hy-po-cri-ti-cal?' I asked, trying to get off the subject.

"'Maybe you can look it up along with your other spelling word tonight,' she snapped back. 'Don't you have a spelling test this Friday?'

"'At other times, my mom would teach me the values of good and fair, and belief in dreams. 'You've got to take the good with the bad,' she said, 'the bitter with the sweet. Life on this earth is always going to have those four things coming at you, no matter if you're the president of the Unites States or a street sweeper in front of the White House.'

"'I need help now,' I whined, 'not when I am in the White House.'

"'Then take care of it now.' She got up and took my bowl to the sink. 'Take care of that problem or it will take care of you.'

"Those words ring in my ear to this very day, but they even helped me when I got my butt handed to me as an eight-year-old going to an all-white school. I grew smarter, but even though I was smart, it never changed what the kids called me, and it hurt worse than a punch in the face. I grew hard and that got me through later in life as I went to college through the Naval Academy and even when I became an officer in the Marines.

"The worst was coming after me and the memory would go down in the core of my soul. I had to deal with the name half-breed for that day until I had to learn some stupid secret that gave me the rite of passage to be a part of humanity.

"When my mom died, I was only ten years old, and after the funeral I was sent to my uncle's home at the White House. He paid little attention to me, and that was when I met Raymond. I began to lose my sense of where I was, and felt the pain.

"I was becoming trouble and not keeping my grades up, so I was sent to the Military Naval Military Academy in Portsmouth, Virginia, because my dad was a Medal of Honor recipient and they knew my uncle, so I got favor with the director who worked at the Department of Veterans Affairs regional office.

"At the Naval Academy in Annapolis, Maryland, I was Lieutenant Vicar going to war in Iraq, and when I was Captain Vicar, I extended his tour over in Afghanistan, where I was given the Medal of Honor, and that's how I got this arm.

"After my career was over, because they didn't have bionics in 2009, they gave me hydraulic titanium steel legs for a while until one day. When I was working over at the VA in Reno, a doctor asked me if I would like to take part in an experiment on bionic limbs.

"I agreed, and while going through the surgery, they had to transfuse my blood and filter it. Because I had a rare blood disorder, I would break down in thirty years. Therefore, they gave me a blood transfusion of normal A-positive and I have lived with these things ever since."

"Man," she said, getting dressed the next morning, "you're a very strong person to endure such hardship."

"Thank you," he responded.

Then she said, "I've been thinking that maybe we could meet at the Amendment Twenty-One Club."

"I thought you wanted to see me again." Natal grinned as he walked her to her car.

"I would like that," she said. "You would think the way you were acting you were going to marry me." Then he kissed her goodbye and she drove down the driveway.

When Natal Vicar became the elected senator of Nevada, his main concern was to stop the rumor about a civil war breaking out. President Charles Pullman was later assassinated by Caspar Reno Jared's White Aryan Race group, who were about 150,000 strong. He was breaking the Constitution of the United States by going into a fifth term to try to end the war in Afghanistan. He tried to unite the countries of Mexico and Canada with the United States of America, losing the privileges of being America. The former United States split into five countries.

The second civil war was called the War of the Roses and Thorns because many of the Christians who were massacred were cremated and buried under rosebushes by anarchists led by Caspar Reno Jared. He was the descendant of the great General Reno, who was in the first Civil War under General Grant. The Christians were feeding homeless people in the park on the river who were fleeing from the battle of Hickory Creek seventeen miles from the front lines.

In addition, in the twelfth year of the twenty-first century, the second civil war of the United States of America began at the Mississippi River. The front lines were East Coast states that were against the West Coast states.

As the mighty general at the front of the hill looked

down at an open wheat field in Kansas, he looked at the approaching army. Knowing that they were trying to take the dominion of the eastern side of the Mississippi River, the general took up his position. Looking on his right and the open spaces of the plains country of Kansas, and on his left, he knew he must make his stand here or the union would be divided, and the state of the Old Republic would perish.

In the foreground of Kansas City, Missouri, were the smoldering ruins of what had once been a blooming metropolis. Natal was using these events to propel him into a bid to be the senior senator of the United States of America. On one occasion he spoke at a joint meeting of the members of Congress, condemning the rebels of the White Aryan Race States of America.

"This treason was not done in some corner of the world," Senator Vicar said. "It was plotted by a Judas who once served this country right here. We must answer for the death of my beloved uncle and the death of innocent civilians with war. Their very name tells us of their intention of the heart."

The roar of the senator's speech could be heard all the way back to his office in Reno as the letters flooded his office. Another meeting in his private suite in the northern part of Winnemucca, Nevada, was taking place, and it was here where the real deal about the White Aryan Race State known as W.A.R. was made known. As Natal was sitting in his office talking to the newly sworn-in president of the United States, he rocked in his executive chair.

"Yes, yes. Of course, sir," Natal said as a well-built, balding Caucasian man came in. Natal motioned for him to have a seat. "Mr. President, I'm sure you will get a full report on the investigative report on the WARS militias. Goodbye, Mr. President." As the senator hung up the phone, the Caucasian man said, "Very moving speech you made on C-SPAN yesterday."

"I knew Caspar Reno would like it," Natal said, smiling.

"He wants to know what our next move is."

"Tell him that the new president, vice president, and secretary of state must be all killed if I am going to be president." He threw a large manila envelope on the desk and said, "That's for both jobs, okay?"

The man responded with a smile, "Gee, thanks. I like your administration already."

As he counted the money, the two of them were looking for an end to this very uncomfortable conversation. Suddenly the phone rang with the vice president on the other line. "You will be picked up tonight," Natal said to him, "so don't be late."

"Okay. You ex-Marines are all the same," the man answered roughly to the senator. "Hurry up and wait."

"Yes, Mr. Vice President, I was just thinking about …" Senator Natal said as his guest left.

Meanwhile, Senator Natal was helping to organize a third militia to fight the W.A.R.S this was the starting place of the airstrike that was the spark of the second civil war. These atrocities began the age of darkness for the people of North America and were done per Natal's design. They put the Christians under harsh persecution and made them a remnant of the church era of the Laodicea's going into hiding.

Standing on a podium in the Nevada National Guard that was destroyed by the W.A.R.S. he began his speech with a lie that was from hell. His chess-like moves reminded me of when I taught him how to play the game, which gave him an advantage over his surprise back-room deals.

"You young men and women are the pride and joy of

the great state of Nevada," he said boastfully, "and now our republic commands you to be her pride and joy." Like Christ this seed of Satan was fulfilling his own share of prophecies. However, he was still doing it by the power of the spirit of prophecy, which is the testimony of Jesus Christ.

Now that he had set the pawns on both sides in play, he would move to checkmate the kings and queens in this second war of the United States. The witness of Christ Jesus, my master, had kept us as his children under the faithful and true chief of the creation of God. The wicked churches of the era of the Laodicea's had caused God to move his sheep to the slaughter as it is written in the book of the Watchman Ezekiel:

"The lost I seek, and the driven away bring back, the broken I bind up, and the sick I strengthen, and the fat and the strong I destroy, I feed it with judgment. Moreover, you, my flock, thus said the Lord Jehovah: Lo, I am judging between sheep and sheep. Between rams and he-goats is a little thing for you to eat the good pasture you will enjoy.

"However, as it was foretold the remnant of your pasture ye tread down with your feet, and a depth of waters ye do drink, And the remainder with your feet ye trample, And My flock the trodden thing of your feet consumed, And the trampled thing of your feet are drinking? Therefore, thus said the Lord Jehovah to them and lo, I, even I, have judged between fat sheep and lean sheep. Because with side and with shoulder ye thrust away, and with your horns push all the diseased, till ye have scattered them to the out-place."

This happened when an Arabian and African-American general, Ishmael Ben Mohammad, who was in the Nation of Islam, and the half-brother of Mustafa, the one I killed in an attempt to try to overthrow the United States by kidnapping Natal's late uncle, gathered an army of 175,000 and seceded from the United States by massacring and enslaving 24,000 Christians in the southern portion of America.

Therefore, God overturned the church by enslaving my people in the Southern African Islamic States of America. Because we acted continually to be neither cold nor hot, but lukewarm, did not Christ Jesus warn us to choose whether we would be cold as sinners or hot as angelic seraphim at the altar of God? However, we were lukewarm, and Christ our king vomited us out of his mouth because we, the church of God, said, "We are rich, and have grown richer of the world, and have need of nothing because we see like Christ," but Christ Jesus in his wrath said, "You are wretched, miserable, poor, blind, and naked."

I stood in the chambers of the chapel of the Watchmen that were five thousand strong to be anointed a prophet and sergeant of arms. I was told by Elder Juniper, "Raymond, you must give the cry of your heart, so speak as the Spirit of God leads you." Then she stood and came before the council of intercessors, saying, "You who stand here today vote whether our new brother is worthy of his office."

I rose to the pulpit and cleared my throat, reaching for a glass of water. Shaking, I drank a small sip. Then I cleared my throat and opened my mouth, "For nearly one thousand four hundred and ninety-five years, we were warned and needed to buy from him the gold of the gospel of Jesus Christ by the word, which was tried by the fire of the Holy Spirit of God. Then we could have been made rich and have treasures in heaven, and the words of Jesus would become the words of God.

"However, Christ has washed us in the water of the word and would have given us white garments that we may cover our nakedness. The Lord has promised to anoint with oil his body with the Holy Spirit, and would open our eyes because the soul's blindness cannot see our sinful nature.

"As many as knew his love, Christ began to convict and chasten, and Christ Jesus, shouting by his New Testament prophets, warned us to be zealous and move toward the Holy Spirit's transformation. The Lord and shepherd of our so-called tradition was put out of the churches of North America, and the doctrine and philosophies of men put the counsel and might of the Holy Spirit of God outside his own blood-bought assemblies.

"As the underground remnant, the body of Christ overcame and sat down with my Father on his throne. He who has an ear, let him hear what the Spirit said to the worshippers of God Almighty.

"In this age from the ashes of the Reformation and civil war arose two churches. The mother religion apostolic church slowly crept into the limelight, and members of this mother of whoredom called themselves the true worshippers of the church of our Lord Jesus Christ. The other was the repented virgin church of the underground remnant of the body of Christ. The thing that we were, the body of Christ must know. We had to understand that God didn't need man to help him with false doctrines of the devil's and lying wonder.

"We will learn all over again to trust God the Father, and will learn to seek the face of God, which will begin to teach us to believe all over again this truth of being the body of Christ who is on Jesus Christ as God without the fables and false doctrines of the worldly televangelists of the Christian Broadcasting Channel. The Christ of humanity only needs to read the true word to get the real picture of who God is. But soon others will not listen to the wolves in sheep's clothing. They are nothing but false prophets; they come to you dressed as sheep, but inside they are devouring wolves.

"This is the burden of love, and I have only one thing to say to this body," I screamed as I looked toward heaven. "REPENT."

The cries of throngs of men and women falling toward the floor took my breath away as I fell on my face. Revival came to that little group as they began to worship God the Father in spirit and truth. The moment lasted only one hour, but the effect would last for eternity, and then they unanimously voted me in as their sergeant of arms.

CHAPTER 19

🏯 🏯 🏯

The Dragon's Breath

The hidden leaven among us was the mysterious Black Pope, who was the dark moon that rose to the light. Neither I nor any of the Watchmen could ever be unloosed from Natal's grip, because the Reverend Maximus Coven was no ordinary man. Like the eyes of Rasputin and the speech of an elegant pope, something about Coven was mystical and yet familiar. I have never seen Natal so afraid of any man, but when he came into the room, I could literally see his knees shaking.

Nevertheless, they were lovers, and I knew this because I was trapped in a fanatical predicament. I was then imperial press secretary, and every morning, I walked through the palace rose garden into the press room and printed out the dailies. I made sure Emperor Vicar could personally censor the news before I delivered it.

Now at two in the morning not a child should be stirring, but the Secret Service the reported while Natal was sleep in an unholy embrace. As I heard two people kissing behind the door, I thought Tiffany and Natal were up early. Then suddenly I heard the old cracking voice of that snake. "Let me be everything to my lord," said the voice of Maximus as I heard him kiss Natal. Then I knocked on the door and heard Natal's voice on the other side. "Yes, what is it?"

"My lord, your dailies are ready for your view."

"Do with them as you would always, Raymond."

"As you wish, my lord."

Daniel's prophecy—the one that said, "Of the gods of his father's he shall take no notice, nor of the beloved of women; neither shall he pay respect to any other god; for he shall exalt himself above them all"—came true. Later that day, as in many days to come, their arguments broke more than dish if not the sound barrier.

"Sleeping with you is a lie," Tiffany yelled. "It is like sleeping with the devil himself."

"You know I am not that rough," he barked back.

"Not that rough? You pulled my hair out by the roots," she screamed, pointing at her head.

Natal tried to grab her hand. "Oh baby, you know …"

"No, Natal. I'll be your arm candy for the public," Tiffany said sharply, walking toward the door, "but you find yourself another sex toy."

Emperor Vicar did, and the man known as the Black Pope was his new sex toy, and they never were apart from that point on. Tiffany was found guilty of adultery with one of the Secret Service men, and both were shot the next morning; I think the man's name was Agent Summers.

I know this was the end of my influencing the only son I had in this world. From that point on I had to watch my step around the emperor. For every five steps Natal made, the Reverend Maximus Coven took six at his heels. I need more proof that Natal's new master was in fact the archbishop of Spain, Louis El-Deon Ignatius, who is now the feared Black Pope of the Society of Jesuits. I remembered the vision told to me back in Orlando, and why Elder Zarepath shared her vision. Lord Charlemagne Vicar was dying, and he called for his friend Archbishop Ignatius. As he sat down with his friend for the last time, Lord Vicar was holding a small vial in his hand and began to call for Archbishop Ignatius.

"What is thy bidding, my lord?" Archbishop Ignatius asked

"It is you that I should be calling lord, Your Grace," Lord Vicar exclaimed while coughing.

"Nonsense, old friend. I have made a pledge to you," Archbishop Ignatius said.

"I need the thorns in my side removed," Lord Vicar said. "All of them threaten my line. Thus I will release you from your pledge and reward you with this devil's brew."

The archbishop asked, "What is it?"

"Take this and mix this blood with your wine," responded Lord Vicar, "and the Count of Transylvania will be in your blood and you will be of the undead."

"How did you get this?" asked Archbishop Ignatius.

"I was in his region as a young priest, and they had slain the Count Vladimir Dracula, and I saw him on the battlefield dying, so before he died, I gave him his last rites. He told me these words before he died: 'On a red full moon, take my blood and drink it,' Count Vladimir Dracula said in a raspy voice. 'You will be as the undead, my boy.'"

Lord Vicar said, "This is my gift to you, my old friend ..."

When Archbishop Ignatius drank that potion, I began to see that he was in fact a demoniac and not some mere man. He became as the undead and was discovered to be the False Prophet that will live and rule with the Antichrist.

Then a tall man with the same goat's head came forth from the cave. The apostle John wrote about him, saying, "He exercises the full authority of the first beast in his presence, and he makes the earth and those living in it worship the first beast, whose mortal wound had been healed. He also performs impressive miracles; for instance, he causes fire to descend from heaven to the earth in the presence of the people. By means of the wonders he can perform in the presence of the beast, he leads those living on the earth astray, telling the earth's inhabitants to erect a statue to the beast that had the wound by the sword and came back to life."

In the dark lower regions of the palace a witch's coven met on a hill as the red moon rose in the distance. I saw crosses with bodies on them hung upside down, and as each priest walked over to them, they lighted them. The bodies burned with that familiar smell, and from the bowels of hell they brought in a nude virgin girl.

"You, my dogs of war, make ready the sacrifices of the young virgins of all mankind and get rid of the enemies of the prince of darkness," Maximus said as he held the knife over a young girl's unconscious body. These were Natal's new armies as the Antichrist and the False Prophet made the Dregs his storm troopers so his whorish war machine could come after us. Then I saw Natal come in and sit on a black marble throne. Maximus mixed the blood of the girls in the chalice and gave this devil's brew to Natal. Maximus then cut his own wrist and let the drops fall into the cup.

"On a red full moon take my blood and drink it," Maximus Coven said in a raspy voice. "You will be as the undead, my lord."

As Natal Vicar drank the potion, his countenance changed, his teeth grew into fangs, and his eyes were like the blood-red moon. Natal Apollyon Vicar was like the one I saw in my vision when I was dead that accursed me before my Lord and Christ. This was Satan now walking among us.

"The heavens I will go up, above stars of God I will raise my throne." Natal took the sword of a dragon and shouted these words. A lightning bolt struck the sword while his red eyes glowed. "I will sit in the mount of the meeting place in the sides of the north."

I could not stay his hand in anything he did. I could only watch in the war room of the Pentagon as he made his plans for conquests, and I had to stay neutral as more of his plans were made public. As one would wipe his blade clean from the sword of combat, so did he wipe the Watchmen from the face of the earth. As these words echoed from his lips, the world turned into a dark place to live in: "I will go up above the heights of a thick cloud. I am like to the Most High."

The tattoo of a million men with the symbol of the clan of the Green Clover Dragons was the Reverend Maximus Coven's tool of conflict. Moreover, he killed the whole council, wiping clean the dagger from his bloody past, or so it seemed to the emperor; three got away to warn me of my fated end. Nevertheless, was this man too late? I was thinking everything was all right when I sent my final message to the Watchmen's Council. Only three would survive in this stalemate of chess, and I had to move before it was too late for me. I began typing this message, which brought me to the end of my story:

January 1, 2058
Volume 3 of the *Watchmen Chronicle*
Subject: The rise and fall of the American breadbasket
Body: What began with the constant growing of this freed monster of this seven-headed leviathan that is ruling the people of the world with fury and brutality? As I stood in front of this vision that brought my knees to quake, I asked God the question. Who is covering and watching this

government or trying to stop this great beast from killing off the innocent? In addition, those who were assigned to watch over this deadly beast as it rose its heads were all in a deep slumber, and when they awoke, it began its pursuit of me, which dumbfounded me even more.

The gigantic leviathan started its pursuit of me long before I was ever born in the sixties of the twentieth century. I couldn't leave while I had the chance to save my own skin.

I was abiding in the sea of the melting pot of my land of fruitful grains, and then I spied a view behind a certain purple mount, climbing to the point of that peak. Suddenly this monstrous beast arose from the seas of democracy and false harmonies of the elders from every temple and villages told me they scorned my vision as I tried to warn them.

"It is but a dream or a vision or ..." The elders of the cities all yelled at me. "He is a bad bit of undigested pork."

That was the last echo I heard as the beast destroyed them all to the last. While I ran from it, watching the viper before me conquering those same cities while hiding behind a cloud of fire, there was lightning and hail. It swept away all those cities that had mocked me by fanning the winds of war with its venomous tail.

When I saw from the height of the safety of the mountain the twirling tornado of demonic violent flow, I feared and worshipped God, who is the creator of us all, and there came blasts of lightning and hailstones. Their weight was that of a quarter-ton truck and crushed the running people trying to escape. Nevertheless, this dragon appeared from out of the dying shaded cloud, and the beast of a translucent color of purple came to steal, kill, and destroy all who had the sign of death.

Although the transgender monster had blue and sea-green armor-like scales, the beast would speak lies that were formed from the centuries of lies it had told the people to lull them into a slumber, and it callously spoke, which made it grow every time it blasphemed God. I saw in the distance a young woman with blond hair, and she was coming up this hill. As she struggled up the hill, the beast who was far away from her saw that she was trying to escape the city below her. In addition, a blast of fire blew up near her and almost killed her, but she moved out of its way.

As she got closer to the top, I went and tried to save her myself, and when I did, the beautiful woman called to me, "Help me, please." As I reached to pull her up, I saw a red mark on her forehead, which looked like the Hebrew character Taf "ת" and the character looked red as crimson, as if it had been burned into her flesh with a branding iron. The symbol and its evil glimmer nearly blinded me as I tried to save her from death. Then the monster came and grabbed her. As she screamed, it devoured her, eating her whole.

I could not believe my eyes when I saw the judgment that came upon that woman, and I fainted from the ghoulish way in which she was destroyed. As my life began to flash over this long walk I was taking, revenge rose in my soul, and I prayed.

Resting on these facts, I asked myself, *Who would punish this sextuplet-headed brute that has walked over all those small towns and cities?* At the same time, each head rose from the birth pangs of the steaming acid eggshells. The gigantic granite-colored eggs were formed very strangely from a creature that was not a female but was a malefactor of past presidents and worsened by the posterity of craved repeated historical mistakes of the woman of mythological origin. The snake-haired demoniac in the tail of the *Odyssey* was nothing compared with this dappled being. The culture that America spawned from the womb of the pit rebellion was the creature of all children's nightmares.

The leviathan that rose from the sea, which had a name engraved in blood-red scales, was called Republicus. The being had smaller names engraved on its seven heads, and was worse than any beast in my nightmare. Intended for deception, the leviathan would be engulfed and be hidden in its tornado-like cloud blowing fiery strikes of lightning to scare others away, and would fool even some of the saints of our country.

Now that this hideous beast had appeared, it would only turn back the furious dragon slayer, calling and screeching for our doom. Nevertheless, the beast called *Republicus* had seven heads; the first was called Bogus Chrio Nāgîd and would draw all false dreamers into the fog.

"This is Camelot," echoed the bottomless voice from the clouds.

Because the poor, the dreamer, and the slothful would believe his lies, they would work endlessly for the dragon as he drove them into an insane frenzy to steal anything. The dragon would whisper from the fog that would form them into zombies, and they became the walking dead for their master of the cloud. Trying to keep from being fed to the monster from the deep, these white zombies went to the cities and villages and traveled into the farmland to enslaved black men and women who were used as pawns to do the dragon's bidding.

The children of these cities hid from the great leviathan so it wouldn't eat them, but were terrorized as they helplessly watched their parents being devoured. Nothing could stop the beast called Bogus Chrio Nāgîd that drew all false dreamers from every generation into the fog from getting the one to come, because it would use a sweet, soft voice like the victims' parents and put it into their minds.

The head called Rivalry, whose crown was in the shape

of a dome-like crest, came into a shape of battle horns, jagged for battles. The horns had worn human skulls and bead-like nodules around the skulls, which represented fourteen of the wars it had fought. Moreover, when this molten-steel-like helmet figure smashed into any metropolis, the monster would devastate any populace with which it came in contact.

The jaded, jagged teeth of blinding stainless steel would devour first the men of the cities, town, and villages, and later the women, who were given as sacrificial offerings by the leaders of the United States. The fiery blast alone of breath of the rumors of war would blaze any hope of coming away unmarred.

The skull-like head called Famine would make the strongest of men wince and gag in revulsion. Its head had a swarm of flies and maggot-like sores around its mouth and nose that dripped out puss like slime on the babies and young children, and then turned into a pile of maggots, killing all the firstborn, whether rich or poor.

Screaming and cries of anguish would come from the cities, towns, and villages as sufferers from the wrath of war wept for the unborn. Every time the beast raged in war, these two heads would eat the most on the carcasses of the unborn and the dead. The sight of this beast would make any nonbeliever choose to pay it substance that they had worked for, and would give gladly or until they felt guilt, which brought more anguish on those who received the charity. They would put the chains of poverty or the spirit of bondage on those victims of famine, and the long chains of addiction would drag them around like slaves until they died, and then the tail of the beast would crush their bones into powder.

The beast of Pestilence was a fog of smoke and flames whose head could not ever be seen. If you saw the mother who bore it, you would be turned into stone by its gaze. A head of the last dragon was called Mayhem and Chaos. It had twenty horns but no mouth to feed it, but when it struck, civil war burst into the cities and villages, destroying the very fabric of any continent and raising its wake of destruction and doom.

The dragon of which I speak is nothing more than a man I have protected who would like to be not just an emperor but your god: that man's plan is to take over the world. His name is Natal Apollyon Vicar, and his accomplice is the Reverend Maximus Coven. They plan to assassinate and strike the first blood on the world with the plans I have attached in this letter on the European Union Conference delegates tomorrow in a conference of peace.

This will end the faceless rule of bipartisanship and begin his domination of the world, and the dragon will feed on power and we will sacrifice freedom to feed his lust for being the god of force …

When I pressed Enter, the door was broken into, and I was arrested.

CHAPTER 20

♨ ♨ ♨

The Tower of Babel Is Rising

February 26, 2058

This will be my final entry, seeing that I wrote early in my first blog post to my underground brothers and sisters to warn them of the coming judgment. We are now the exporters of a homegrown terrorist police state for the world in what was once the United States of America, where we live as a people who have become prisoners of the rights we have forgotten. Our land is but a breath away from another civil war. We pray for peace that comes at the price of being policed, but shall we pray for war that may bring the coming of the Lord?

I wish my fate were so easy, because I have become one of seven men who have been posted around the world by God. I am the Watchman of the city of New Philadelphia, which became the new North American capital city. The old republic is no more, but the new republic was born out of the ashes of racial and religious wars.

The North America Alliances have split the old United

States of America into six rebel states, never to be the glorious nation I remember as a young boy; there was the White Aryan Race States in the Northwest, and then there was the Natives Indo-Mexicana Clan in the Southwest.

There's the Christian States of America in the central Midwest, and the Afro-Islamic Revolutionary States that tried take over the south. Now the New Republic States of America are the homegrown terrorist police states of the world. But they are all no more, because these civil wars were toys in the emperor's arsenal to create the chaos we have today in the form of ROMES, which stands for the new Republican Occupied Majority European States.

This is my final post for the *Watchmen's Chronicle* because I must flee for my life or face charges of espionage if I am to keep my cover as a reporter for the *New Republic Journal*. Reporting for the *Watchmen's Chronicle* blog, this is Naba Zaphah.

The Reverend Maximus Coven read the transcript out loud to the emperor: "'Body: What began with the constant growing of this freed monster of this seven-headed leviathan that is ruling the people of the world with fury and brutality? I question whether I should keep my cover and watch this government kill off the innocent or leave while I have the chance to save my own skin. In addition, there was the watching over this deadly beast as it raised its heads and began its pursuit of me long before I was ever born in the sixties of the twentieth century.

"'I was abiding in the sea of the melting pot of my land of fruitful grain, and then suddenly this monstrous beast arose from our seas of democracy and false harmony, all the while fanning the winds of war with its venomous tail. From this tornado of demon fire and smoke, a dragon appeared, translucent purple in color, but the transgender monster with blue and sea-green armor-like plating was formed from the centuries of lies, and it callously spoke, which made it grow every time it matured.

"'As my life began to flash over this long walk I was taking, revenge rose in my soul, and I prayed. Resting on these facts, I asked who would punish this sextuplet-headed brute that has walked over the small towns and cities in its way. At the same time, each head rose from the birth pangs of a steaming acid-like substance of stone resembling eggs, with three eggs that were one.

"'The gigantic granite in which the egg was formed was very strange in that it wasn't from a female. Its mother was a malefactor of past presidents worsened by mythological snake-haired demoniac in the tale of the Odyssey. The culture that America was spawned from the womb of eternity of the pit of a nightmare had created this creature.

"'This leviathan was born and rose from the sea. Its name, Republicus, was engraved in bloodred scales, and smaller names were written on its seven heads, worse than any other beast in my nightmare. Intended for deception, the leviathan would be engulfed in flames and hidden in its tornado-like cloud, blowing fiery strikes of lightning to scare others away. It fooled even some of the saints of our ...'"

Natal said with a sigh, "Do we have to go through this again?"

The Reverend Maximus said sharply, "And I quote: 'the leviathan is none other than Emperor Caesar Apollyon Vicar,' end of quote."

"Yeah, and your point?" Natal bellowed, and then sighing, he flung the papers to the floor. "I have read mendacity reports like these for months, and you have not given me one head yet."

"Ah, but I do have one head, my lord," the Black Pope said as he grinned.

As the door opened to the room, Natal looked up, smiling. Then his eyes met mine and his amused grin turned to an angry frown of distrust and unbelief. He turned to Maximus, frowning at him, and I thought for a moment that my freedom was at the door.

"Is this some cruel joke?" Natal asked. "You want me to fly into some raging tyrant's fit?"

"This is your traitor, my lord," Maximus said, calm and smirking.

Natal screamed, "Then take him away."

As the guards were marching in twos down the corridors coming toward my cell, I knew that my end was near. I can only write this last letter and hope as I etch the message on this wall that posterity will receive it in the kingdom to come.

February 27, 2058

This is the final entry of my journal, and I am glad to see this day that I have waited so long for. I am one hundred years old, and I am and I will be done with my life, because I have seen my sorrows of life, and even though my pain in not in body, I wish my heart could say the same. I am going to be led out and instead of being put to sleep in the chamber, as should be done for a hero. I will be shot as if I were the real criminal. It is starting to drizzle, and I can see lightning in the distance on the hill at the post where I will be executed. I will be seeing my God soon.

Goodbye, Natal,
Raymond Mitchell Moore
Chief Elder of the Watchman

It's a funny thing about lightning: when it hits a man on a chained wooden pole, it leaves no trace of a body. When 175,000 gig watts of power hit a post and you see an angel, break your chains. It does something to a man's faith toward God through it. Suddenly, right before the lightning struck me, I saw a ten-foot angel break my chains. As I fell through a trapdoor, in front of me was a shadowy figure that looked very familiar.

I knew him as Michael Jones, but he was my long-lost brother, De'Angelo Michael Jones or in Hebrew it would be Jonah. My baby brother De'Angelo was adopted by Jews and taken back to Israel. He served two years in the Israeli army and then came back to the United States after marrying a New York girl visiting his parents. He became an electrical engineer officer in the Marines. That was how we reunited at the Marine Corps ball at the reunion for those who had served in Afghanistan, and the rest is history.

"Hey, you gonna sit there on your blessed assurance?" De'Angelo whispered.

I knew that whisper, although I had not heard it in more than ninety-one years. As I tried to see the familiar face, I saw only an older De'Angelo, the man Michael I knew in the Marines. I wanted to hug him and let him know I knew who he was, but I couldn't form the words. Instead, tears came to my eyes, blurring my vision for a second.

"You know, it's not going to be long before they figure out that you're not dead," De'Angelo said.

"How is our sister Imani?" I asked.

"She … is … fine," he said, stunned. "You know." He hugged me as if we had forever. He had had the other troops build the track system that was at the end of the tunnel a mile away. The whole year, the Watchmen had been building it to rescue me while I was doing my job.

"Is he dead?" Natal asked.

"Yes, my lord, burned in a lightning strike. There is no trace of his body," Maximus said gleefully.

Then Natal closed the door to his private study. I was going to finish something that should have been done ninety-one years earlier. I had my brother, De'Angelo, my liberator, do one thing for me before we left for Israel. I had him wait at our mother's and stepfather's old grave site where Port Norfolk is now part of the city of Portsmouth. I could see the ship at the dock, and it was here I found peace and it was here I made peace with both God and my murdered parents and finally said goodbye.

"Hey, tell Elder Zaphah we must go," the frightened captain said. "We've got to catch this tide going out."

"In a minute," my brother said as he bowed his head.

"Our father, which art in heaven; hallowed be thy name. Thy kingdom come, thy will be done; on earth as it is in heaven. Give us this day our daily bread, and forgive us our trespasses as we forgive those who trespass against us. Lead us not into temptation, but deliver us from evil. This is a word, Lord, I couldn't say back when I was a little boy. Back then that man was evil, but now you have delivered me and my family. I can finish this prayer … For thine is the kingdom and the power and the glory, forever and ever," I whispered softly. "Amen."

As he looked at their tombs, where they were buried together as they had lived, Raymond could finally close this chapter in his life. Moreover, there in that somber place he was able to bury all the demons of his past.

Raymond said to me as we walked away, "It's always curious about a fresh start."

"What's that, Raymond?" he asked.

"You never get any younger," Raymond said, and we laughed and continued talking.

As I walked away from the place in old Port Norfolk where my brother and I had lived for our childhood, I gave him the start of a new chapter with my new friend and brother, but then again, he had always been a friend. I got Raymond to see that you can't pet a dragon, nor can you tame a wolf.

As Raymond's hero, I often looked up to him as my big brother, and now I was his liberator and I would try to bring the people of God. The world needs to see who Emperor Caesar Apollyon Vicar was: the dragon that came from the sea of this cosmos, or for you regular talking people, the world.

Now my brother, Raymond Moore, stood in Jerusalem in Sanhedrin Hall of judgment to make a speech to the twenty-four elders of the Council of the Watchmen and the elders of Israel. As he got up, there was a standing ovation. He was unanimously elected the 356th chief elder of the Watchmen Intercessory Council as their new leader. He said, "We must begin to walk in the Old Testament and the New Testament in the Holy Bible, and be in the Holy Spirit's purifying fire. We must be a united force, both Jew and Gentile, for we are making white the gown called the body of Christ, till the end of time. Intended for a time appointed, and through the underground newspaper called the *Watchman's Chronicle* there are hidden code words in online Internet newsletters for the Christians who were in hiding from Emperor Vicar. The Tower of Babel is on the rise."

I am the real writer of the *Watchmen's Chronicle*, and I am hoping you will come and join us in Israel. However, I cannot tell you personally who I am as Raymond Moore's liberator, because you may try to get me captured by the empire. Then again, you would have to do that over my brother's dead body. I hope you already know what the outcome of that foolish attempt would be.

The End

BIBLIOGRAPHY

1 De Rosa, Peter. 1998. *Vicars of Christ: The Dark Side of the Papacy.* New York: Crown.
2 Papal Sin; Gary Willis; "On the Dignity of the Priest." Cited in Peter Damian. Ranke-Heinemann; pp. 108–110; Doubleday; New York. © 2000
3 Tsaphah, Michael. 2008. *A Tree Called Morality.* Baltimore: PublishAmerica.
4 *King James Authorized Version Study Bible.* Aharoni, Yahonan, and Michael Avi-Yonah. 1964Chicago: Thomas Nelson.
5 *New King James Version 1611.* Gideon Bible Society. Nashville; 1865.

Printed in the United States
By Bookmasters